ATTRACTION

THE LEPIDOPTERA VAMPIRE SERIES

BY
SUSAN HODDY

First published in 2016

Copyright © Susan Hoddy 2016

ISBN 978-0-9954134-2-9

Cataloguing-in-Publication details are available from the National Library of Australia.

Website: www.susanhoddy.com

Prologue

SIXTEEN YEARS AGO

The tears welled in Talitha's eyes when she looked upon the face of her newborn daughter. The thought of having to give her up for adoption bothered her immensely, but she knew it was necessary to keep her child safe.

"Can I take her now, or would you like some more time with your child, Talitha?" asked William, standing next to Talitha and watching the baby sleeping in her cradle.

"Give me one minute, William. Wait outside," said Talitha, authoritatively.

"Yes, Queen."

William nodded once, leaving her to spend what precious moments she had left with the child. Shutting the door to her room, William stood guard outside and waited.

Talitha placed her finger into her daughter's tiny hand, and without hesitation, the child curled her little fingers around Talitha's and opened her darkened newborn eyes.

"You sure are beautiful," said Talitha, tracing every inch of her facial features and trying to hold onto the only memory she might have, as she knew she may never see her again.

Swaddling her firmly in a pink, blue, and yellow striped baby blanket, Talitha bent over and picked her child up out of the cradle. Holding her in her arms, she bent forward and kissed her forehead, lingering to take in her sweet smell, that only babies have.

"Good bye, my sweet child. I love you dearly. I hope we get to meet again one day."

As she opened the door, Talitha found William waiting, as usual, to take the child to safety. Handing her one-day-old daughter over to William was not only heart wrenching, but comforting as well. Even though she would never watch her child grow into a strong, capable woman, Talitha knew it was the only thing she could do to keep her baby safe from the Debauched. She had carried her for nine months and wished, with every inch of her body, that she could keep this precious gift. But if was not to be.

With a heavy heart, she watched William walk up the stairs and out of sight, with her child. As the tears streamed down her face, Talitha retreated back to her basement room, and closed the door. Hugging herself as she slid down the door, she sobbed uncontrollably into her lap. The pain of losing her child had taken its toll on her today, more so than any other child she had given birth to.

Like many previous times, Sister Mongose, who was from the Bagnolet parish, was waiting in the foyer of the Gramaze mansion to take the child to a loving family for adoption. Standing when she saw William approach her, she asked, "Boy or girl?"

"Girl," said William, handing the baby over.

"Right," said Sister Mongose, with raised eyebrows. "First girl for a while."

"Yes… this one must go to a family who will keep her safe," said William, authoritatively.

"Yes, sir. As always, Mr Gramaze," said Sister Mongose, kneeling on the floor and tucking the child into a wool-lined calico bag. This would keep the child warm enough for her journey to the church, which was a couple of blocks away from the Gramaze mansion. "Thank you again, Mr Gramaze."

"Just make sure she is kept safe," said William, wanting to believe he would see the child again one day, to strengthen and increase his Lepidoptera coven.

"I will. Err, umm, well… good night, Mr Gramaze," said Sister Mongose, swallowing hard, picking up the calico bag from the floor and walking to the front door. Even though she enjoyed placing the children with families, over the many years that she had dealt with the Gramaze family, she had always found William to be intimidating. She knew something wasn't right in that house, but wasn't about to ask questions for fear of reprisal.

"Good night, Sister," said William, opening the front door for her.

Chapter One

PRESENT DAY - JANUARY

The heavy rain sounded like horses' hooves on the tin roof, as the thunder and lightning crackled and lit up the night sky. With the fierce winds rattling the windows of their friends' small house, the lights flickered every now and then, which virtually made it impossible for Violette and Danielle to study whilst they waited for their parents, who had stayed at work late to help with a presentation.

At around 10.30, there was a knock at the door. Thinking it was their parents, Danielle and Violette packed up their books to go home. But when they opened the door, two police officers were standing on the step.

"Good evening… may we come in?" said the oldest police officer, showing his badge.

Pulling the door completely open, their friend's dad, Brian, let them in.

"What is this all about?"

"We have some news that we wish to discuss with you, regarding Mr and Mrs Castell," said the oldest police officer.

"Right. Come this way," said Brian, gesturing towards the lounge room.

Swallowing hard, Violette's felt a cold chill fan out over her body. Grabbing Danielle's hand, she held it firmly, as they both looked at each other with concern. Placing their school bags on the floor, near the front door, the girls followed Brian to the lounge room.

"What is this all about officers?" said Brian, as he sat on the couch across from the officers.

"I am afraid we have some bad news," said the oldest police officer as he looked towards the two girls standing in the doorway. "There is no nice way to tell you this... this evening at around eight, Mr and Mrs Castell were shot by carjackers and have passed away."

"No... no... you're lying!" shouted Violette, sliding down the wall and collapsing on the floor in disbelief. "I know they will be here soon to collect us."

Sobbing, she looked over at her sister for reassurance. But all she saw was Danielle in a sitting position on the floor, rocking herself back and forth and crying uncontrollably.

With her tears flowing freely down her cheeks, and her heart pounding in her ears, Violette thought she was going to pass out. She couldn't comprehend that she wasn't ever going to see her parents again.

Awakened by the captain's voice over the PA system, Violette caught the tail end of him saying that they would be landing soon. With her heart pounding in her chest, she realised she had been dreaming about the night her parents had been killed. Holding back her tears as they formed in her eyes, she took a few deep breaths and tried to calm herself. Looking out the small window, into the filtered clouds, she turned her thoughts to LA and of how much simpler life had been before this move to Bagnolet. Back then, the only thing she had to worry about, besides long, brown hair that never sat right, was graduating from Beverley Hills High School. Feeling for the button on her arm rest to place her seat back in its upright position, Violette's ears popped as the plane started its descent.

"Violette," said Emily. "Would you like some gum or candy?"

Smiling, she shook her head slowly. "No thanks, Emily."

"How about you both?" said Emily gesturing to Danielle and Emily's husband Adrian, sitting across the aisle from them.

Violette leant forward, and watched Danielle look up from her book, and reach across the aisle to take the gum from Emily. Noticing the elegant gold ring, which had been left to Danielle by their mother, on her slim, right ring finger, Violette remembered the day Danielle was given the ring at the reading of the will by the lawyer. The look on Danielle's face was one of shock and disbelief as she accepted the ring and wept.

"Thanks," said Danielle. Jostling her long, blonde hair to one side, she put her glasses on to continue reading her book on France.

"Can you pass me some over?" said Adrian opening his blue eyes and pushing his short brown, greying hair to one side.

Taking the gum from Danielle, he leaned back in his seat and turned his attention out the window to see land below through the clouds.

"I have enjoyed LA and the business opportunities that eventuated," said Adrian. "But I sure am glad to be going home. I have missed Bagnolet and our friends."

"Hmm. I will miss LA, and my friends," said Danielle picking at her finger nails. "But I'm also looking forward to the move. If I haven't said it before, Adrian, thank you for taking us to Paris. We know this is a great opportunity. It might take us some time to settle in though." The concern on her face was apparent.

"That's OK, Danielle. We expect that. Just give it time. It will get easier for you both as you start to settle in," said Adrian. He knew what it was like firsthand, to be unsure of a new adventure. He, too, was fostered as a child and moved from his home town to a different city. "Just remember Emily and I are always here for you and Violette."

Hearing Danielle and Adrian's conversation brought back memories for Violette, of the first day Emily and Adrian had met them in the group home. Within minutes of meeting them, Adrian and Emily had curbed Danielle and Violette's shyness and nerves, with their calming nature and distracting jokes. Violette couldn't believe how they had become close in such a short time since her parents' death, four months before. *I think Mom and Dad would be happy to know we have been fostered by a wonderful couple, who care for us really well.*

"Everything alright?" said Emily.

"I was thinking about Mom and Dad," said Violette, fidgeting with her fingers and staring out the window.

Emily placed her hand over Violette's.

"Oh, OK. I am sure they are watching over you, Violette. Is there anything you want to talk about, dear?"

"I was thinking about all that has happened in—what? Four months?"

Her parents' funeral, moving to a group home and then being fostered by Emily and Adrian. She shook her head.

"And now, we're moving to Bagnolet."

She wanted to go home. She wanted it to be like it was. Violette tried to hold back the tears as she looked to Emily for comfort. Emily squeezed Violette's hand.

"It sure is strange how life can change with a click of your fingers. But one thing I am sure of is, life will get better for you both. The pain you are feeling now will get less as time goes by. Time is a great healer."

She handed Violette a tissue out of her bag.

Sniffing into the tissue and placing her head on Emily's shoulder, Violette said, "I know you're right, but some days are worse than others. I am looking forward to the move to Bagnolet and hoping to settle into some sort of routine with you and Adrian. I have missed being part of a family."

Emily nodded and held Violette's hand. As the plane descended, Violette lay her head on Emily's shoulder, thinking about the past and what might lie ahead for her future.

The flight from Los Angeles took around ten hours, and when they arrived at the Charles De Gaulle Airport, a black stretch limousine was waiting to collect them and take them to their new home. Initially they had left LA at eleven in the evening to catch their flight and were now exhausted. Walking onto the tarmac, Violette took in a deep, cleansing breath and looked out into the sky. The air was different. It seemed cleaner and cooler in Paris.

After a long drive, with lots of old buildings and busy highways, they pulled up in front of a large property with a high limestone brick wall and electric wire along the top. The driver punched in a code on the key pad located outside. As the wrought iron gates opened, he drove along a winding white pebble stone driveway, with manicured green lawn and colourful gardens on both sides. When the house came into view, it too was made of large limestone blocks, with a black gabled roof, and double door windows with balconies. Smiling with excitement, Violette couldn't wait to see inside, as she guessed it would be just as spectacular, like something you might see in the magazines for the rich and famous. Looking over at Danielle, Violette wondered what she was thinking of the house and grounds so far, as she wasn't showing any emotion on her face. In fact, Violette thought Danielle looked nervous as she watched her straighten her clothes and pick at her cuticles.

Pulling up outside the house, their driver got out and opened their door and helped Danielle and Violette alight from the limousine. Waiting to greet them outside the front doors of the house were two men dressed in black.

They look dressed for battle, thought Violette. She guessed they were security guards because of their muscular bodies and crew cut hair style.

"Come inside, girls, and we will show you around our house." Emily led the way.

Walking into the foyer, Violette saw that the house was just as magnificent on the inside. With her mouth open and her eyes darting from the ceiling to floor, she noticed a huge clear glass chandelier hanging from the ceiling and a white marble staircase straight in front of them, with doors and walkways either side of it. *French Provincial. I love it.* In awe of her surroundings, she tried to take it all in, until she was interrupted by Emily.

"I want you to meet someone," said Emily pointing toward the rear of the house. Waiting for them was a woman who looked like she was in her fifties, tall, with brown hair, which was tied back in a bun. "This is our cook."

"Bonjour," she said taking each of Danielle and Violette's hands in hers. "My name is Lamiae." She had the most beautiful French accent. "It's a pleasure to finally meet you both. I live in the little cottage at the back of the property with my family. Please don't hesitate to call on me if you need anything cooked."

"Thank you, Lamiae," they both said together.

"Lamiae, can you please show Danielle and Violette to their bedrooms upstairs whilst we get ourselves settled in?" said Adrian.

Lamiae nodded and the girls followed her up the marble staircase to where their rooms were situated.

"Are you hungry?" Lamiae asked, standing in the hallway. "I can bring back some dinner, if you like."

Danielle and Violette looked at each other and both nodded.

"Yes, please," said Danielle instantly. For a girl with a gorgeous figure, she was always hungry.

"Good. I have made you something special, and was hoping you would be hungry. Well, I will let you get settled into your rooms now," said Lamiae, indicating to Violette and Danielle which room was theirs. "Your cases will be bought up to you soon by the chauffeur."

She left them to look around their rooms.

Wow. We have a chauffeur. I am already starting to like this place, thought Violette.

Coming from a home where both parents worked, but didn't have a considerable amount of money to waste, Danielle and Violette were used to sharing a small bedroom, with just the bare necessities. But in their new home, in Bagnolet, Emily had previously informed them that they had separate bedrooms. Secretly, Violette was grateful to have her own space and to be able to place her shoes, clothes, and makeup wherever she wanted, without Danielle complaining.

After Danielle left Violette's doorway to go and settle into her own bedroom, Violette took a couple of steps into her room. With her mouth open in astonishment, and her eyes welling up, she looked around the exquisite room in disbelief. It had high 18th century decorated white ceilings, grey plush carpet, with grey background and pink flower wallpaper on the top part of the walls and a blue grey paint on the bottom. An antique light fitting glistened from the ceiling and lit the room perfectly. There was a four poster, queen-sized bed that had a red and pink floral quilt on it with lots of pillows.

I would never have dreamt in my wildest dreams that I could have a bedroom like this. So exquisite, thought Violette as her eyes filled with wonderment.

As she was admiring her new bedroom, her luggage turned up. At the opposite end of the bedroom doorway was the walk-in wardrobe. It had white shelving, plenty of white drawers, and a few rails for hanging her clothes on. There was even a separate shelf for her shoes.

After she opened her luggage, Violette folded and placed her clothes in the wardrobe. They appeared lonely on the single shelf she had chosen. Her two favourite pairs of shoes seemed to cower in the corner of the massive space provided. Violette sighed as she remembered the day she and Danielle were taken to the group home, and how they were told they couldn't take any more than a few clothes and shoes with them. She wished she knew what had happened to the rest of her clothes that were left behind. Especially the dress that her mom had bought for her sixteenth birthday.

As Violette walked out her wardrobe, she noticed an elegant 18th century white dressing table she could use for her jewellery and makeup. It even had a stool for her to sit on in front of the oval mirror. Looking at herself in the mirror, she thought about her old bedroom. Violette had slept in a single bed, which had a multi-coloured, knitted blanket her mom had made, to keep her warm, at the foot of the bed. Being a small room, which she shared with Danielle, there was never enough room in the wardrobe or chest of drawers, so they always stored some of their clothes in the attic and swapped them depending on the season. She sure was appreciative of the space her new bedroom had, even if she didn't have enough clothes to fill it.

Opening the curtains of her bedroom and looking out the French window double doors, she drank in the view outside of the luscious green lawn and stunning gardens. Looking into the sky, Violette watched in wonderment as the majestic red, golden sunset at the back of the property filtered through the sombre clouds.

Hmm, it's still light out. What time is it? Frowning, Violette took a quick glance at the digital clock next to the bed; it read 7.04pm. *That's different. Back home it would be nearly dark by now.*

Over on the right hand side of the lawn area, Violette spotted an opal-blue lap pool which had a large, white gazebo next to it with a dark-coloured table and chair setting. *Cool.* Jumping up and down on the spot with glee, she hugged herself. For the first time in months, her world was a happier place.

Then, appearing from what seemed like nowhere, Violette spotted the figure of a guy in the grounds outside. Six-foot tall or more, and dark haired, with his tight t-shirt outlining his muscular body, Violette wondered who he was. He was standing there, just looking straight at her. His look was so intense it sent a shiver down her spine. Something about him made her feel uneasy.

Startled by knocking at her door, she turned to see Danielle running into her room. By the time she had looked from the window to her bedroom door and back again, the mysterious man had disappeared.

Where did he go? I will ask Emily about him later, thought Violette.

"Do you believe this place? Your bedroom is as awesome as mine," said Danielle, looking around Violette's bedroom. "How lucky are we, sis? Come and have a look at my room; it's beautiful."

Excited, Danielle pulled Violette by the hand out the door and into her own bedroom, which was right next to Violette's.

Standing inside her doorway, Violette couldn't believe how beautiful her sister's room was. It looked very similar to hers except for the colour of the carpet and wallpaper, which were all in cream and pink. As they sat on Danielle's bed talking about how amazed they were that their foster parents owned a place like this, and how hard they must have worked to get this awesome house, there was a knock on the door.

"Come in," said Danielle looking up to see Lamiae standing at the doorway.

"Here we go, girls. I have made you a roast beef dinner and some pudding as well for later. Would you like me leave both trays of food here in your room, Danielle?" asked Lamiae, walking in.

"Yes, please," Danielle and Violette chimed in at the same time. Violette's stomach rumbled. She hadn't eaten much on the plane, so she was grateful to Lamiae for the food.

"Thank you, Lamiae. You are so thoughtful. It smells absolutely scrumptious," said Violette.

"You are welcome. As I said, girls, anytime you need something cooked, please don't hesitate to ask me and I will make it for you," said Lamiae placing the dinner trays in front of them.

"Lamiae… I… I wanted to ask, do you mind if we use the kitchen to cook ourselves something from time to time? It's just that we are used to making our own food, where we come from. Our parents taught us all we know about cooking," said Violette, picturing her mom bustling about the kitchen, and her dad pouring a glass of wine. As her vision of them blurred, Violette's mood shifted. She wondered if she could ever feel happy again, without feeling guilty.

Lamiae studied Violette's face. She seemed to know how unhappy Violette was at that moment.

"I am very sorry for the loss of your parents, my dears. If there is anything I can do to make your time here easier or pleasurable, please don't hesitate to ask me. And, yes, you are most welcome anytime in the kitchen to cook something you like."

"Thank you, Lamiae. That is so kind of you," said Danielle.

"You are welcome. Well… I will leave you both to eat your dinner. Good night, girls. I will see you in the morning for breakfast," said Lamiae, walking towards the doorway.

"Good night," they both said together.

After Lamiae left Danielle's room and closed the door behind her, Violette said to Danielle, "She seems really nice."

"Yeah… I can't believe she made this nice dinner for us. Talk about spoilt," said Danielle, picking up her knife and fork. "Mmm, this food looks delicious. Let's eat. I'm starving."

Sitting crossed legged on the floor, with their trays in front of them, eating dinner, Danielle said, "God…how long was that plane trip? I thought it was never going end."

"Yeah. I know… right. Talk about a numb butt," said Violette, cutting her meat.

"Do you believe we're now living in Paris? And this house…how amazing is it?" said Danielle, excited at the prospect of finally being able to live comfortably. She had hated living at the foster home and thought it was beneath her.

"When we drove onto the grounds, I couldn't believe what I was seeing. Emily and Adrian had shown us pictures, but I didn't realise it was this beautiful. We are very lucky to be living here, sis… but I miss LA already. I miss my friends too. It's just not going to be the same. Is it? Ever…" said Violette, holding back the tears.

Placing her arm around Violette's shoulder, and resting her head on Violette's head, Danielle said, "Don't worry, sis. Everything will get better. You'll see. And we still have each other."

"I don't want to ever lose you, Danielle. You are all I have left. God, I miss Mom and Dad," said Violette, placing her arm around Danielle's shoulder.

"Yeah, I miss them too…but, you know, I am very grateful Emily and Adrian fostered us. They have been wonderful. We sure have been lucky," said Danielle, looking around her room.

"Knock, knock. Can I come in?" asked Emily.

"Come in," said Danielle, sitting up straight.

"How are you girls settling in?" Emily asked, as she entered the room.

"Good, thanks," said Violette quickly, wiping her eyes, with a false smile.

"Good. Thanks, Emily. Your house is so lovely. Thank you for bringing us here," said Danielle.

"Well, this is now your home too, and we are hoping you both will eventually like it here. I was thinking, after you have finished your dinner, why don't you both take a shower and make it an early night? Because of the time difference between the two countries, you may get a bit of jet lag for a couple of days," said Emily, kneeling in front of them.

"Not a bad idea, sis," said Violette looking at Danielle. Her body ached to lie down.

"Yeah. You look as tired as I feel," said Danielle.

"Finish up your meals and I will show you where your bathrooms are," said Emily, standing. "Actually... I will be back in a minute. I need to make sure your bathrooms have towels."

After they had finished their meals, Emily took them to their bathrooms. Both were laid out basically the same, with a huge clear screen shower, large white claw-foot bath tub, and a long white vanity cupboard with a large mirror on the wall. Violette's bathroom had been painted antique white with light grey wallpaper and white tiles, and Danielle's was painted in light fawn, with brown and white wallpaper, and fawn colour tiles. The girls couldn't believe how enormous their bathrooms were, let alone that they would have a bathroom all of their own.

"So now you have seen your bathrooms, I will leave you girls to have your showers and get ready for bed. We will see you in the morning and show you around the rest of the house and grounds," said Emily, turning off the light in Danielle's bathroom.

"Thanks, Emily," said Danielle appreciatively.

"Yeah, thanks Emily," said Violette, walking over to Danielle's bed and sitting down.

"Hope you both sleep well," said Emily. Leaning in, she gave them a loving kiss good night on their foreheads.

As the door shut behind Emily, Violette said, "Hey...do you ever think about Stephen?"

When Emily had kissed Violette on her forehead, it had triggered a memory of her brother kissing her forehead when he left home. She hadn't thought about him in a while.

"Often. I still can't believe we weren't able to contact him when Mom and Dad passed away. I guess he must have been gone for about eight years now," said Danielle, remembering the good times she'd had with Stephen when they were younger. He always like to play hopscotch, or hide and seek. She definitely missed him.

"Yeah, I wonder if he even knows. And now we have moved here, I wonder if we will ever see him again?" said Violette. "I remember when we were younger, him leaving to find work when he had just turned seventeen and he never returned. And Mom and Dad hardly ever spoke about him either. I sure miss him, sis."

"Me too," said Danielle. "Not much we can do about it now Vi, until I turn eighteen next year. Then I am at a legal age to start proceedings for his search. Not unless we ask Emily and Adrian for their help now."

"Maybe we could speak with them tomorrow and ask if they could look into this for us?" said Violette, sounding hopeful.

"Sounds like a plan. In the meantime, I'm going to have a shower and catch up on some sleep," said Danielle, yawning.

"Yeah, me too. Have a good sleep, sis. See you in the morning." Violette gave Danielle a hug and headed to her bedroom.

Wiping the steam from the mirror with a hand towel, Violette tried to flatten the bags under her eyes with her fingertips and wipe away her sleep deprived appearance from the plane trip. *Hmm, not a good look. Can wait for tomorrow though.* With her old comfortable flannelette pyjamas on, Violette turned off the light in her bathroom, and headed for her new bed.

Lying in the darkness, Violette spread out her arms and legs, to feel the enormity of her bed and how soft the sheets were. *Mmm, heaven. Just what I need.* Her body was weary and she enjoyed the comfort of her new bed, but Violette couldn't stop thinking about all she had been through in the last four months. She kept going over and over the details in her mind. But what kept her awake the most was the thought of finding out who that good-looking guy was outside her window this evening. Very intriguing…

With her body finally giving into exhaustion, she finally fell asleep.

Chapter Two

As her eyes opened, Violette became disoriented. Taking a few moments, she realised she was in her new bedroom. Yawning, she lay there for a minute staring at the ceiling, and wondered what the day would bring. Illuminating the darkened room was a digital clock on her bedside table, which displayed the time of 7.30am.

Why am I awake at this ungodly hour of the morning?

The tiles were cold under her bare feet as she stood in front of the basin to wash her hands. Looking in the mirror, Violette knew she would have to wear makeup concealer today. She remembered she had tossed and turned most of the night and didn't feel like she'd had much sleep at all.

Deciding to have a shower, Violette quickly retrieved her clothes from the wardrobe. Placing her neck and shoulder blades under the steaming hot water, for a few minutes before she washed herself, had always relaxed Violette in the past.

Rejuvenated, she reluctantly turned the faucet off and stepped out the shower onto a fluffy, white floor mat. Looking around the bathroom, she spotted some white towels, which were rolled up, next to the bathroom cabinet. *Hmm, so soft. I could get used to this type of luxury.* Once she brushed her teeth, put her hair up in a ponytail and was dressed, Violette decided to proceed down the marble stairs and have a look around the house.

With each step she took, Violette smelt the delicious aromas of coffee and bacon coming from an area near the back of the house. Following her nose, it led her to the kitchen.

As she stood in the doorway of the kitchen, Violette watched Lamiae moving about, busily making breakfast. Taking in her surroundings, she noticed that next to the stove were lots of pots and pans hanging from the ceiling on steel rails. The kitchen was enormous, with white wall tiles, black marble bench tops, and white cupboards along each wall. In the middle of the kitchen was a long black marble island bench top with white cupboards underneath, and some stools around the outside.

Violette was overwhelmed by the vast size of the kitchen and couldn't comprehend how lavish it was, compared to the small kitchen in the house where she grew up.

"Good morning, Lamiae," said Violette, walking into the kitchen.

Lamiae turned around to greet Violette.

"Good morning. Are you an early riser?" said Lamiae, as she continued to whisk the eggs.

"No. Not usually. I think I am still getting used the time difference. What are you making for breakfast?" said Violette, sitting down on the black, leather-topped stool at the island bench.

"Waffles, ham and cheese croissants, toast, scrambled eggs, fried tomatoes and bacon. This will be served with percolated coffee, English tea and hot cocoa."

"Mmm, that all sounds so delicious. Can I help you make anything?"

"That would be lovely dear. Do you know how to make waffles?"

"No I don't. But I am happy to learn."

Lamiae showed her how to prepare the mixture and then how to make the waffles with the waffle iron. Violette found it easy. She loved to help in the kitchen. By the time Violette had finished, everyone was up in the house and ready for breakfast.

"Good morning Violette, Lamiae. Did you sleep well Violette?" said Emily walking into the kitchen.

"Bonjour, Madame," said Lamiae looking over her shoulder.

"Morning. Slept like a log," said Violette wiping up the mess she had made making the waffles.

"Oh, that's good. Well, it looks like breakfast is ready to be served. So why don't I show you where the dining room is, Violette?" said Emily.

Adrian and Danielle were already seated at the dining table waiting for them, when Violette entered the Parisian style dining room with Emily.

"Sit anywhere you like, dear," said Emily gesturing to the wooden table, which had ornate carved legs and would have sat about thirty people. There was an embroidered rug under it.

"Oh. OK," said Violette noticing it was set up for the four of them at one end of the table, with white lace placemats, and lots of silver cutlery. *Goodness knows why there is so much cutlery. I only need one of everything, not three.*

Sitting down next to Danielle, Violette looked around the room in amazement. Painted in an antique cream colour, with a polished bronze texture outline around the wall inserts, with a few Parisian style artwork hanging on the walls, the room was well-designed. The two crystal droplet style chandeliers hanging over the long table, lit the room elegantly. As Violette was taking in her surroundings, she noticed the spectacular view of the blue morning sky out the double glass doors, which also opened up out onto the back lawn and gardens. *Can this house get any better? Everything is so extravagant.*

"How are you this morning, girls?" asked Adrian.

Violette and Danielle said, "Good," at the same time, then looked at each other and giggled. Truthfully, they all looked like they could use more sleep.

Adrian chuckled. "Yeah we all look like we need a decent night's sleep, no? The jet lag usually takes a few days to get over."

It wasn't long before the food was brought in by Lamiae and placed into bain-maries, which were situated on a sideboard, next to the dining table.

"Help yourselves to breakfast, girls. You can have anything you want," said Emily.

Danielle was first out of her seat. She was always hungry.

"Mmm, this all looks so good. Thanks Lamiae," said Danielle.

"You are welcome, dear," said Lamiae. She left them all to enjoy their breakfast feast.

"What are you going to have?" said Violette, trying to deciding what to eat.

"Maybe some waffles first," said Danielle, eyeing them off.

"I made the waffles this morning," gloated Violette.

"Right. Well in that case... I might try something else. Don't want to get sick," teased Danielle with a smirk on her face.

"Hey..." said Violette, bumping her sister's shoulder.

"Only kidding, sis," said Danielle, selecting a waffle and taking it back to her seat.

"Once we have finished breakfast, we will show you around the house and grounds, girls," said Adrian cutting up his bacon.

"Cool," said Violette.

Secretly she was really looking forward to seeing outside the most. Maybe she would come across that mysterious guy again.

"I can't wait to see what the rest of the house looks like," said Danielle, excited. Never in her wildest dreams did she think she would ever live in a house like the Lachance residence.

After they had finished their breakfast, Danielle and Violette picked up their plates to carry them to the kitchen.

"Girls, you don't need to take your plates out. Lamiae will do that. Leave them on the table," said Emily.

"Are you sure, Emily? We're not used to leaving our dishes for someone else," said Danielle.

Emily and Adrian smiled at each other.

"Yes, that's OK, dear. Lamiae will be back soon to take all of this out. Come on, why don't we show you around the house?" said Emily, gesturing toward the doorway.

I am not complaining, but this will take some getting used to, thought Violette.

As Emily and Adrian showed Violette and Danielle around the house, they watched with delight the girls' facial expressions of excitement as they entered each room and discovered its history. Each room had high elegant ceilings, beautiful Parisian paintings and tapestries.

"I love this room," said Violette, looking around at the wall to wall assortment of maps, books and magazines for them to peruse.

"Yes. It's one of my favourites too," said Adrian. "I love to read and basically anything to do with history."

"Let's go upstairs and show the girls your office," said Emily to Adrian.

"You have an office here?" queried Danielle.

"Yes. As you know I am a dealer in cultural and historical artefacts. I often work from home. But most mornings I work at the Louvre," said Adrian proudly.

"Truth be told girl, it's a bit of a mess up there," joked Emily.

"Don't believe a word she is saying. Plus, we have been away for a few months, so I haven't had time to go through everything. Anyway, come take a look," said Adrian.

By the time Violette and Danielle had toured through the whole house and discussed each room in detail with their foster parents, it was mid-morning. Lamiae had already prepared for them an assortment of cakes with all different types of fillings, which was waiting for them back in the dining room.

With a look of concern as she sat down, Emily said, "You girls are very quiet today. Is there anything wrong?"

"No…there is nothing wrong Emily. It's… well… we are not used to such a lavish lifestyle and it will probably take us a bit of time to get used to all this," said Violette looking at Danielle for support. "I can't believe how lucky we are to be in such a lovely house like this."

Danielle nodded in agreement, as she fumbled with her napkin under the table.

Emily looked at Adrian and held his hand, and then back at the girls.

"I thought as much. I remember feeling the same way when I first moved in here after we got married. We are hoping that once you both have been here for a while, the house will feel like home to you. Please, just give it some time. Always remember this is your home too, and you can use any room you want," said Emily.

"Thank you both for helping us both to feel at home here. I am sure that in time, Violette and I will start to feel comfortable living here," said Danielle, looking from Emily to Adrian as she spoke. "We do love you both dearly and appreciate everything you have done for us, though."

Emily and Adrian got out of their seats and walked around the table to give Violette and Danielle a hug.

"We have grown so fond of you girls over the past four months, and we really love having you around. If you ever need to talk over anything about your parents or anything at all, please don't hesitate to come and see one of us," said Emily.

Danielle and Violette both nodded.

After morning tea, Emily and Adrian showed Violette and Danielle around the grounds. With sculptured bushes and trees lining the grey concrete pathways on either side, and a statue in the middle of a fountain at the end of the luscious green lawn, Violette and Danielle looked at each other and smiled as they walked hand in hand together admiring the view. They had only seen grounds like this in magazines previously, and couldn't believe how fortunate they were now.

"This is beautiful, Emily and Adrian. I feel privileged to be here," said Violette, looking around the grounds.

"Ditto. I am in awe of this place," said Danielle.

"It sure is wonderful. I will never tire of this view. I love it out here," said Emily.

"Come on, why don't we show you both down the back of the property?" said Adrian.

"There's more?" asked Danielle, surprised.

"Yep. Follow us," said Emily, as she started to walk arm in arm with Adrian.

As they neared the back of the property, Violette's neck started to throb. *Hmm, my neck feels tight. I mustn't have slept right,* thought Violette as she twisted her neck from side to side and massaged the back of it with her hand. Continuing to follow Adrian and Emily, and walking around the back of a steel and wooden gazebo which was painted white with a greying tin roof, Violette heard Adrian say, 'good morning' to someone. Looking up, she saw who Adrian was talking to. It was the same guy as the night before, who had been standing outside her window. With her brow furrowed, she stared at him as he walked on by, with his rifle in hand. At least this time Violette got to have a good look at him before he disappeared on her again. With his short, brown, curly hair, tall build, muscular body and good looks, she couldn't keep her eyes off him.

"Bonjour, Mesdemoiselles," said the stranger, smiling and bowing his head slightly.

"Bonjour," said Violette and Danielle together.

Watching him walk toward the house, Violette thought, *Emily and Adrian only have one groundskeeper, and he's a middle aged man who lives on the property with his elderly mother. So who is this mystery man that I keep seeing?*

"Adrian. Who is that?" asked Violette.

"Oh, that's Michael. He lives with his family, who are good friends of ours, not far from here," said Adrian. "He often comes over to shoot the vermin we have down at the back of the property."

"Oh. OK," said Violette, continuing to follow Emily and Adrian. *Hmm, Michael. Nice name. Wonder what he is like? Not into guns, though.*

In the early afternoon, Emily and Adrian requested their chauffeur to drive the four of them to Danielle and Violette's new school, Lycee International, where the girls would enrol in their classes and organise books and uniforms. The drive from Bagnolet to Saint Germain-en-Laye would take forty minutes, and Adrian wanted the girls to become familiar with the route to school.

"You girls excited about starting at the new school?" asked Adrian.

"Excited. Not the word I would describe," said Violette, as she looked to Danielle for support. She had been struggling to get enthusiastic about starting at a new school and trying to fit in.

"I had a look on the internet at Lycee International yesterday, when we were on the plane. It's very old. I suppose the best thing about it is that it has the same curriculum as Beverly Hills High," said Danielle.

God, I hope we haven't fallen too far behind. I still want to be a teacher when I graduate, thought Violette, as she heard Danielle blabber on about making new friends.

"We are nearly there," said Emily looking out the side window to the huge building which was situated in front of them.

"Wow," said Danielle, with her eyebrows raised.

"Looks like a castle," said Violette, looking out the driver's front window. *This should be interesting.*

Stepping out of the limousine, Violette looked up at the sides of the building, towards the roof, and took in her surroundings. Made up of a reddish brown brick, with cream bricks as a feature around the windows, and a dark grey metal roof, the front building looked fit for kings and queens.

"Let's go inside and see the principal," said Emily gesturing to the front door.

"Come on, sis," said Danielle, excited. Placing her arm around Violette's shoulder, they walked inside together.

With her foot tapping the floor, and her anxiety building whilst they waited for the principal, Violette decided to look around the reception notice boards with Danielle.

"Cool. They have drama classes here, Violette," said Danielle pointing to the pamphlet on the notice board.

"Great. No thanks," said Violette, unenthusiastically. Rolling her eyes, she sighed at the thought of starting anything new.

"What's wrong, sis?" said Danielle placing her arm around Violette's shoulder.

"I miss my old life. I wish we were back at Beverly Hills High. You know I don't make friends easily Danielle. Look at my anxiety rash I have on my stomach," said Violette pulling her top up a little for Danielle to see. "I feel sick in the stomach, you know? I just want to get this over and done with and go back home."

"Jesus, Vi. That rash is terrible. Is it itchy?" said Danielle, looking at Violette's stomach.

Before Violette could answer Danielle, the principal opened his office door.

"Danielle and Violette Castell," he said, looking around the reception area.

Pulling her top down, Violette and Danielle walked over to the principal.

"Yes, that is us," said Emily standing up. "Come on, girls."

"Come in," gestured the principal, as he shook their hands and they entered his office. "Take a seat, everyone."

Closing his office door, the principal took his seat on the opposite side of the wooden desk, which was overflowing with manila folders and paperwork.

"Good morning. My name is principal Lopez. Welcome to Lycee International. I believe you two girls are wanting to enrol at our school today."

"Yes, sir," said Violette and Danielle together.

"Do you have your paperwork from your old school?" said the principal.

"Yes," said Emily, handing over the girls' reports and exam results.

"Thank you. Just give me a minute to have a look at your grades," he said, placing the documents on his desk. A few minutes later he said, "Hmm, you both have done very well at Beverly Hills High. So are you both wanting to carry on with the same type of classes here at Lycee?"

"Yes, sir," said both girls.

"OK. Well, why don't we organise a tour of the school for you this afternoon and sort out your books, and uniforms etcetera? I will have my receptionist draw up your time table and give to you before you go home."

"Thank you," said Emily, standing up. "I wanted to speak with you about the fees as well. If you don't mind."

"Oh yes. The fees. I will ask my receptionist to speak with you about that, whilst I organise for someone to give Violette and Danielle a tour. Was there anything else you wanted to ask?"

"No. I think that is all for now," said Emily, looking at Adrian.

"OK. Right this way, Mesdemoiselles," said principal Lopez, opening the door.

"That was pretty full on," said Violette, watching the school disappear from view as the limousine pulled out the parking lot. "But the best news is that we don't start at Lycee for another week."

"What about if we do some sight-seeing this week, sis?" said Danielle.

"Sounds good. As long as it's OK with Emily and Adrian," said Violette looking in their direction.

"Course it's OK with us. You girls need to become more familiar with the area anyway," said Adrian.

Pulling into the driveway of the Lachance residence, the driver parked next to the front doors of the house.

"Did you know in France you can drive a moped when you are 14 years old?" asked Adrian.

"No," said Violette and Danielle at the same time.

"Well, guess what... these are yours to ride whenever you want," said Adrian pointing to the two mopeds parked near the front door.

"Really... oh wow! Thank you Adrian and Emily. You are so kind to us," said Danielle. Tears of happiness welled in her eyes, as she gave them both a hug, and ran off to have a look and try out her moped.

Violette screamed with joy. "Thank you so much!"

She jumped out the car and ran over to have a look at her moped. Excited, she swung her leg over the moped and took a seat. Pretending to start it up and rev the engine, Violette then unfastened the helmet from the moped and tried it on for size.

"We are also going to give you a monthly allowance of one hundred Euros so you could buy fuel for your mopeds or any other items you wish to purchase," said Adrian, standing in front of the mopeds with Emily.

Talk about spoilt rotten, thought Violette.

"Thank you Emily and Adrian. This is so kind of you."

"Yes, thank you guys. I can't believe I am so lucky to have one of these babies," said Danielle smiling and tapping her moped.

"You're both very welcome. There is just one thing I ask. And that is to drive carefully," stated Emily, looking from Violette to Danielle.

"Without a doubt," said Danielle.

"You won't have to worry about me. I will drive carefully," said Violette, smiling.

Later on in the afternoon, Adrian drove Violette and Danielle to the local police station to acquire their licenses to drive the mopeds. In France, it was a requirement of the local government for anyone driving a moped at a young age, to sit lessons prior to their licenses being granted. But because the two girls could prove that they had passed their moped licenses at their old school in LA, then they were able to obtain their licenses that day. Most days they would be chauffeur driven around in the limousine, but when they wanted to go off on their own and explore they could use their mopeds.

The rest of the afternoon was spent leaning how to defensively drive the mopeds with Adrian. He wanted the girls to become confident drivers before they left the property. With the sun setting, Adrian showed Violette and Danielle where to park their mopeds in the back shed at night.

"Here," said Adrian handing the girls some road maps and turning on the shed lights. "Before we go inside, I want to teach you how to read these road maps of the area and where to find specific places. Bagnolet is a small town, so you shouldn't find it too difficult. Then once you are confident, you can venture out into Paris further."

"Oh, OK," said Violette.

"Sounds like a good idea," said Danielle, looking over the maps on the bonnet of the limousine with Adrian. Within minutes, the girls had worked out the road system, and soothed Adrian's concern for their safety.

Chapter Three

As she wiped the sleep from her eyes, Violette sat down in front of her dressing table mirror to check her complexion. Whilst brushing her tangled hair, she had the strangest feeling that she was being watched. Feeling uncomfortable and anxious, she kept turning around in her seat to see if someone was behind her, even though she would have seen them in the mirror. Eventually walking over to the window, she pulled back the curtain, just to see if anyone was out there on her balcony. But no one was there. Just the clear morning blue sky.

Violette took a deep breath, and rubbed the back of her neck with her fingers to ease her tension, as she stared out into the garden and tried to relax her thoughts. *Paranoid much...? What is wrong with me? Girl, you watch way too many scary movies.*

After having a much needed hot shower, Violette decided to go and see if Danielle was up. Putting her head around the corner of Danielle's bedroom doorway, she noticed Danielle was sitting up in bed, yawning.

"Good morning, sleepy head. Are you getting up soon?" teased Violette, walking into the room and sitting on Danielle's bed.

"I still feel tired this morning," said Danielle, yawning. "I might just stick around the house today and catch up on some sleep and relaxation. What about you…what are you going to do today?"

"Well… I was thinking I might take a ride on my moped and have a look around France. Would you like to come along with me? Please…you can read road maps better than me. Come on. Say yes," pleaded Violette.

Rolling her eyes at Violette, Danielle said, "Oh, alright… we don't want you getting lost now, do we? Meet you in the dining room in say, thirty minutes. After breakfast we can go out all day if you like."

"Are you sure? I thought you were tired," said Violette, with a smirk on her face.

"Funny, aren't you… we may as well go enjoy ourselves whilst we can. I can relax and sleep tonight anyway," said Danielle.

"Great. I'll meet you in the dining room in thirty."

Violette ran off to get her bag from her room and then continued downstairs to the kitchen.

Entering the kitchen, Violette could see Lamiae was busy as usual making breakfast.

"Good morning, Lamiae. How are you this morning?"

"Hello, my girl… I am going really good this morning, and would love your help, if that is ok."

"What can I do for you?"

She handed Violette the waffle making machine.

"Thanks Violette. You're a lifesaver."

"No problem," said Violette. pouring the waffle mixture into the hot waffle iron. She was becoming quite the expert.

"How are you this morning Violette?" asked Lamiae.

"Yeah, good. I think," said Violette. But all Violette could think about was how she felt uneasy for the past two mornings. Luckily these feelings always seemed to subside after a while.

"Everything ok?" asked Lamiae.

"I think so... it's... just... well, since I have been here... oh don't worry, it's silly what I am thinking anyway," said Violette, annoyed at herself for even bringing it up with Lamiae.

"I don't think it's silly, Violette. Something is bothering you," said Lamiae, looking up from whisking the eggs. "If it helps, I am a good listener."

"Nah, it's nothing Lamiae. Everything is alright. So...what are we having for breakfast this morning?" asked Violette, trying to change the subject.

"The same as yesterday morning, my dear," said Lamiae, pouring the mixture into a hot fry pan.

"Oh, OK," said Violette. *Should I tell her I feel like I am being watched? Don't be stupid Violette. Lamiae is going to think you are imagining things.*

After Violette made the waffles, she helped Lamiae carry the breakfast into the dining room, where Danielle, Emily and Adrian were sitting at the dining table chatting.

"Oh, here. Let me give you ladies a hand," said Emily, pushing her chair back and standing up.

"We have it covered here Emily. You sit," said Violette, waving her away.

"Alright," said Emily sitting back on her chair. "Thank you."

Placing the food in the bain-maries, Lamiae said, "Thank you for your help, my dear."

"No problem. Anytime," said Violette, walking over to the table.

"Breakfast is served," said Lamiae. She then left them to enjoy it.

"From what Danielle tells us, it sounds like you girls are going to have a great time today sight-seeing," said Emily, turning to Violette. "Just promise us that you will be careful driving around."

"We will be careful. Don't worry," said Violette, sitting down at the table.

"You both seem refreshed this morning. How did you both sleep last night?" asked Emily, looking from Violette to Danielle.

"I slept really well. But I am still trying to get used to having people around us. I could have sworn this morning that someone was outside my window. I think it's all the different people you have working here," said Violette.

"Who would be outside your window, sis? You are just being paranoid," said Danielle. Violette gave Danielle a dirty look.

"Yeah, it takes a bit of getting used to having all these servants around," said Emily, placing her hand on Violette's. "I remember what it was like when I first moved into the house. It took me a while to settle in."

I hope that is all it is. Because this is starting to creep me out, thought Violette.

After breakfast, and some final instructions on the traffic in France from Emily and Adrian, Violette and Danielle walked down to the back garage and collected their mopeds.

As they neared the front door, Adrian and Emily were waiting for them.

"Don't forget these," said Adrian, handing Danielle the road maps.

"Whoops. Thanks Adrian," said Danielle. "Here, Violette."

Taking the maps from Danielle, Violette placed them in her backpack and then put on her helmet.

"See you later Emily and Adrian," said Violette.

"Bye. Have a good time today girls. Don't hesitate to ring us on our cell phones if you get stuck or need anything. By the way—we are having a special dinner tonight. A few guests will be coming over who have been dying to meet you both. So make sure you are home by say… 5pm? That will give you plenty of time to shower and get dressed into something really nice for our guests," said Emily.

"OK," said Danielle, nodding.

"Oh, right. See you at 5pm then," said Violette, sighing. She wasn't ready to meet new people yet. "And thank you once again for my moped."

"You are most welcome. Drive safely, girls," said Adrian.

With the sun shining through the clouds, and the feeling of freedom as the wind blew through their hair, Violette and Danielle rode confidently side by side each other, pointing out statues, monuments, and sometimes giggling at the sights they come across as they checked out Paris.

Navigating the roundabout at the Arc De Triomphe was a nightmare, and they had many cars beeping them to move out the way, because they used the wrong lanes to exit off. This, they would have to master another day. After the ordeal of the busy Paris traffic, Violette and Danielle decided to stop off for lunch at a quaint café which was on their way to the Petit Palais.

Taking a seat at an empty veneer table, which was in the far corner of the café near the window, Violette waited for Danielle to return with their lunch. With the café packed to the rafters inside and out, and the ordering counter three deep with customers, including Danielle, Violette decided to get out the maps from her backpack, to try and plot out their next sight-seeing expedition that afternoon. Looking out the window, across the asphalt road, Violette tried to get her bearings as to which street they were on. Sighting a street sign on the side of a building, she looked back at the map, then worked out how they would get to the Petit Palais.

Not bad for someone who couldn't read a map before, thought Violette, quietly hugging herself.

Looking toward the counter, Violette could see Danielle finally getting served. *About time.*

Whilst waiting for her food, Violette looked around the decoupage style café, and noticed that a lot of young people were dining there. *Looks like we lucked out here. Maybe this is a popular place for people our age.* Scanning the room, she did a double take when she spotted across the other side of the room her mysterious guy, Michael. *What is he doing here?*

Seated at a table with another guy and girl who looked around his age, he was chatting and laughing. Ruggedness and confidence radiated from him, as Violette watched him run his hand through his curly black, shoulder length hair. The more Violette looked at him, the more she liked what she saw. Looking away quickly and blushing with embarrassment, her heart skipped a beat. But she had to look back. Something about this guy attracted her to him. Taking a deep breath, she glanced at him once again.

But this time he was actually looking her way. Nodding he mouthed the word 'hello' and took a sip of his coffee.

Violette nodded and smiled back. With her heart racing, she could feel the blood rushing to her face. *So good looking. Look away. Look away.* Fumbling with the road map, she pretended to study it. And when she took a sneak peek, a few minutes later, he had turned back to his friends and was chatting again.

By the time Danielle had arrived with their lunch, Violette was beside herself. Folding up the road map Violette said quietly, "Hey… you know that guy we met at the house, Michael? He is over there with some friends."

"Where?" said Danielle, putting the tray on the table and sitting down.

"Over there," said Violette pointing. When she looked, he was gone. With a furrowed brow she shook her head in bewilderment.

Danielle shrugged her shoulders, dismissed the idea and sat down.

"This must be a popular café. I can't believe how long it took me to get a couple of sodas and our lunch."

"Yeah, you were gone a while. Lunch looks good though. I am starving. Let's eat," said Violette, taking her lunch off the tray.

"Hey…did you want to go out to a night club tomorrow night? I have been looking online for what's in the area for entertainment, and they have a few good night clubs in Bagnolet. Apparently the band 'Train' is going to be playing at a night club called 'Fire and Ice' tomorrow night," said Danielle.

"I would love to go," said Violette. 'Train' was one of her favourite bands.

"So it's a date then. We can ask Emily and Adrian when we get home today and see if it's OK for us to go. Maybe we can get the chauffeur to drop us off and collect us later," said Danielle, flipping the lid on her soda.

"Sounds like a plan," said Violette, picking up her tuna and salad sandwich.

After they finished their lunch, Violette showed Danielle the route she had marked out on the road map so far.

"Looks good, sis. Let's head out," said Danielle, standing up.

Nodding and placing the maps in her back pack, Violette and Danielle headed across the busy road, to where their mopeds were parked.

"I'll follow you," said Danielle, looking around at the busy traffic and realising that they wouldn't be able to ride side by side.

"OK," said Violette, pulling on her helmet and starting her moped. Violette had marked out on the map the Petit Palais, the Eiffel Tower and the Louvre Museum for them to see that afternoon. And anything else that they might see was a bonus.

Walking out of the Petit Palais, Violette checked her phone to see if she had any messages. "Geez, it's 4.13, Danielle. We had better head off home," said Violette.

"Really? We haven't been here that long, have we?" said Danielle pulling her phone out of her pocket and checking the time.

"Yep. Looks like the traffic is quite heavy, so I will follow you on the way home," said Violette.

"Sure," said Danielle, nodding. "Hey… I wonder who the dinner guests are tonight that Emily and Adrian have coming over to meet us."

"Hmm. Hopefully they're nice," said Violette. *Probably some boring oldies, with the same old questions for us.*

On the ride home, Violette watched the sky become grey and gloomy and felt the air start to chill. Turning into their street, the wind whipped past her and made her shiver. *Wish I had bought a jacket. Lucky we are not far from home.*

With the mopeds coming to a halt at the front gate of the Lachance residence, Danielle tapped in the code on the key pad to open the gate.

"Looks like it might rain," said Danielle, as she felt a few drops hit her skin and looked up into the clouds.

"Yeah. I think we made it home just in time," said Violette.

Riding around the back of the house, Violette and Danielle parked their mopeds in the shed.

"Ooh, I feel a bit stiff and sore from riding all day," stated Danielle, as she got off her moped.

"Yeah, me too," said Violette, rubbing her inner legs. "I had such a fun day though. What about you?"

"Same. I can't believe how awesome Paris is. Some of the museums and sights we have seen today… wow, sis. How lucky we are," said Danielle, hanging her helmet on the moped's steering grip.

"Yeah… I wish we could have seen the Eiffel Tower today. Maybe we can go out another day and have a look," said Violette.

"Mmm, but now we live here, we can see it anytime we like," said Danielle.

"Yep. Well I suppose we had better head inside and get ready for tonight," said Violette, placing her helmet on the moped seat. "I wonder what's for dinner? I'm starving."

"Hmm. Hopefully something nice," said Danielle, with a furrowed brow.

Walking through the back entrance to the Lachance residence, Violette and Danielle didn't notice anyone about, so they went straight up to their bedrooms to get ready for their dinner guests.

Violette pushed open her bedroom door, and fumbled for the light switch. When her eyes focused on the room, she first noticed that her bed had been made and the curtains were pulled closed. *I wonder who made my bed?* She then noticed something hanging near her walk in wardrobe. With surprise, she realised that it was a dress. Running over to it, she felt the soft material of the exquisite blue gown with her fingers. *Oh, wow.* It had thick straps, a love heart bodice with a flowing skirt, which was knee length. Taking it off the hanger, she placed it up against herself and whirled around the room with it. *This is beautiful. I must show Danielle.*

With gown in hand, she ran next door to Danielle room. "Do you believe this. Emily and Adrian have brought me this beautiful gown to wear?" She then noticed Danielle's dress as well. It was very similar to hers in style except Danielle's was floral.

"I can't believe how lovely and elegant they are," said Danielle, noticing Violette's gown as well. "I can't wait to try mine on." Excited, Danielle placed it against herself and twirled around the room with it.

As they were looking over their gowns and chatting about how much they must have cost, Emily walked into Danielle's room.

"Hi girls. So…what do you think of the gowns? Do you like them? These were made by a famous French designer especially for you both," said Emily, watching their expressions.

"Thank you Emily. I love mine," said Danielle, as she gave Emily a hug.

"This is so exquisite Emily. Thank you so much," said Violette, hugging Emily.

"You are welcome. I am glad you like them," said Emily. "They are to wear for dinner tonight."

"How was your day of sight-seeing?" asked Emily, sitting on Danielle's bed.

"Paris is so beautiful Emily. I can't believe how lucky I am to be here, let alone live here," said Violette.

"And the food is to die for. I believe I will fit in perfectly here," said Danielle, dreamily smiling.

"That's great, dears. You will have to tell me all about your day later on. But now you had better go have your showers and get ready for our guests, who are arriving at 7 o' clock," said Emily.

"OK. See you later on," said Violette, walking towards the doorway.

"Thanks once again for my dress. I love it," said Danielle, giving Emily a hug.

"You are welcome. Now off you go and get ready," said Emily.

Whilst Danielle and Violette were getting ready, it was all hands on deck downstairs. Lamiae and her family were in the kitchen preparing the meals for the night, and setting the dining room table. Everything smelt so good as it wafted through the house.

When the doorbell rang, Violette and Danielle ran down the stairs to greet the guests at the front doors.

Opening the door, Adrian said, "Come in, come in, my friends. Before you get wet."

As everyone walked in, Adrian took their coats and hung them on the coat rack next to the door.

"Violette, Danielle, these are our very dear friends Mr. and Mrs. Gramaze—Renee and William," said Emily.

The girls both said, "Hello," and shook the Gramazes' hands.

"Nice to meet you both," said Renee.

Violette and Danielle smiled politely.

When Violette looked behind Mr. Gramaze to greet the next guest, she couldn't believe who was standing there. It was the guy she kept seeing in the gardens, and again that day at the café. Michael. Violette couldn't take her eyes off him. *Wow... He is so cute in those tight jeans. Oh and the way that striped shirt looks on him. Hmm... sizzle. Breathe, Violette, breathe.*

"Girls, this is Michael, Grayson and Annabelle, and they are Mr. and Mrs. Gramaze's cousins," said Emily.

Michael took Violette's hand and said, "Bonjour mademoiselle. Finally, we are properly introduced." His eyes were a mesmerising blue and his touch made Violette feel warm all over. With her heart beating fast, she started to blush when he didn't let go of her hand.

Forgetting that Violette and Danielle had briefly met Michael in the back gardens, Emily turned to Violette and said, "Have you two met already?"

"Yeah. Remember in the gardens? And today I saw them in a café when Danielle and I stopped for a lunch," said Violette, pulling her hand away from Michael's grasp.

"Oh, that's right. Silly me. Forgetful memory. I am not surprised though that you saw each other in a café today. Paris is such a small place," said Emily smiling.

Annabelle and Grayson shook Danielle and Violette's hands and Grayson said, "It's nice to meet you both."

"Hello. It's nice to meet you too," said Danielle, shaking Grayson's hand, but not letting go. Her eyes were fixated on him.

"Hello... sorry, Grayson, you will have to excuse my sister. She is a bit of an incurable romantic when it comes to men," said Violette, forcing Danielle to let go of his hand.

Rolling her eyes at Violette, Danielle blushed and then shook Annabelle's hand.

"That's OK," said Grayson, politely.

"Let's all go into the dining room, and I can pour everyone some drinks," said Adrian.

"Something smells really nice," said Mrs. Gramaze, smiling.

"We are having something special tonight. Lamiae is surprising us," said Emily, taking Renee by the arm.

"Looking forward to it," said Mrs. Gramaze, walking into the dining room arm in arm with Emily.

As they walked into the dining room, Michael turned to Violette and said, "You look very lovely tonight. Is that dress new?"

"Um...thanks. Yes, it's a new dress that Emily brought me today. Back home we never had clothes like this," said Violette, feeling special.

"Where are you from? You have an American accent?" asked Michael, as he pulled out a chair for Violette to sit on.

"Los Angeles. We used to live near Century City," said Violette, taken back by his gentlemanly gesture. "Err... and now we live here." Taking her seat, she nervously fiddled with the cutlery, as Michael sat next to her.

"Oh, OK. I know where that is. I have been to LA a few times. Umm...I want to say that I am sorry for your loss of your mother and father. Must have been a horrible time for you both," said Michael, looking into Violette's eyes with concern.

"Thanks...you never know when your world is going to be turned upside down by something like that happening. It wasn't the best time in my life; that's for sure," said Violette, looking down at her hands.

"If you ever need to talk, I am a good listener," said Michael.

"Thanks," said Violette. But she was done talking about her parents' death. She just wanted a normal life and to be happy again.

Once everyone was seated at the dining table, which was set up in all its fine china, silverware and glassware for their guests, Lamiae and the servants served the dinner.

At dinner Mrs. Gramaze, who sat across the table from Violette and Danielle, asked, "Where will you be going to school, girls?"

"We are starting at Lycee International next week. Both of us are hoping to become teachers," said Danielle.

"The school also has the same curriculum as LA. So we can continue on with our studies. Hopefully where we left off," said Violette.

"That sounds great. I have heard Lycee International is a really good school, especially for the graduating students. They have a great programme there that helps you either apply for universities you like, or to help you acquire a job after you graduate," said Mrs Gramaze.

"What type of teacher did you both want to become when you graduate?" said Annabelle.

"Either an English or a Social Studies Teacher," said Violette.

"Sports Teacher. But I need to get my grade average up, so I can apply to a good University," said Danielle, knowing she had a lot of hard work head of her.

"Yeah... it sure will be interesting to see what we need to catch up on, as we haven't been to school for the past four months," said Violette remembering the emotional roller coaster they went through after their parents' funeral. "When we went to enrol yesterday, the assistant principal at Lycee International said to us that they would help us in any way they could so that we didn't fall behind. But I am looking forward to a challenge."

"So have you girls seen any of Paris yet?" asked Mrs. Gramaze.

"We went out on our mopeds today and did a bit of sight-seeing. It was fun. I can't believe how beautiful Paris is," said Danielle.

"France is such a lovely place. I am sure that Annabelle, Michael and Grayson can take you out sight-seeing soon. They are around your age, you know. So they may be able to show you some interesting things."

"Cool… that would be great," said Danielle, excited.

"I would like that," said Violette, hoping to spend some more time with Michael.

After dinner, everyone gathered in the sitting room. Renee, William, Emily and Adrian sat in the back of the room on the lounge chairs, and caught up on social issues and local gossip that Emily and Adrian had missed out on in the last four months whilst in LA. They seemed to enjoy each other's company immensely.

Standing near the window, Violette looked across the room and noticed Danielle was talking her head off to Annabelle. *She always makes friends easily. Such a socialite.* Even though Violette and Danielle were close as sisters, Violette was always envious of her sister because she was the opposite to Danielle. Violette was shy and awkward, whereas Danielle was outgoing and confident.

Startled by his voice, Violette jumped when she realised Michael and Grayson were standing beside her and she didn't even know they were there.

"Sorry… what did you say? I was off in a bit of a dream world," said Violette.

"That's OK. I was asking what are you and Danielle doing tomorrow night?" said Michael.

"Umm, we were thinking about going to a night club here called 'Fire and Ice'. My favourite band 'Train' is playing there. Why do you ask?" said Violette.

"We were wondering if you both would like to see some sights of Paris. They are really beautiful at night," said Michael.

"That's very nice of you both to offer. I will talk it over with Danielle and let you know," said Violette.

"Do you have a number I can contact you on Violette?" asked Michael.

"Umm... yes," said Violette. *He asked me for my number. Me... calm yourself girl. Calm yourself.*

They exchanged numbers.

"I have heard 'Train' is playing at 'Fire and Ice' all week long. So maybe you could go there another night. Anyway, let us know," said Grayson.

"Oh, OK. I didn't know that," said Violette. "It looks like it has stopped raining. Would you guys like to go outside for a bit of fresh air?"

"I won't. I wanted to speak with Adrian about the painting he is appraising for me. But you two go ahead," said Grayson. "I'll catch up with you both later."

"So was it you I saw here last night?" said Violette, walking out into the garden.

"Yes, it was me. Sorry if I startled you. We live only a few houses down, and I just love the gardens here. So sometimes I come and admire the view. When I saw you standing at your window, I didn't know who you were, until I asked Renee, Mrs. Gramaze. She told me about how you and Danielle have come to live with Emily and Adrian," said Michael.

"Oh, OK," said Violette. As she listened to him speak, Violette felt her heart thumping in her chest. She was glad that they were in the dark, otherwise he would have seen how rosy her cheeks were. The more she spoke with him, the more she became comfortable, and even learned that they had a lot in common.

He sure is a sweet guy. As she looked into Michael's soulful eyes, she felt a piercing pain in the back of her neck, which travelled up to her head and gave her an instant headache.

"Uh, all of a sudden I have a splitting headache and I don't feel well. Sorry Michael, but I need to go and get some type of medication to stop the pain. I will be back soon," said Violette, putting her hand up to her forehead.

"I will come with you," said Michael, as he took her hand and led her into the kitchen.

"Lamiae…could we get some medication for Violette? She has a really bad headache," said Michael as they walked into the kitchen.

"Sure."

Lamiae handed Violette some painkillers which she retrieved from the top drawer of the island bench, and a glass of water.

"Thanks, Lamiae. I can't believe how fast this pain came on. That has never happened before," said Violette, rubbing the back of her neck.

"You're welcome my dear," said Lamiae, looking at Michael, worried.

"Are you OK, Violette?" said Mrs. Gramaze, as she walked into the kitchen. She had noticed that Violette wasn't feeling well and followed them to the kitchen.

"Bit of a headache, that's all. Thank you for asking," said Violette, overwhelmed by the attention.

"Oh, that's no good. Hope you are feeling better soon, dear. Michael, we are all going home now," said Mrs. Gramaze.

"OK," said Michael.

"Thank you for a lovely dinner, Lamiae. As usual, it was delicious," said Mrs. Gramaze.

"Yes. Thank you, Lamiae," said Michael.

"You are most welcome," said Lamiae.

Walking back to the dining room, Michael said, "How are you feeling now?"

"Better…it's just about gone," said Violette.

"Well, thank you for a great evening, Violette. I am glad you are feeling better. Don't forget to ring me later about the sight-seeing tomorrow night," said Michael.

"I won't…but…do you have to leave now? I was really enjoying your company," said Violette.

Mrs. Gramaze overheard their conversation and said, "Sorry, dear, to drag Michael away. He is needed at home. I believe from speaking with Grayson that you might be going out sight-seeing with them tomorrow night. So maybe Michael can stay a bit longer then."

"OK," said Violette, as she neared the front doors, where everyone else was waiting.

"Good night Violette," said Michael, warmly.

"Thank you for a lovely evening, Emily and Adrian. We must do it again soon. Next time at our house," said Renee, giving Emily a hug goodbye.

"That would be great. We look forward to it," said Adrian, shaking William's hand.

"Was nice to meet you Violette and Danielle," said Mrs. Gramaze.

"Thanks. It was nice to meet you both too," said Violette.

"Was nice to meet you, too. Have a safe drive home," said Danielle.

After they all said their goodbyes to their guests, Danielle and Violette said their good nights to Emily and Adrian, and went upstairs to their rooms.

"Hey sis, would you like to go night sight-seeing with Michael, Grayson and Annabelle tomorrow night instead of the night club? Grayson told me that 'Train' are playing here all week, so it wouldn't matter if we went another night this week," asked Violette.

"Oh, OK. Sounds good. I suppose it's a way we could get to know them a bit better, as well as doing some more sight-seeing," said Danielle.

"Yeah. I'll give Michael a ring later and let him know we will be coming… I might go and have a bath to relax. I still have a little bit of a headache and it doesn't seem to be shifting," said Violette, rubbing her neck.

"OK." Danielle gave her a hug and said, "See you in the morning Vi."

"Night, sis," said Violette.

Lying in her warm bath tub, with bubbles all around her and her head resting against the cushion at one end, Violette hashed over the conversations she had had with Michael earlier, and how he had made her heart race when she was near him. Violette was excited about seeing him the next night, but a little bit apprehensive as well.

When Violette finally got into bed, she rang Michael to let him know that they would be coming the next night, but his phone went to voicemail. So she left a message. Turning off the lamp, Violette lay there staring at the ceiling and thinking about the night, and Michael. She hoped he liked her just as much as she liked him.

Chapter Four

Michael watched the moon, which was low in the sky, disappear behind the clouds, through the window of the black limousine. He thought about the enjoyable evening he had had at the Lachance residence. Most of all, he remembered Violette. The soft touch of her hand, her beautiful blue eyes, the sweet smell of her perfume; Frangipani. But why did he suddenly feel attracted to a human?

"Hey… did you see what happened to Violette tonight?" said Michael, leaning into Grayson who was sitting beside him.

"Nope. What happened, bro?" said Grayson, with raised eyebrows.

"She said that all of a sudden she had a pain in the back of her neck and had a splitting headache."

"Was she alright by the time we left?"

"Yeah. She took some headache medication and the pain went away as quickly as it started," said Michael, shrugging.

"Humph. You know women bro; they are different," said Grayson, as he bumped Michael's shoulder.

Sitting across from Michael and Grayson, with her head on William's shoulder and eyes closed, Renee listened to their conversation about Violette. Recognising the symptoms that a female Lepidoptera vampire had when she met her life partner,

Renee sat up straight and said, "She did seem attracted to you Michael. More so than a human would."

"What are you saying, my love?" said William, curious.

"Maybe Violette is a Lepidoptera vampire. I remember feeling the same way about you, William. When I met you, the attraction was instant," said Renee, looking at William.

"Come on, Renee. I think we would all know if she was a Lepidoptera, don't you?" said Grayson.

"A female Lepidoptera… there hasn't been one born for years. I think Grayson is correct. We would know if a new female was around us," said William, dismissing the idea. Placing his arm around Renee, he pulled her in close and kissed her forehead. "You are such a romantic."

Renee tried to dismiss her thoughts. She knew this could all be one big coincidence. But she made a promise to herself to check Violette's neck for the butterfly tattoo that was known to their kind, the next time she saw her, just to be certain.

"I thought that Danielle and Violette seemed very nice… you two boys have you work cut out for you though. From reading their thoughts it looks like they have the hots for you both," teased Annabelle.

"Hmm, I heard," said Grayson, rolling his eyes. His life was chaotic enough and he didn't need a human ogling over him.

"I hope they will come sight-seeing tomorrow night. It's fun showing new people around France. I just love to watch their faces as they see some of the sites for the first time," said Annabelle excited.

Michael smiled. Even though Annabelle was a warrior, she still had the feminine side to her, and liked to shop and chat like most women.

"Hopefully we don't come across any Debauched vampires tomorrow night. They could ruin everything for us, if they make a play for the humans. I am starting to wonder whether it was a good idea asking Violette and Danielle to see the sights with us. We don't need them finding out about our kind," said Grayson.

"Yeah... it's been a long time since we have taken any humans out with us. We just need to keep our eyes and ears open," said Michael, anxiously.

"If we get into trouble, we can always call for back up. We should be alright," said Annabelle, shrugging.

"I don't want any trouble when you take them out. Heads will roll if any human finds out about our kind; you all know this," said William, authoritatively to his family.

"What was of concern to me tonight was when Violette told us that she and Danielle were going to that night club 'Fire and Ice'. That is vamp city and the Debauched vampires hang out in huge numbers there. I think it might be a good idea if we go with them to keep them safe," said Grayson.

"Good idea Grayson. As these girls are new to France, you will need to point out to them where are the safe places to go. I will leave that in your capable hands," said William.

Grayson nodded.

"Yes, Sire."

Arriving home, William was first out the car with Renee, and the others followed. Opening the front wrought iron and wooden architectural doors, William said, "Before you three head out tonight, we need to check in with Brock."

Brock was their IT specialist, whom everyone relied on when it came to finding the Debauched vampires and the trouble they caused each night. It had been quiet lately, which usually meant something big was about to go down. The Gramaze family knew they needed to keep their eyes and ears open.

"There will be a meeting in the operations room in five minutes. We need to find out what the Debauched are up to prior to you all going out tonight. I want these fuckers stopped," said William, with his features tightening as he walked off.

William was the leader of the Lepidoptera vampires in France, and was one of only a few, of the eldest vampires, left around the world. Descendent from the very first blood line of the Lepidoptera, he was well respected amongst their kind for his strength and integrity.

With his family assembled at the long, wooden table in the operations room, and waiting instructions from their leader, William said, "Tonight when you are out on patrol, I want you to go down to the docks, the night clubs, and the warehouse districts. Your assigned areas will be put up in the combat room, on the whiteboard. By checking out these locations we should at least come across some Debauched to exterminate. Or better yet, torture for some information on what these mothers are up to. They are too quiet for my liking and I know from experience that they are up to something."

"Whilst you were out at dinner tonight, I have been going over CCTV footage in these areas, and it seems quiet," said Brock, standing up and plugging his laptop cord into the monitor on the wall, to show his family the areas he had searched. "But it's only early, and as we know, they do tend to come out later in the evening."

"Right… that's all for now. Be ready to go in ten minutes," William grunted.

Checking the whiteboard in the combat room, Michael, Grayson and Annabelle noticed they had been placed together that night to patrol the city centre. Bumping fists with the other two Annabelle said, "What game did you want to play with any of the Debauched tonight?"

She always like to play cat and mouse games with the Debauched when they caught them, before she decapitated them.

"We have to find the bastards first," stated Grayson, collecting his weapons of choice.

Shoving his sword into its sheath on his waist, Michael's thoughts were distracted, if for only a minute, by the vision of Violette in the beautiful dress she had worn earlier. Shaking his head, he knew he needed to focus on the task at hand, and that was to protect humans from the Debauched.

"Tunnel or pavement tonight?" said Michael to Grayson. As Grayson was second in command, it was his decision to make.

"We haven't been down the tunnels for a while. Maybe we might find some action down there," said Grayson hopeful. He was always in the mood for a decent showdown with the Debauched.

The tunnels they were about to enter were more like sewers. The stench of faeces and the skinny little rats running everywhere kept most humans out of the tunnels. Walking down the cobbled stone steps that led to the concrete lined tunnels, Grayson put his hand up to stop Annabelle and Michael from walking any further. Listening for a few seconds as they stood on the steps, the Gramaze knew all too well what the sound was. Waving Annabelle forward to check out what was going on further down the tunnel, Michael and Grayson stayed out of sight, but close enough for back up.

Quietly running down the side of the tunnel, trying to keep out of the putrid water, Annabelle came across a Debauched who was feeding on a human. Annabelle stood in the shadows watching the human thrash his legs about as the Debauched vampire held him down on the ground with one hand and savagely suck the blood from his forearm. As she got closer to the action, Annabelle noticed four more Debauched standing around. They each seemed to be waiting for their turn at draining the human.

"What the fuck do you think you are doing, asshole?" said Annabelle, coming out of the shadows and getting closer to them with her hand on her sword.

"Fuck off, Lepidoptera. He is ours," said the tallest of the Debauched vamps, looking up from his prey.

"Yours. Humph. I don't think so," said Annabelle, rushing toward him with her sword drawn to behead him.

Thinking that they could take one lonely Lepidoptera down, four Debauched ran toward her swinging their swords. But when they saw Grayson and Michael coming toward them as well, it stopped them mid-flight. Holding their stance, the young inexperienced Debauched vamps didn't realise they didn't stand a chance against the Gramaze.

With sword drawn and running toward them, Annabelle took out the first Debauched. When his headless body fell to the ground, it disintegrated. Running at the second one, she found he wasn't so easy to terminate and was a great adversary. The other two were no match for Grayson and Michael. With the power and strength which the Gramaze family had gained from many years of combat and from generations of Lepidoptera knowledge, the two Debauched were obliterated from society in a split second. The look on the inexperienced Debauched vamps' faces as they were beheaded was one of surprise. When Michael turned to see Annabelle struggling, he ran toward her and put his sword through the Debauched vamp's back. With the young Debauched now distracted, this gave Annabelle an opportunity to decapitate him.

Watching his mate fall to the ground and disintegrate, the Debauched who was feeding on the unconscious human, decided to flee. Running for his life down the middle of tunnel through the stinking water, he soon was confronted by Grayson, who was waiting for him as he turned the corner. With sword drawn still, Grayson ran the blade through the Debauched vamp's chest, and then cut his head clean off with his knife. As his body fell to the ground and disintegrated, Grayson pulled the sword from his chest and wiped the blood on the leg of his black jeans. Watching his ashes flow down the sewer water, Grayson looked up to see Michael coming toward him with the human in his arms and Annabelle walking beside him.

"What would you like me to do with the human, Grayson?" asked Michael.

"Is he alive?"

"Barely."

Checking the young man's weak pulse, Grayson noticed that he was dressed in what looked like battle gear. His senses were telling him that the human was not a vampire, even though he had a belt that carried knives and a sheath for a sword. But they were all missing.

"Lay him down over there," said Grayson, pointing to flat piece of board on the sewer floor.

Nodding once, Michael carried the human over to the side of the sewer. Kneeling down beside the young man, Grayson checked his pockets for some identification. Pulling a wallet from his jeans, Grayson found an identification card from a local college.

"Daniel Fletcher," said Grayson, holding it up to the light coming from the tunnel entrance. "He is only seventeen years old. What is he doing down here and dressed like this?"

Pulling his own mobile phone out of his pocket, Grayson rang William.

"Yes," said William, abruptly answering the phone.

"Sire…we may have a new Lepidoptera male here. He is barely alive. What would you like us to do with him?" said Grayson.

Before William replied, Michael, Annabelle and Grayson heard footsteps coming towards them. Hanging up his phone and putting it back in his jeans pocket, Grayson drew his sword. Michael and Annabelle did the same but stood guard in front of the human. When the footsteps grew louder, William came into view.

"Let me take a look at the human," said William, as he pushed passed them. Kneeling beside him he noticed the bite marks on his forearm. "Debauched?"

"Yes, Sire," said Grayson.

"I will take care of this situation. You three need to carry on with your patrol. I want a full report though when you return," grunted William, as he checked the boy's neck for the butterfly tattoo.

They all nodded once and walked off in the direction of the city.

Picking the boy up in his arms, William ran, with vampire speed, through the tunnels back to the Gramaze house. He had alerted the medical team back at the house of his return with the young man.

Why is this boy out here on his own? I wonder who his master is? His butterfly hasn't fully formed yet, so maybe he doesn't have a family yet, thought William, anxious to find some answers.

Laying the boy down on a bed that had been prepared by Renee, the medical team stepped in and hooked him up to a blood drip. Checking him over, they ascertained that he had a stab wound to his abdomen, and that his right leg was swollen, due to it being broken.

"I want a guard on him 24/7," said William, turning to Brock.

"Yes, Sire."

"Advise me when he wakes," said William, to the medical team as he walked out the room.

"Yes, Sire," said the doctor knowing the boy would heel quickly, being a vampire.

Following William out the room, Renee closed the door behind her.

"William... wait up," said Renee, chasing after him.

"What can I do for you my love?" said William.

"This boy... I wonder how long he has been on the streets? Does he have a master?" asked Renee, with raised eyebrows.

"I don't have any answers yet. As soon as he wakes, I can question him. One thing I do know is that he hasn't fully transformed yet. But I don't know whether he has a coven or not. From the look of his weapon holster that was around his waist, I would say he has been in combat before. Anyway, my love, I don't want you worrying about this," said William, running hand down the side of Renee's face.

Leaning into his hand as it brushed the side of her face, she said, "He is one of us William. So I would like to think that you are considering taking him into our coven. That's if he doesn't already belong to another," said Renee.

"Quite right, my love," said William kissing her forehead. "I need to go and attend to some coven business. See you later on."

"Alright," said Renee, watching him walk away.

That night out on patrol, not much else happened for Grayson, Michael and Annabelle. Besides some heated arguments between drunken humans outside the night clubs, and a few intoxicated young women falling over in the streets, it was pretty quiet. No Debauched in sight.

Waking, Violette rolled over and checked her phone to see if Michael had replied to her message from last night. Sure enough, there was a text message from him saying, '*We will pick you both up at 6.30pm.*' With a smile from ear to ear, she lay there, excited at the prospect of seeing him again.

By the time Violette decided to get out of bed, it was mid-morning. She had been surfing the internet and chatting to her friends back home on social media all morning and had lost track of time. Remembering that Adrian was at work that day, and Emily had said she was going shopping, and Danielle was sleeping in, Violette decided to stay in her room to label her books and get her new laptop ready for school the next week. Within an hour, she had finished and could feel her stomach starting to rumble from lack of food.

Opening her bedroom door, the delicious aroma of food hit her nose. Walking down the stairs, she followed the smell to the kitchen. Entering the kitchen Violette spotted Michael sitting at the island bench chatting with Lamiae.

"Hello Michael. I didn't know you were here," said Violette, sitting next to him at the bench.

"Bonjour Violette. I often come and see Lamiae as she is the best cook in Bagnolet. I have known Lamiae since I was a small child. She is like a second mom to me," said Michael.

Lamiae smiled with appreciation of what Michael had said.

"Good morning Violette," said Lamiae.

"Morning Lamiae. I hope I wasn't interrupting anything… I can come back later if you want to speak with Lamiae by yourself. It's always nice to have someone to talk with about things," said Violette, trying to be polite.

"No that's OK. I can talk with Lamiae later. Anyway, I am sure Lamiae is busy, so I shouldn't interrupt her whilst she is making lunch," said Michael.

"That's alright, Michael. Come down to my cottage later and we can have a chat then," said Lamiae.

"OK. Thanks Lamiae," said Michael. "What have you got planned for the rest of the day, Violette?"

"Well, after lunch I was going to take a walk in the gardens. Would you like to join me?" said Violette. Her heart was beating so fast when Michael was near. *He will probably say no anyway.*

"I would love to, but sorry, I can't. I have some errands I need to run for Renee and William. But I will catch up with you tonight for our sightseeing tour. Make sure you wear something comfortable and warm," said Michael.

"Oh, OK," said Violette sighing in disappointment.

"Well, I had better be heading off. See you later Violette," said Michael heading towards the door. "I will catch up with you later on Lamiae."

"OK, my boy," said Lamiae stirring the sauce.

"Bye, Michael," said Violette.

From the look of sadness on Violette's face, Lamiae sensed that Violette would have preferred Michael to stay.

"Isn't he such a lovely boy?" said Lamiae.

"He sure is…can you keep a secret Lamiae?" said Violette.

"Yes. But why do you ask, child?" said Lamiae, looking up from cutting the vegetables.

"Umm… I know I only met Michael last night, but I keep dreaming about him, and wondering what he is doing. Do you think that is silly, Lamiae?" said Violette.

"No I don't think that is silly, dear. In fact, you will probably find that he feels the same way about you," said Lamiae, raising her eyebrows. "I shouldn't be telling you this, but this is what he came to talk with me about."

"Really?" said Violette smiling.

"Yes. But he is not sure if Emily and Adrian will let you see him, as he is a couple of years older than you, and because you are still at school," said Lamiae. "You are the first girl Michael has even liked in a long time, you know."

"Why?" She was curious to find out why such a good looking guy like Michael didn't already have a girlfriend.

"Since Michael's parents died a few years ago, he hasn't been the same and has kept to himself. Not going out much to meet nice girls like yourself. Their death really hit him hard. You are the first girl he has even looked at in a long time," said Lamiae. "Please don't tell Michael I said anything about any of this, will you Violette? I don't want to betray his talks with me. I just thought you would like to know."

"Your secrets are safe with me," said Violette, putting a finger to her lips. She was excited to know he felt the same way as she did. "Lamiae… I haven't had a real boyfriend before. Can you give me some pointers?"

"You just need to be yourself, dear. When the time's right for things to happen, it will. Michael is a lovely boy and he won't hurt you. In fact, you won't find a better boy than him," said Lamiae.

Just as Violette was about to say something about Michael, Danielle walked into the kitchen. Violette didn't want to discuss Michael in front of her, so she didn't continue with their conversation.

"What smells so good? I can smell it all the way to my bedroom," said Danielle sniffing the air.

"I am making Chicken Stir Fry for lunch. That's probably what you can smell. You both must be very hungry. Give me a few minutes and lunch will be served," said Lamiae.

"Can we eat in here with you today Lamiae?" asked Danielle.

"Of course you can. It would be so nice to sit and eat lunch with you both," said Lamiae stirring the sauce through the chicken and vegetables.

As Michael walked through the underground, brick walled tunnels that led from the Lachance house to the Gramaze house, he was thinking about Violette. He couldn't stop thinking about her. But one thing he was worried about was William, and what he would say if he found out Michael was thinking about Violette as being anything but a friend. He had to try and keep his thoughts to himself, so no one could read his mind. William had always forbidden any romance between humans and vampires in his coven. Amongst the Lepidoptera vampires in the Gramaze house, it was common practice for the males to take a mate that was one of their own kind, because there were so many complications for humans and vampires to have any sort of life together. And Michael knew this, but he couldn't help himself, when it came to Violette. She was different.

Chapter Five

"Stop being ridiculous, Annabelle. We don't want to hear your thoughts on Violette and Danielle, and what they think of us," said Grayson, waiting for the door to open. It was six-thirty in the evening and Michael, Grayson, Annabelle and Taiven were waiting for the door to open at the Lachance residence.

"Why not? You know I am right," teased Annabelle. "Humans, hey?"

"Just drop it," said Taiven, his lips pursing. He was tired of listening to her.

"Can you smell it? Here they come," said Annabelle jokingly, just as the door opened.

"Come in, come in," said Emily, pulling open the door. "The girls won't be a moment."

"Thanks, Mrs Lachance," said Michael, as he walked in with the others.

Taking one last glance in the mirror in her bedroom, Violette made sure she looked alright. She had changed at least four times that night, before she finally picked out jeans, a cream blouse and a fleecy jacket.

"You ready to go?" said Danielle, standing in the doorway.

"Yep. Do I look OK?" said Violette, fidgeting with her jacket zip.

"Course you do. What about me? Do I look good?" asked Danielle, twirling around.

"You always do," said Violette, looking her up and down.

"Let's go then," said Danielle, impatiently.

Walking down the stairs with Danielle, Violette felt her heart skip a beat when her eyes met Michael's.

He sure looks good wearing those jeans and a blue t-shirt with his leather jacket, thought Violette.

"Hi everyone," said Danielle, as she got to the bottom of the stairs.

"Hi Danielle and Violette… this is our cousin Taiven, who you both wouldn't have met yet. Hope you don't mind, but we asked him if he would like to come along with us tonight. It's a bit boring at home sitting with the oldies, if you know what I mean," said Annabelle.

"Yeah. That's all good. Hi Taiven. Nice to meet you," said Danielle, eyeing him off and smiling sweetly.

Prior to becoming a Lepidoptera, Taiven had been a magazine model who was sought after by a lot of talent agencies. Tall, athletic, and well built, he had black, curly hair, with blue eyes that pierced though your heart.

Putting her hand out in front to shake his, Violette said, "Hello Taiven. Nice to meet you."

"Thanks. It's good to meet you both as well," said Taiven in his Spanish accent.

"We are taking the mopeds for transport tonight. Is that's OK with you both?" said Michael.

Danielle and Violette both nodded and smiled politely.

"I was thinking that maybe you can ride with Taiven, if you like Danielle, and Violette can go with Michael," said Annabelle, smiling.

"Sure. No problem," said Violette.

Adrian and Emily joined them in the foyer.

"Good evening," said Adrian, addressing everyone.

"Good evening Mr and Mrs Lachance," said Grayson.

"Hello Grayson. You all ready to go?" asked Emily.

They all nodded in agreeance.

"We hope you all have a good night. Please take care of our girls and don't bring them home too late," said Adrian, looking from Michael to Grayson.

"We won't, Adrian. Please don't worry; they will be alright," said Michael.

"Yeah, they will be safe with us. I am sure they will enjoy the night lights of Paris," said Annabelle.

"Well, we had better get going as we have a lot of sightseeing to do tonight. See you later, Mr and Mrs Lachance," said Grayson.

"Bye Grayson. Drive carefully everyone," said Emily. "Take care girls."

Stepping onto the moped, Michael said to Violette, "Make sure you hold on tight, as I don't want you to fall off."

"You don't have to ask me twice," said Violette, smiling and placing her arms around his waist. *If he only knew how happy I was to put my arms around his waist. Cloud nine.*

"Hang on, Danielle," said Taiven, as he pushed the start button on his moped.

"OK," said Danielle, doing the strap up on her helmet quickly and placing her hands onto Taiven's hips.

Emily and Adrian stood on the front porch and waved them good bye as they rode off.

Pulling up to the front gate behind everyone else, Violette watched the overhead lights turn on and the front gate open slowly. Feeling a drop of what she thought was rain on her nose, Violette looked into the sky and saw a huge kaleidoscope of multi-coloured butterflies hovering above them. Tapping Michael on the shoulder, Violette pointed towards the sky and said, "Wow. Look at all those colourful butterflies. Aren't they beautiful?"

Turning around, Michael watched the wonder on her face. "They sure are… so graceful."

"Why are they out so late?" asked Violette, knowing butterflies only usually flew during the daylight, because their wings needed the warmth.

"Not sure," said Michael pursing his lips. "Maybe it's going to rain."

"Yeah, maybe. I did feel a drop on my nose, just now," said Violette, looking towards the sky again.

Michael knew it was strange that the butterflies were out this late in the evening and wondered why they would be showing themselves to humans, especially Violette. Shaking off his questions, because he knew there would be a logical answer to them, he put the moped in gear and followed everyone else out the front gate.

Riding through Paris, Violette leaned in close to Michael so that he could hear what she was saying.

"The night lights are like a million jewels all shining at once. So beautiful, Michael."

Michael nodded and smiled as he continued to drive. Michael had lived in Paris for a long time and knew the history of each monument and the architecture, and was able to tell Violette in detail about each one of them. Violette noticed that Taiven was doing the same with Danielle as they drove along.

After about two hours of riding and sightseeing, Violette said, "Can we stop somewhere for a while Michael? I would like to get off and stretch my legs."

"Sure. I am starting to get a bit stiff myself. Maybe we can get a coffee somewhere to warm us up," said Michael, looking around.

Michael signalled the others to pull over and see if they wanted to do the same. But they all wanted to keep going.

"We will meet you all at the Eiffel Tower in about one hour, if that's ok," said Michael.

"OK," said Grayson, wondering if he should leave Annabelle with them. But something told him they would be fine. "Ring us, if you need us."

"Sure," said Michael, nodding once.

"See you later on, sis," said Violette.

"See you. Don't do anything I wouldn't do," joked Danielle, as she rode off with Taiven, Grayson and Annabelle.

Noticing a quaint little café, Michael and Violette parked the moped across the road from the Eiffel Tower and texted the others their location, so they could meet up later.

"You want to choose a table and I will get the coffees?" said Michael, opening the wooden and glass door to the café.

"OK. Could I have a weak café au lait?" said Violette.

"Sure, Violette. Did you want a cake as well?"

"No thanks. But thanks for asking."

Violette stood in the entrance to the fifties-style café looking for a table, until she spotted one in a secluded corner, next to the window. Taking her seat, Violette noticed that it hadn't fully turned dark yet outside. *Sure is strange.*

"Penny for your thoughts," said Michael, placing the coffees on the table.

"Huh? Sorry, I didn't even see you standing there," said Violette, startled by his presence. "I was wondering if I would ever get used to it being light outside, when its past six in the evening."

"Takes a while. But you'll get used to it," said Michael, smiling and taking a seat at the table. "I remember feeling the same way when I moved here years ago." As he looked into Violette's eyes and read her mind, Michael realised the attraction they felt for each other was immeasurable. When he was around Violette, she always made him feel calm and like nothing else mattered, except them. Even though Michael knew he was forbidden to have any feelings for a human, he just couldn't help himself, when it came to Violette.

"What are you smiling at?" asked Violette, twitching her lips and wondering why he was staring at her.

Reaching for her hand, he said, "You... do you have a boyfriend?"

"No. Why do you ask?" Violette felt her face blushing as she enjoyed the touch of his hand on hers.

"I have really enjoyed tonight with you and I would like to take you on a date tomorrow night. Just the two of us," said Michael.

"I'd like that. But I would have to ask Emily and Adrian first before I say yes." Violette's heart was beating so fast she thought it was going to jump out of her chest.

"I really do enjoy your company, Violette, and would like to get to know you some more. So hopefully Emily and Adrian will say yes."

"Where did you want to go on our first date?"

"I was thinking maybe we could have dinner at a cosy little restaurant I know, and then maybe see a movie. What type of movies do you like?" asked Michael.

"I like all types of movies, especially the action or romance ones."

"Me too. When we get back to your house tonight we can have a look at what's showing and decide what one we want to see."

"Sounds like a plan then," said Violette, excited at the prospect of seeing Michael again the next night.

The hour flew by fast and before Michael and Violette knew it, Grayson, Annabelle, Danielle and Taiven had parked up out the front of the café and were waiting for them to go home.

"You look worn out, sis," said Violette as she approached Danielle.

"Yeah. All this fresh air has made me tired," yawned Danielle.

"Well, we had better head off. It's a thirty-minute ride home," said Grayson looking around. *Heads up Gramaze… Debauched at 2 o'clock.*

"Right," said Michael, calmly stepping onto his moped. "Hop on Violette."

Looks like we got here at the right time. Let's get the fuck out of here, thought Annabelle to the other Lepidoptera's. As she pulled away from the kerb, Annabelle noticed in her side mirrors, three Debauched standing outside the cafe, just watching them ride off.

On the way home, Violette couldn't help herself. She texted Emily and asked her if it was alright to go out to dinner and watch a movie with Michael the next night. Emily texted Violette back: "Yes." Violette smiled.

With their mopeds coming to a stop in front of the front doors of the Lachance residence, Danielle said, "Would you all like to come in for a coffee?"

"Grayson and I are feeling tired, so we will head off home. Can we take a rain check?" said Annabelle.

"No problem. Maybe we can catch up again soon," said Danielle, taking off her helmet.

"I'd like that," said Annabelle.

"Thank you for taking us out sight-seeing tonight. I had a wonderful time," said Danielle, giving her helmet to Taiven to fasten back onto the moped seat.

"You're welcome. Well, we had better be off now," said Grayson. "See you at home later on, Taiven and Michael." *Not too long guys. You have patrol tonight, don't forget.*

Michael and Taiven nodded.

"Bye Annabelle and Grayson. Thanks for tonight. Catch up with you both again soon," said Violette, placing her helmet on the moped seat.

"Bye Violette," said Annabelle.

"Yes. See you soon," said Grayson, as he started his moped back up.

After they left, Danielle, Taiven, Michael and Violette went into the kitchen to make the coffees and to see what there was to eat. Luckily, Lamiae had made some strawberry jam and fresh cream doughnuts.

As they ate their doughnuts, Danielle said, "Hey, did you guys have to go home yet, or would you like to stay and watch a movie with us?"

"Yeah… OK," said Taiven, and Michael agreed.

"What type of movie do you guys like?" said Danielle.

"I like action movies," stated Taiven.

"You pick. I am not too bothered about what movie we watch," said Michael.

"What about the new Tom Cruise movie?" said Danielle.

"Hell yeah… that sounds great," said Taiven.

The Lachance theatre room was the size of a small movie cinema, and was decked out with lots of single and double seats and couches. With deep blue carpet and dark, emerald green curtains that went around the four walls from ceiling to floor, and speakers mounted on the tall walls for surround sound, it was perfect for watching movies in.

Michael listened to Violette's thoughts as he followed her into the theatre room. He wasn't surprised to hear that she wanted him to sit next to her on the double seater couch, in the back of the room. As he took his seat next to Violette, Michael wondered why his attraction to Violette was so intense every time he was next to her. He wasn't sure how much longer he could hold back his feelings for Violette, before he acted on them, even if it was forbidden.

"Give me a minute guys. I need to find the DVD and put it on. Take a seat, Taiven," said Danielle politely gesturing to the couches and noticing Violette and Michael sitting in the back together. "Ah, here it is." Pushing the DVD into the machine, and taking the remote with her, Danielle took her seat in the front row, next to Taiven on the long lounge.

Whilst watching the movie, Michael moved closer to Violette and held her hand. Nervous, but glad he had taken the first step, she looked up to find his mesmerising blue eyes, looking back at her. Leaning in, he kissed her lips tenderly.

With his kiss intensifying, Violette felt like her body was floating, and her heartbeat quickened. She couldn't ever remember feeling as happy as she did in that moment. Pulling away from his lips to get her breath, she felt a sharp pain in the back of her neck.

"Hmm, I have the same pain in my neck as last night at dinner," said Violette, frowning and moving her head from side to side.

"Really?" said Michael. "That's not good. Do you get these pains often?"

"No. I'll be back in a minute… I just need to get some medication from the kitchen," said Violette, massaging the back of her neck with her hand.

Searching the kitchen, Violette found some painkillers in the top drawer of the island bench. Pouring some tap water into a glass, she took the medication and waited for it to take effect, whilst rubbing her neck. *Wonder why I keep getting these pains in my neck? Really annoying.*

"How is your neck pain?" said Michael, standing in the doorway of the kitchen.

"Still there. Just waiting for the medication to kick in," said Violette, massaging her temples with her fingers.

"Maybe I can help," said Michael walking in. Coming around to where she was standing at the island bench, Michael kissed her forehead, and then her eyes, one by one.

Violette felt the tension in her neck ease and her body relax, as she kept her eyes closed and took deep breaths in and out slowly. "That's better."

With her eyes closed, Michael leaned in to steal another kiss from her sensual lips.

His lips are so soft and inviting. His touch… mesmerising. Slowly she melted into his arms and could feel the pain dissipating with every kiss they took.

Reading her mind, Michael pulled away quickly from her.

"I think we should slow this down a bit before we do something we might regret." He knew life could get a whole lot more complicated than it had to be.

"Huh…" said Violette opening her eyes and blushing. "Sorry Michael. I can't seem to control myself." *God, what is wrong with me.*

"Don't be sorry. I feel the same way Violette. But we have only known each other for a couple of days and I think we should take it slowly."

Before they could talk any further about their feelings, Taiven and Danielle walked into the kitchen. "Hombre… You ready to go home or are you staying a bit longer?" said Taiven. His Spanish accent was apparent.

"I will be coming home with you, Taiven. Renee and William will be expecting us home soon," said Michael.

"OK. I will wait for you out the front. Good night, Violette and Danielle. It was nice to meet you," said Taiven, walking towards the door. Secretly he was glad to be going home. Reading Danielle's thoughts in the theatre room, he realised she wanted more than just friendship, and he wanted no part in that.

"It was nice to meet you too, Taiven. Maybe we can all catch up again soon," said Violette, politely.

"Sure," said Taiven.

"I will walk you to the front door, Taiven," said Danielle, placing her arm through his. Always the flirt.

Violette held Michael's hand as she walked outside with him to his moped. The night had gone by quickly and she had enjoyed his company, but she didn't want him to leave yet. She had never felt like this about a boy before.

Embracing her in his arms, he gave into his feelings once more, with a long passionate kiss.

"Good night," said Michael, pressing his forehead against hers.

"Bye," said Violette, dreamily, as Michael pulled away from their embrace. Saddened by his departure, she watched him hop onto his moped, put his helmet on and started up his moped.

Both girls waved Taiven and Michael goodbye as they rode off home.

"You two look like you are getting really close. What is going on there?" said Danielle, walking inside with her arm around Violette.

"I really like him, sis. We seem to have a lot in common... and... well... I have it bad for him," said Violette, as she showed Danielle the selfie they had taken that night at the café.

"Good on you, Vi. He seems very nice. You deserve some happiness in your life," said Danielle, giving her sister a hug.

As they walked up the staircase, Danielle and Violette said their good nights to each other and then went off to their bedrooms.

Shutting her door behind her, Violette sat on her bed and checked her mobile for messages. There was one from Michael. 'I had a good time tonight. I can't wait for tomorrow night. Will pick you up about 7pm.'

Smiling, she thought, *I can't wait to see you again too.* Placing her mobile down on the bedside table, she decided to go brush her teeth and get into her pyjamas.

Lying on her bed, she once again looked at the photo of her and Michael at the café. Enlarging the picture on her mobile screen, she studied his face and smiled, remembering their conversations and just how much they had in common.

Startled, she heard a soft tapping noise at her window. With the curtains drawn, she couldn't see who or what was there. Eventually the tapping got the better of her and Violette got up to see who or what the noise was. With her heart racing, she opened the curtains quickly. To her surprise, Michael was standing on her window porch.

"Can I come in?"

"You frightened the life out of me. What are you doing here?" Violette whispered, as she opened the window.

"Sorry… I couldn't wait until tomorrow night to see you again Violette. I really like you a lot and if it's OK… I would like to come in and talk," said Michael, quietly.

Stunned and excited at the same time that he was there, she hesitated at first. Violette knew she would be in a lot of trouble if Emily and Adrian found a boy in her room. But the attraction she felt for Michael was overwhelming.

"Of course you can come in. But we will have to be quiet, otherwise someone will hear us."

"OK," whispered Michael, stepping into her bedroom. It was then that he noticed her bedroom was in complete darkness except for the bedside lamp.

Violette must have been getting ready for bed. This should be interesting, thought Michael.

As Violette sat on the edge of her bed, Michael said, "Do you mind if I sit on the bed next to you?"

"That's OK… come… sit down," she said patting the bed.

"Violette, I didn't come here tonight to do anything but talk, and if possible, just hold you in my arms. I can't stop thinking about you. I haven't felt this way for a girl in a long time." said Michael nervously. He was talking too much. He needed to find a way to calm himself.

Violette put a finger to his lips.

"Shhh... it's OK. You don't have to explain anything... we could turn the TV on and cuddle up on the bed, and maybe even go to sleep?" said Violette, trying to reassure him. But at the same time, Violette was nervous for inviting him to stay. She just hoped that Emily or Adrian didn't check on her during the night or in the morning.

"Are you sure?" queried Michael. *Are you sure... God, what am I doing.*

"Yes. I am sure," said Violette.

"OK," said Michael, taking a deep breath and feeling somewhat relieved.

Violette switched her TV on and lay down on her bed next to Michael, who had already propped himself up with some pillows, and grew comfortable. Putting his arm out, Violette cuddled into his shoulder and watched Michael flick through the channels for a good program. As her mind and body relaxed, she fell asleep.

When Michael arrived home from Violette's house, he was confronted by William at the front door. "Where the fuck have you been, Michael? We tried calling you on your mobile, but it went straight to voicemail. Did you have it turned off?" grunted William, authoritatively.

"No... out patrolling," said Michael, matter-of-factly.

"Don't bullshit me... oh I see, you have been with Violette," said William. No matter how hard Michael tried to block him out, William read Michael's thoughts.

"Yes, Sire... but please let me ...," said Michael.

But William didn't let him finish his sentence.

"You are forbidden to see any human romantically, you know that. So why are you pursuing this? You know our laws on human and vampire interaction," said William, heatedly.

"Yes, Sire. But for some reason I am really attracted to this woman. I can't stop thinking about her," said Michael.

"Attraction... what would you know about attraction? You have never had a mate before. So what makes you think she is your life partner?" said William, with his hands on his hips.

"Since the day Violette arrived into France I have been attracted to her scent. I know humans and vampires don't mix, but I feel this is different William."

William always knew what was best for his coven, but when Michael mentioned scent, it triggered something in his memory.

"Hmm... it's funny you should mention scent. I noticed at the Lachance house the other night, there was a scent in the room of a new female Lepidoptera. As I haven't smelt that scent for centuries, I just wasn't sure if what I was smelling was correct and who it was. Do you think that it maybe Violette?"

"I don't know. But I can check it out tonight, if you permit me, Sire."

"I want you to report back to me when you get home tonight on what you find. If she is a female Lepidoptera transitioning, we will need to keep an eye on her. To think that we have not seen a new female Lepidoptera vampire for hundreds or years. This is exciting," said William, rubbing his chin in thought.

"Yes, Sire. May I go now?" asked Michael, nervously.

"Be gone already," said William, waving him away.

Waking to the morning sun coming through her windows, Violette turned over to see Michael had already gone home.

Looking at the pillow beside her, she noticed a piece of paper. It was a note from Michael.

'See you tonight beautiful lady. Can't wait.'

Violette smiled and knew just how lucky she was. Michael was a great guy and a true gentleman. She was sure her parents would have really liked him.

Her warm thoughts were interrupted when she heard a knock at the door. She quickly placed the note under the covers.

"Can we come in?" asked Emily.

"Sure," said Violette, sitting up.

"Good morning, sleepy head," said Emily, walking in with Danielle behind her.

"Good morning. Morning sis. What's up?" said Violette.

"Well... I was thinking we could all go clothes shopping today. What do you think?" said Emily, hoping she was just as excited as Danielle about going shopping.

"Yes please. I would love to. Which shops are we going to?" asked Violette.

"It's a surprise. The quicker you get ready and have breakfast, the quicker we can go," said Emily.

"You don't have to ask me twice," said Violette, climbing out of bed, and heading for her bathroom.

Standing next to the tinted windowed limousine with the back door open, the chauffeur waited patiently for Emily, Danielle and Violette. When the front door of the Lachance house opened and the three woman walked toward the limousine, the chauffeur smiled and said in a French accent, "Bonjour Madam, Mesdemoiselles. Lovely day for shopping."

"Bonjour," said Violette and Danielle together, nodding eagerly as they climbed into the car.

"Bonjour Louie. Here is a list of shop addresses we would like you to take us to today," said Emily, handing him a piece of paper.

"Yes, Madame," said Louie, taking the list and helping Emily into the car.

As the limousine pulled out the driveway, and the security gates closed, Danielle said, "Where are we going first?"

"Well, I was thinking we could go to my favourite salon and have our hair and nails done first. What do you think?" said Emily smiling.

"Mmm… shopping or salon. That is a hard choice to make," teased Danielle, smirking.

"I choose salon," said Violette, looking at her fingernails in disgust.

"OK. Salon it is," said Emily. Looking at the driver in his rear vision mirror, she watched as Louie nodded in acknowledgement of where to take them first.

"Emily… um… What can we have done to our hair?" asked Danielle.

"What would you like to do, my dear?" said Emily, looking from Danielle to Violette.

"Will it be OK to have some highlights put in?" asked Danielle.

"Sure… what about you Violette?"

"Just a wash and style for me," said Violette.

"Come on, sis. Try something different," said Danielle, teasing Violette. Danielle was very adventurous when it came to hair colours and styles.

"Maybe… I will have a look in some hair magazines when we get there. So what colour high lights are you thinking about?" asked Violette, trying to get the attention off herself.

"Not sure. Maybe a pink, or... I don't know. I am sure the hair dresser will be able to help me."

"Just remember, ladies, that you have school next week, and they won't allow any outrageous colours or styles," said Emily, with a raised eyebrow.

"Forgot about that... oh well, maybe not pink then," said Danielle.

"What about you Emily?" said Violette.

"Well... I have had a fringe now for so long, that I was thinking about growing a side fringe. And also I was going to have some blonde highlights put into my hair. I am getting a bit sick of just being brown," said Emily, playing with her hair.

"Yeah, I could see that would suit you to," said Violette.

Parking the limousine outside the salon, Louie hopped out quickly to open the door and help them alight from the car.

"We will be here for around three hours Louie. Whilst you are waiting for us, I would like you to collect these items for me," said Emily, handing him a piece of paper.

"Yes, Madame," said Louie, taking the list from Emily and having a look at what needed collecting. "Will there be anything else, Madame?"

"No, thank you," said Emily.

"I will be waiting here when you come out, Madame," said Louie.

Looking all around as they entered the salon, Danielle and Violette were approached by a lady dressed in a bright blue dress. "Bonjour Mesdemoiselles. How can I help you this morning?" said the assistant.

"We would like to have our hair and nails done," said Emily, as she walked into the salon and overheard what the assistant was asking.

"Oh... good morning, Mrs Lachance. I didn't see you there. Welcome," said the assistant, noticing Emily, who was a regular client, for the first time. "So... hair and nails for all. Come this way ladies."

The assistant led them to a back room which was painted antique white, and set up with deep blue furniture and black leather chairs. Each station had its own individual mirror, complete with magazines for each customer. "Here we go... please take a seat. Margot, Shayne and Alison will take care of all your requirements today ladies."

"Thank you," said Emily.

As Emily, Danielle and Violette took their seats, the assistants enquired about what treatments they were looking at having done, and then went about setting up their individual stations accordingly.

I sure have enjoyed all the pampering and special treatment this morning, thought Violette sitting on the black leather couch at the front of the salon, whilst she waited for Emily and Danielle to finish getting their nails done.

Glancing up from the beauty book she was flicking through, Violette noticed a man, about six-foot tall and wearing a long black leather coat, through the salon window. He seemed to be standing there in the shadows, just watching her. She didn't recognise him and his body language gave her the most unnerving feeling. Even the hair on the back of her neck was standing up and she didn't know why. Getting up out of her seat, she went over to the window to get a better look at him. But when he noticed that she saw him watching her, he quickly got into his black SUV, spun his wheels, and drove off. With a furrowed brow, she watched him drive off into the distance, weaving throughout the traffic, like he was in a hurry. *That's strange.*

"Violette," said Danielle, taping her on the shoulder.

Jumping, Violette turned around to see Danielle and Emily standing behind her.

"You ready to go shopping?" said Danielle, excited.

"Um...yep... sure," said Violette, secretly glad that Emily and Danielle were ready to go. The strange looking man had creeped her out and she just wanted to get out of there and go back home, where she felt safe.

"Are you OK dear?" asked Emily, noticing Violette had gone a bit pale.

"Yeah. Just a bit tired, that's all," lied Violette.

"We can go shopping another day dear, if you like," said Emily.

"I am OK Emily. Anyway I am sure Danielle wouldn't agree with you," said Violette, looking at Danielle.

"You're right. I don't agree. So let's go," said Danielle, walking toward the door of the salon with her arm around Violette.

Emily sat next to Violette in the limousine. Patting Violette's hand she said, "Are you sure you are OK dear?"

Looking at Emily with a raised eyebrow and thinking she must have read her mind, Violette said, "Um... I'm not sure... it's... you know when I was waiting for you and Danielle to finish up in the salon... well... I could have sworn that a man whom I didn't recognise was watching me from across the street. He looked creepy and it made me feel uneasy."

"Maybe he was waiting for someone and it looked like he was looking at you," said Emily, placing her hand over Violette's hand.

"Yeah, you could be right," said Violette, looking out the window. But that didn't make her feel any better about it.

"You know Violette, you have always had an overactive imagination," teased Danielle.

Violette gave Danielle a sideways glance that said, *mind you own business, sis.*

"But just to be on the safe side, I will let security know at home and I will have the driver follow us around the shops this afternoon. Will that make you feel safer my dear?"

"Yes. Thanks Emily," said Violette, letting out a sigh of relief.

The afternoon of shopping was uneventful. Emily, Danielle and Violette tried on lots of clothing and shoes and eventually Violette relaxed and enjoyed herself. Violette even found the most beautiful dress to wear out for dinner that night with Michael.

"You girls ready to go?" said Emily, as she paid for the last item.

"Yes please. I have sore feet," said Danielle, holding the bags of shopping she had chosen to carry.

"Sounds good Emily," said Violette, smiling.

"Let me take those bags, Mesdames," said Louie, approaching them as they walked out the store. He had played security guard and waited outside the shop for them patiently.

"Thank you, Louie. You can take us home now," said Emily, handing over her bags.

"Yes, Madame," said Louie, bowing slightly.

"Thank you for today, Emily," said Danielle, stepping into the limousine and taking her seat. "I really love my new clothes and shoes, and I just love these highlights in my hair."

Opening her handbag, Danielle took out a pocket size mirror and checked out her new look.

"You are welcome, dear," said Emily.

"Yeah, thanks Emily. I can't wait to wear my new dress tonight for my date with Michael," said Violette, sitting next to Emily and giving her a hug.

"You are most welcome dear," said Emily, embracing her. Truthfully, Emily loved going shopping and having her nails and hair done regularly. Now she didn't need an excuse, as she had two foster daughters, whom she loved dearly, to go with.

On the way home, Violette stared out the window contemplating her date with Michael that night. As the city buildings turned into family homes, the car pulled up to what was now a familiar limestone wall and security gate. Excited, Violette couldn't wait to get inside to spend the rest of the afternoon getting ready.

Violette walked into her bedroom and placed the bags of clothing down on her bed. As she was taking the gifts that Emily had paid for out of their bags, her mobile phone beeped with a message.

'Hello Violette, something has come up and I can't go tonight. So sorry I won't be able to attend our date. Will contact you later to see if we can rain check. Again... sorry.'

"What... rain check? Humph," said Violette, sitting on her bed with rolled shoulders. Watching the back light on her phone disappear, Violette decided to call Michael. But when she rang his number, it went straight to voicemail. Ending the call without leaving a message, she placed her mobile on her bedside table and lay on her bed.

"You decent?" asked Danielle, knocking at the door.

"Yep. Come in, sis," said Violette, sitting up.

"I thought you would have been getting ready by now?" said Danielle.

"Michael has cancelled. I received a text message saying, he couldn't make it," said Violette, with a saddened face.

"Sorry, sis. That's a bummer," said Danielle, sitting next to Violette. "I know how much you were looking forward to going. How about we do something instead?"

"No. That's OK," said Violette sighing, picking at her cuticles and looking at the floor.

"I am not going to let you sit here all night long and mope… and anyway I am not taking no for an answer," said Dannielle. "We could go see a movie."

"Yeah… that sound good. Thanks Danielle," said Violette, placing her head on Danielle's shoulder.

"OK. Let's have a look at what is on at our local theatre then," said Danielle, taking her mobile phone out of her jacket pocket.

"Knock, knock," said Emily, peeping around the semi closed door.

"Come in," said Violette.

"So what time is Michael picking you up tonight?" asked Emily.

"He's not. He just sent me a text message cancelling," said Violette.

"Oh, sweetie. Sorry," said Emily, sitting next to Violette.

"It's OK," said Violette. "Danielle has asked me to go to the movies. Will that be OK with you?"

"Of course that's OK," said Emily, placing her arm around Violette's shoulders. "So what are you going to watch?"

"Not sure yet. We were just going to have a look at what is on now," said Danielle.

"OK. Well… you girls choose and I will go and let the driver know he is taking you both to the movies tonight," said Emily, standing up.

"Thanks, Emily," said Violette.

Arriving at the Cin'Hoche movie theatre, the girls collected their tickets and decided to buy some popcorn and sodas. Settling into their allocated red velour seats to watch the movie, Violette scanned the old theatre and thought she saw Michael sitting in the back row. Turning back to the advertisements which were playing on the screen, Violette nostrils flared as she sighed heavily. *What is he doing here? And why hasn't he returned my earlier call. Busy, my ass.*

Turning around, for a second time, Violette looked back to where she thought she had seen Michael sitting. But he was no longer there. Frowning, and shaking her head, Violette started to question if she had even seen him at all. With the movie finally starting, Violette decided to put it out of her mind and just enjoy the movie.

"I told you not to sit there. You idiot," said Annabelle, slapping Michael's arm.

"She didn't see me. Don't worry. I can hear her doubting what she saw now," said Michael, listening to Violette's thoughts.

"We are just meant to guard the girls. That's all," said Annabelle, with her hands on her hips.

"Yeah, yeah," said Michael, sighing. "It's fine."

"So… where to now?" asked Annabelle.

"Up there," said Michael, pointed to the rafters of the theatre roof. "We can sit up there and guard them."

"Right. Let's go," said Annabelle, walking towards the stairs.

Taking their seats in the back corner of the rafters, Annabelle watched Michael sit in a cat-like stance, ready to pounce upon anyone who would dare touch the girl he liked, Violette.

"Why are you blocking me from your thoughts?" asked Annabelle.

"I don't answer to you... just do your job," said Michael.

"Someone is grouchy tonight," teased Annabelle. "You like her... correct?"

"Yes... no... it is forbidden to fraternize with humans... you know this," said Michael, watching Violette's every move. "But for some reason, that I can't explain, I am attracted to her scent." *Frangipani.*

"You must fight this attraction, Michael. She is not one of us, and you know how much trouble you will be in with William. So why do you persist?" said Annabelle, shaking her head.

"What... you don't think I already know this?" said Michael. "Anyway it looks like they are leaving. The movie must have finished. We just need to make sure they get home safely. And don't even think about mentioning this to William. Are we clear, Annabelle?"

"My lips are sealed homme," said Annabelle.

Arriving home, Violette and Danielle were greeted by Adrian at the front door.

"Good evening, girls. How was your movie?" asked Adrian.

"It was OK," said Violette, shrugging.

"It was a good movie. Lots of action," said Danielle yawning. "We are going off to bed now. See you in the morning Adrian."

"Oh, OK. Good night. Sweet dreams," said Adrian, giving them both a hug good night.

Her dimly lit room was quiet as Violette lay on top of the quilt, thinking about Michael. Wondering why she hadn't heard from him that night, she then remembered that she hadn't taken her mobile phone off silent since the movies. As she reached over to her bedside table and opened it up, much to her delight, was a message from Michael. 'Sorry about tonight... had to work. I will make it up to you.'

Smiling, she hugged the phone to her chest. Sitting up, she decided to call Michael.

"Hello," said Michael answering his phone.

"Hello. What time do you finish work?" asked Violette.

"Around 2am," said Michael.

"Oh. OK. Did you want to meet up tomorrow, somewhere?" said Violette.

"I will probably be sleeping most of tomorrow, Violette," said Michael, remembering he had been told by William that he was to fly to Rome to help out with some Debauched problems they were having over there the next day.

"What about tomorrow night?" said Violette.

"Well... I have to work again. William has put me on to work nights for the next two weeks. So it means I won't be able to see you," said Michael.

"Oh. OK," said Violette, sounding rejected.

"Sorry, Violette. I don't have a choice," said Michael.

"It's OK. I understand," said Violette.

"Violette… I have to go now. If I get a break I will try to call, but I can't promise," said Michael. Truthfully, he was outside her bedroom window guarding her. For reasons Michael couldn't comprehend yet, he had been instructed by William to guard only. No contact allowed.

"I understand," said Violette. "Bye."

Hanging up her phone, she placed it on the bedside table again. *I wonder if he really does like me… we seemed to have a good time last night, so I wonder why he is busy all of a sudden.* Violette knew she would be starting school the next week and that this would take up a lot of her time. So maybe it was a good thing that he didn't have time for her and that their friendship hadn't developed any further.

Turning off her bedside light, Violette lay there, for what seemed like ages, thinking about Michael, until her body finally gave into sleep.

As the days slipped into weeks, Violette's only contact with Michael was over the phone. He was always pleasant with her, but could never commit to seeing her, and now she had started school, Violette was busy with assignments and homework too.

With June nearing an end, and the weather heating up, Violette sat quietly in the limousine on the drive home from school. As it pulled up to the Lachance residence front door, she noticed an unexpected, yet familiar figure waiting for her on the doorstep.

As her door opened, Michael helped Violette alight from the car.

"Bonjour, Violette," said Michael, pulling her in close.

"Bonjour…," said Violette, looking into his eyes. Her heart beat quickened as his arms drew her in close and softly kissed her forehead.

"How are you?" asked Michael.

"Good. What… how are you here?" mumbled Violette, fumbling her words.

"Umm… I… I came to tell you that William has now rostered me onto work night shift until the end of September," said Michael, his shoulders drooping, and a disappointed look on his face.

"Oh… right," said Violette, her eyes looking towards the ground. Sighing heavily, with a downward turn of her mouth, she wondered what he was going to say next.

"Sorry, Violette… I don't have any control over when I will be rostered on. William has told me, apparently we are busy for the next couple of months and that I and everyone else are required to work double shifts as well. There isn't much I can do about it at this point," said Michael, with a furrowed brow.

"It's OK… I understand," said Violette, quietly.

"I can still ring you though," said Michael, pulling her chin up to look into her eyes.

"I would like that," said Violette, as she looked into his beautiful blue eyes. "I am sure I will be busy with school anyway… And Emily and Adrian have said to us yesterday, that we are going back to LA in August for a holiday."

"Oh, really? That will be nice for you. Hopefully you may be able to catch up with some of your old friends," said Michael. *Hmm, I will have to alert William to this.*

"Yeah, I am hoping to," said Violette, remembering her best friend, Rebecca. She hadn't spoken with her since she had left LA and was looking forward to spending some time with her.

"Well… anyway, Violette. I have to go," said Michael, listening to her heart beat fast. Brushing his hand down her hair, he memorised every detail on her face. "I sure will miss seeing your lovely face."

Pulling her in close to his body and enveloping his arms around her, he leaned in and stole a sensual kiss from her lips. Eventually peeling himself away from her frangipani perfume, which he loved, he said, "Au revoir."

Violette opened her eyes, and tried to steady her breathing.

"Au revoir," whispered Violette gently. As she watched him walk away and through the front gates, she felt a tear break free from her saddened eyes. He had only been gone for seconds, and she was missing him already.

As July rolled into August, Violette experienced her first summer in Paris, end of semester exams and the school holidays. With her sister Danielle and the friends she had made at Lycee International, Violette spent the school holidays either swimming, going to the movies, shopping, or riding her moped. Even though she enjoyed herself immensely, her thoughts were of Michael and how she longed for him to return.

The Santa Monica Pier and beach hadn't changed much in the time Violette had been away. This was one of many things that she missed, now that she was living permanently in Bagnolet. Digging her heels into the sand as she sat on her towel, she watched the waves crash onto the shoreline, and families enjoying themselves at the beach.

"You coming in, Violette?" asked Rebecca, taking her dress off to reveal her black bikini.

"Nah… I might lay here for a while and get a tan. You go. I'll come in later," said Violette, looking up at Rebecca and Danielle.

"Ok. Come on Danielle. Let's go. The water is calling me," said Rebecca.

"Ok," said Danielle, picking up the beach ball.

As Violette watched Rebecca and Danielle enter the water, she heard her phone ring. Fumbling through her beach bag, she found it. Much to her surprise, the screen displayed that it was Michael calling.

"Hello," said Violette, with a grin from ear to ear.

"Hello... how's your holiday going?" asked Michael.

"Great. Danielle and I are at the beach today, with my friend Rebecca," said Violette.

"Cool. Have you been for a swim yet?" asked Michael.

"Not yet. Might go in a bit later," said Violette.

"Oh, OK," said Michael, remembering the beaches in LA. "So... when are you coming back to Bagnolet?"

"We fly home tomorrow. I can't believe we have been here for ten days already. The time has flown. I have had such a great time... But I have missed seeing you," said Violette, drawing his name in the sand.

"Yes, I have missed you to, belle fille. Sorry, beautiful girl. What time do you get in tomorrow?" asked Michael.

"Around eight in the evening, I think. Not looking forward to the long flight, though," said Violette.

"Hopefully you sleep all the way, so that the flight won't seem long," said Michael. "Oh, and William has told me that I will be going back to working day shift as of tomorrow, so... I was wondering if you would like to go on a date Friday night?" asked Michael.

"I... I would love to," said Violette. "But I will have to check with Emily and Adrian to see if that is OK first."

"D'accord," said Michael.

"Hmm... what? I am still learning French. What is 'd'accord'?" said Violette, scrunching her nose.

"It means, 'OK'," said Michael, smiling.

93

"Oh. OK. So what time Friday night?" asked Violette, excited.

"Say around 6.30pm," said Michael.

"D'accord," said Violette, smiling.

"Very good… well…give me a text later and let me know if you are able to go," said Michael.

"I will," said Violette.

"I had better go, Violette. William will be wondering why I haven't turned up for work," said Michael.

"Humph… OK," said Violette. "Talk to you later."

"Bye," said Michael, hanging up his phone.

Chapter Six

Excited, and looking forward to their date, Violette watched Michael's car pull into the driveway from the hallway window. He was early, but she didn't mind, as she had been ready for a while, checking and rechecking herself in the mirror. Running down the stairs in excitement, she opened the front door in anticipation of his arrival in his chauffeur driven limousine. As she watched him climb out the car, Violette noticed he didn't look too happy. That is, until his eyes met hers.

"You look stunning in that dress. Is it new?" said Michael, noticing how she filled the dress perfectly.

"Emily brought it recently for me," she said. "Hey…are you ok? I noticed when you got out the car you looked irritated about something."

"Humph… I just had an argument with William," said Michael, taking a deep breath and rolling his eyes, remembering what he and William had talked about.

"What was it about?" said Violette, intrigued.

Shit, what am I going to tell her?

"Well… err… he said that I should be careful about spending too much time with you. He told me that I should find someone of my own age." said Michael, trying to think quickly.

"I can't believe he said that, Michael. Doesn't he like me or something?"

"He thinks you are a lovely girl and didn't want to see you get hurt, that's all," said Michael, knowing he had just made it worse by lying.

"I don't see that happening here. In fact, you have been nothing but a gentleman," said Violette frowning, with a sharp breath. She was annoyed with William for trying to keep them apart.

"Well, he is worried. In fact, I nearly was not allowed to go tonight," said Michael.

"What made him change his mind about letting you come?" said Violette, with her eyebrows furrowed.

"I told William that I really liked you a lot and that I wanted to spend more time getting to know you."

"You said that about me?"

"It's the truth Violette... I do really like you," said Michael, taking her hand in his. "Even though we have not known each other very long, I feel we are meant to be together, not apart. I just hope William doesn't tell Emily and Adrian about all this as they would probably stop me from seeing you."

"I won't let that happen Michael. To tell you the truth, I feel the same way about you. Whether we are together or apart, you are all I think about," said Violette, looking into his blue eyes.

Pulling Violette in close, he leaned into her and kissed her warm, supple lips tenderly. Holding her firm in his muscular arms, he lost himself as he took in the sweet smell of her frangipani perfume.

Hearing Adrian clear his throat to get their attention, Violette opened her eyes, startled.

"Can I see you for a moment, Michael, before you take Violette out?"

Opening his eyes, and pulling away from their embrace, Michael felt a bit apprehensive and red faced. He settled his thoughts and said, "Yes, sir."

Watching Adrian and Michael walk inside, Violette closed the front door, and decided to wait for them in the foyer.

I wonder what that is all about, thought Violette, as she watched them walk away.

Adrian led Michael into the sitting room.

"Please… take a seat," said Adrian, sitting down on the edge of the couch.

"Michael… I want to know what your intentions are, as far as Violette is concerned?"

Michael took his seat on the couch across from Adrian, and thought about what his response would be, before he could answer. He also tried to read Adrian's thoughts, but for some reason, he couldn't. Frowning, he felt uncomfortable and nervous, not knowing why Adrian's thoughts were blocked from his mind.

"Well, Sir… I really like spending time with Violette and would like to get to know her better, if you will allow it," said Michael, looking him in the eyes. His intentions were clear.

"I understand. I am just worried that she will get hurt," said Adrian, in a fatherly manner.

"I would never hurt Violette, Sir. I know it's only early days, but I truly have feelings for her. I know I am two years older than her and a bit more experienced at life, but that doesn't mean I would take advantage of her at all. I can promise you that, Adrian."

"Thank you for being so honest, Michael. I do appreciate it. I just want the best for my girl, that's all," said Adrian. "Now, go and have a good time tonight and please bring Violette home by 1am at the latest."

"Yes Sir. But I am sure we will be home before then. Violette seems to be a real homebody," said Michael, standing.

"She sure is." said Adrian, standing and shaking Michael's hand firmly. "Take care of my girl tonight."

"Yes, Sir," said Michael, shaking his hand back. Looking into Adrian's eyes, Michael tried to read Adrian's thoughts again, but there was nothing. He knew something wasn't right and would need to report this to William later on that night.

Previously, Michael hadn't had much to do with Emily or Adrian, except for the occasional dinners, until he had met Violette. He had never had the need to read Adrian's thoughts before either. What Michael didn't know, because Adrian hid it well, was that Adrian was a warlock. One of Adrian's main goals in life was to protect the innocent and to reunite supernatural creatures with their own kind. Secretly this was why he and Emily had always lived between the USA and Europe, and why he lived so close to the Gramaze household. Adrian and William often had contact with each other. Adrian was aware of the mission of the Lepidoptera vampires, to rid the world of the Debauched and protect humanity, and he helped them to do this wherever he could.

As Violette waited impatiently for Michael in the foyer she saw Emily walking towards her.

"Hello, dear. You waiting for Michael and Adrian?" said Emily.

"Yes," said Violette. "What is taking so long?"

"Why don't we have a chat whilst you are waiting," said Emily. "Take a seat, dear."

"Oh, OK," said Violette, walking over to the cushioned chair.

"I was wondering how you and Michael are going?" said Emily, sitting next to Violette.

"What do you mean Emily?" *This is just a bit embarrassing, to say the least.*

"Are you starting to have feelings for him?"

Violette could feel her face turn red from embarrassment. *Here goes.*

"I like Michael a lot, and when I am around him he makes me feel happy," said Violette, watching Emily's reaction. "Don't worry Emily, he has been a true gentleman so far…we have only kissed and hugged that's all."

"Sorry dear, I don't want you to feel uncomfortable; it's just that I worry for you."

"It's OK, Emily, you can trust us both as we wouldn't do anything like that yet… Actually, Emily can I ask you something, though?"

"Of course dear. What is it?"

"Umm…this is a bit embarrassing… but I have never slept with anyone before. If I was thinking about it, could I come to you for some advice on contraception?"

Shocked, but glad of her honesty, Emily swallowed hard.

"Sure Violette. That is what I am here for. In fact, why don't I make an appointment at the doctor's tomorrow to see if we can get you on some contraception, just in case?"

"Sounds good Emily… thank you for caring so much."

"Hey, that's what parents do. We worry and take care of our children."

"Emily, I really love having you and Adrian as our foster parents. We couldn't have wished for better," said Violette, giving her a hug.

As there were talking, Adrian and Michael came out of the sitting room.

"Are you ready to go? We don't want to be late for our dinner," said Michael, holding his hand out to help her up.

"Sure… we will see you later on Emily and Adrian. We won't be home late, I promise," said Violette.

"Have a lovely time dear," said Emily smiling.

Stepping into the limousine, Violette felt extremely nervous, but at the same time excited about going on her first date with Michael. The connection she felt with him was like no other she had experienced previously. Not that she had many experiences to compare this date to. But tonight it was just going to be the two of them and she wasn't sure if Michael was the type of boy that liked shy girls who had no prior experience. She had decided that she was just going to be herself, as it was no good pretending she was something else.

"What did Adrian want to talk to you about?" asked Violette as Michael sat next to her.

"He asked me what my intentions were towards you. So I told him how I felt. He seemed to be satisfied with that, for the moment anyway." Looking into Violette's eyes Michael sensed his blood pulsating throughout his body and his teeth shift in his mouth. Her sweet frangipani smell and alluring pale skin was intoxicating and all he wanted to do, was envelope her in his arms and never let her go. But he knew he needed to take it slowly and heed William's warning.

"That's funny, Emily asked me if I had feelings for you."

"And what did you tell her?"

"I told her that I actually like you and would like to get to know you some more too."

"Really…" said Michael. But he already knew from listening to Violette thoughts how she felt about him. "Well, at least you have foster parents that care about you and your happiness."

"Yeah… They are so nice," said Violette, nodding and remembering back to the first day she and Danielle had met Adrian and Emily in the Child Welfare Home. "So where are you taking me? I have been looking forward to going on our date all day."

"You'll see when we get there. It's a surprise." He moved closer to Violette on the seat and held her hand.

As they drove along the Seine riverfront, Michael couldn't believe how lucky he was to be going out to dinner with such a wonderful girl, and in the most romantic city in the world. He was also hopeful that William was right about Violette being a Lepidoptera. His world had been lonely since he was turned, and Michael had always secretly yearned that one day he would meet his life partner.

Arriving at the restaurant, Michael instructed the driver to come back in two hours to collect them. Once inside, the owner greeted them, showed them up to the roof top and introduced them to their waiter for the night.

The night air was perfectly still, and the lighting on the roof top was elegantly low and romantic. There was only one table, which was stylishly made up, with a white linen table cloth, fine silver cutlery, sparkling glassware, and a small tea light candle. The view of their surroundings was of some beautiful lights in Bagnolet and they seemed to be twinkling in the distance like jewels. Once they were seated, the waiter gave them their menus and took their drink orders.

"Wow... I see what you mean about it being a surprise. Thank you Michael."

"You're welcome."

As he sat there looking into her beautiful blue eyes and holding her hand at the table, Michael couldn't remember ever feeling this happy and he knew Violette felt the same way from listening to her thoughts.

Once they decided on their food, Michael summoned the waiter to their table, and they placed their orders.

Waiting for their orders to come, Michael said, "So…I know you are from Century City L.A, and that you have a sister, and you are going to school here, but what else can you tell me about yourself? I know so little about you."

"Well… there is probably not much more to tell Michael. I mostly like to listen to music, read or talk with my friends on Facebook… What about you, Michael, what do you like to do in your spare time?"

"Most of my time is spent working security for William. I don't usually get time off to socialize. But I do like to read when I get spare time," said Michael, knowing how terrified Violette would be if she knew he was a vampire. Hunting was not something he could tell her about, just yet.

Security work. Mmm… That's why he is so buff, thought Violette.

"Whereabouts does William send you to do the security work?" asked Violette.

"All over the place. But mainly in the shipping yards, or night clubs. Just recently we have been guarding important people. You know, like actors, singers, or the rich and famous," said Michael, trying to impress her.

"Wow… that must be exciting," said Violette, with raised eyebrows.

"Not really," said Michael. "I don't get to talk with them. Just protect them and secure their premises."

By the time their entrée and main meals came and went, Violette and Michael had talked casually about themselves and found they had a lot in common.

With the night growing old and the air becoming fresh as the waiter took away their dinner plates, Michael watched the goose bumps forming on Violette's arms from the coolness of the night. "Are you cold?" asked Michael. Unlike humans, vampires didn't feel the heat or cold.

"Mmm... a bit," said Violette nodding.

Michael stood up and took off his jacket and placed it around her shoulders to keep her warm. The seasons had just started to change in Paris, so the nights were becoming cooler.

"Thank you, Michael. You are so thoughtful," said Violette, enjoying the instant warmth, as she watched him sit back down and then looked out over the city. "Isn't this view beautiful from up here on the roof top?"

"Yes. But it's not as beautiful as you, Violette," said Michael, leaning in to steal a kiss from her inviting lips. Taking a breath, he pulled his chair closer to Violette and held her hand. "I think I am falling for you, Violette. And if I am not mistaken, I think you feel the same way."

"Really... umm. I do like you Michael. But are you sure you want to be with someone like me?" said Violette, looking down at their intertwined hands.

Frowning, Michael couldn't fathom why she would be questioning his words, until he read her thoughts.

"Yes, I am sure. You are all I have been thinking of since I first saw you at the window," said Michael, looking into her blue eyes.

"Me too. You have certainly taken me by surprise. I can't remember ever feeling this attracted to a guy before," said Violette, smiling. Leaning in, she kissed his lips ever so softly.

Clearing his throat, the waiter hesitated and then placed their mugs of coffee in front of them. "Excuse me Mademoiselle, Monsieur."

Violette's face was crimson red as she pulled away from their kiss. Swallowing hard, she couldn't give the waiter eye contact, and looked to Michael for support.

"Thank you, waiter," said Michael, gesturing him to move away.

Nodding once, the waiter moved away quickly.

Looking down at his watch, Michael realised it was nearly time for the chauffeur to return. He had enjoyed himself and was now wondering where the night had gone.

"Unfortunately, we have to go in a few minutes. The chauffeur will be waiting for us below."

"Is it that time already? It just seems like we arrived here," said Violette, wanting the night to go slower. She wasn't ready to go home yet, let alone say good night to Michael.

Catching the waiter's attention as he came up the stairs, Michael summoned him over.

"Yes, Sir," said the waiter, standing next to the table.

"Could you please do up the bill," said Michael, taking his wallet out of his pocket.

"Yes, Sir. I will meet you down the stairs at the front counter," said the waiter.

"Thank you," said Michael.

Helping Violette out of her chair, Michael placed his hand in hers and they walked down the stairs together. Waiting for them at the front counter was the restaurant owner.

"How was your meal, Sir?" said the owner, handing the bill to Michael.

"Was excellent. And the service was good too. Thank you," said Michael, taking his credit card out of his wallet and handing it to the owner.

"Thank you," said the owner, swiping the card through the machine. Smiling, the owner handed Michael his card and the receipt. "Have a good evening, Mademoiselle, Monsieur."

"Thank you," said Michael, nodding once.

Violette's breath was short as the cool night air hit her lungs when they walked out of the restaurant. Shivering, she was glad to still have Michael's jacket around her shoulders. With his arm around her, trying to provide some warmth, they walked over to the parked car across the road, where the chauffeur was waiting for them with the door open. Climbing in, Violette was instantly pleased to find the chauffeur had turned the heater on for them.

"Mmm, it's nice and warm in here," said Violette, snuggling into Michael's side as he sat down.

"Sure is," said Michael, placing his arm around her. "Did you still want to go to the movies or would you like to do something else?"

Hesitating, she eventually said, "I don't know. What do you have in mind?"

"I was thinking we could go back to my place and watch a movie and err... cuddle up. Does that sound OK to you?" said Michael.

"Umm... Are you sure that will be OK with your family?" asked Violette. Her stomach was doing somersaults.

"Yes. I am sure my family won't mind." Michael nostrils flared as he took in a deep breath, and felt his eyes dilate, when he heard her heart beat quicken. Her frangipani perfume was overwhelming and he wanted to take her there and then. For fear of repercussions from William, he knew he couldn't. He had to keep calm.

Violette nodded quickly. She had never been to Michael's house before and was feeling a little bit apprehensive.

"Driver… change of plans. Take us home instead," said Michael.

"Yes, Sir," said the chauffeur.

As the car pulled up to the front of the Gramaze house, Michael said, "Everyone is out tonight. So we will have the whole house to ourselves."

"Oh, OK." Violette swallowed hard.

Stepping through the front door entrance, Violette's jaw dropped open and her eyebrows raised, when she noticed how extravagant the Gramaze family house was. Just from the first glance, she could tell they were overwhelmingly wealthy, from the crystal and golden chandelier, which hung in the front foyer.

"Your house is beautiful, Michael. You are lucky," said Violette, admiring each room as they walked through the house.

"Thanks. I know," said Michael, knowing luck had nothing to do with it. It had taken a few thousand years for the Gramaze family to acquire and decorate the house as it currently looked.

"This is my room," said Michael pushing the door open to his bedroom, and gesturing for Violette to walk in first.

Not having any expectations, Violette entered his room with caution. The first thing she noticed was the king sized, four poster bed, and its black and grey quilt cover with two pillows. Next to either side of the bed were black, three drawer cabinets with white ceramic lamps on top, which were already on when they walked into the room. The walls were painted a gun metal grey down the bottom of them and the top of the walls were wallpapered in a black and grey metallic colour which matched perfectly. There was even a crystal and wrought iron chandelier hanging from the ceiling. To the right hand side of the room, near the French windows, which were covered with black velvet curtains, was a corner which was set up with a couch and reclining chairs, with a TV in front of them.

"So what movie would you like to watch?" said Michael, interrupting her thoughts.

"Umm, I don't mind. I like mostly anything; except opera."

"What about *Summer Dancing?*"

"I love that movie. I haven't seen it in such a long time."

"What about I go and get some snacks and drinks from the kitchen and you can get the movie going?" said Michael, pointing to the cabinet.

"OK," said Violette, watching him walk to the doorway.

After finding the movie, and working out how to switch the TV and DVD player on with the remotes, she finally found the right channel to watch the movie on. Sitting back on the recliner, Violette waited for Michael to return. As Michael seemed to be taking a while in the kitchen, Violette closed her eyes and became comfortable in the recliner, which she had already extended the footrest on. With the room completely quiet, Violette thought she heard someone calling her name. Opening her eyes, she sat up and looked around the room. But no one was there. *Must be hearing things.* Violette shook her head slowly, closed her eyes and relaxed back into the recliner once more.

'Violette'

With wide, fearful eyes, and a sharp breath inwards, Violette stood up quickly. There seemed to be a whisper of her name this time. With her eyes darting everywhere, she swallowed hard, looking around the dim lit room. But she couldn't see anyone. *Am I going mad?*

'*Violette.*'

Following the voice, she walked towards the doorway. Even though she trembled slightly, Violette was drawn to the voice, which she was sure, was a woman's. In a trance-like state, she followed the voice that was calling her name, out of the bedroom and slowly down the stairs to the basement.

Finding herself in front of a white coloured wooden door, she heard the voice call her once more. Placing her hand on the golden door handle, she turned the knob.

'*Violette.*'

"Violette," said Michael, trying to kept his voice calm. "What are you doing down here?" She didn't answer.

Slowly Violette turned her head towards the sound of his voice. Michael noticed she had a frosted, zoned-out look in her eyes, which looked right through him. Placing his hand gently over Violette's hand to stop her from turning the handle, he steered Violette slowly away from the door. With his arm around her shoulder, he led her back up the stairs to his bedroom.

It dawned on him that he wouldn't have to look at the back of Violette's neck to see if she had the butterfly tattoo forming, because only the Lepidoptera vampires were able to hear the call of the queen and be drawn to her. Michael knew Renee's suspicions were right.

Opening her eyes and yawning, Violette sat up quickly. Looking around the room, she found Michael sitting next to her waiting for her to wake.

"Sorry... I must have been tired," said Violette, feeling a bit embarrassed.

"That's OK. It took me longer than expected to make some snacks and drinks anyway. You only nodded off for a few minutes," said Michael.

If she only knew what had just happened in the basement, and how close she came to meeting our queen, thought Michael.

Michael now knew why he was immediately drawn to her scent when Violette first arrived into Bagnolet. She was meant to be his Lepidoptera vampire partner, and this was why their attraction to each other was very strong. With Michael's ability to read minds, he knew how Violette felt straight away from the first touch, when they were introduced at dinner that night at Emily and Adrian's house.

How am I going to explain all of this to Violette? thought Michael.

He decided he would speak with William and Renee about it, so that they could instruct him on what to do. One thing he was sure of though, was Violette was there with him and he was enjoying having her there.

As he pressed play on the remote and they started watching the movie, Michael cuddled up closer to Violette and started to kiss her passionately. Just as they were about to take it to the next level, there was a knock at the door, which halted any sort of intimacy for Michael and Violette.

"Michael… we are all home now. I was going to make a cuppa. Would you like one?" asked Annabelle, through the door.

"No thanks. Violette is here too," said Michael. But Annabelle already knew that, as she had read Violette's thoughts as soon as she entered the house.

Opening the door, Annabelle said, "Hi Violette. How was your night out with my cousin?"

"Was really good, thanks Annabelle."

"Oh, that's good. Well, I will leave you two love birds alone. See you again soon, Violette," said Annabelle, realising she was interrupting their night.

"Yeah, see you soon."

"Night," said Annabelle, shutting the door.

Annabelle has been in this position previously where she didn't know anything about Lepidoptera vampires. I remember at first she was freaked out by us, but it seems over time that she had just come to accept everything. So maybe there is hope yet for me and Violette, Michael thought.

But Michael realised he would still need to seek permission from William before he told Violette about their world.

When the movie had finished, it was only just after eleven o'clock and gauging by Violette's thoughts, Michael realised that she didn't seem ready to go home yet.

"Would you like to go for a drive and then take a walk down by the Seine river?" asked Michael.

"Would it be safe this time of night Michael? Back in L.A. we would never go walking at night because you could get mugged."

"Paris is not like L.A., Violette. People go out walking all the time at night by the Seine. So we should be safe."

"Oh, OK then. I would love to go."

As they said their goodbyes to Renee and William, Michael said to Renee, "I should be back around 1am."

"OK. Be safe. Have a good time both of you," said Renee. "Oh and here my dear... You will need this jacket, as it's a bit cold out tonight."

"Thanks Renee. Bye," said Violette, taking the jacket from Renee and walking hand in hand with Michael out the front door into the waiting limousine.

Arriving near the bridge, Michael said, "Albert, can you come back and collect us in about two hours, that's if I don't call you any earlier."

"Yes, Sir," said Albert, turning the car off and getting out to open the door for Michael and Violette.

The night air was chilly and as they walked alongside the Seine River with their arms around each other, Violette felt her heart was starting to quicken once more. Approaching the bridge, a couple who looked like they were madly in love, asked Michael for the time. As Michael lifted his arm to tell them, the woman started looking at Violette very strangely. She kept licking her lips and hissing under her breath. Within seconds, the woman grabbed Violette and pushed her up against the metal railing of the bridge. It was then that Violette saw her face had changed, and her eye teeth were protruding out of her mouth. She was just about to bite Violette's neck, when out of nowhere, Grayson turned up and grabbed the woman by the hair and forced her to the ground.

Where did he come from? thought Violette, watching the fight take place.

"Back off bitch. Otherwise you will die," said Grayson, as he held her down with his hands around her throat.

Violette couldn't believe what she was witnessing. With her breath quickening, she felt so frightened and could feel herself shaking.

"The girl is mine," said the woman, trying to fight Grayson off.

As they fought, Violette watched in horror, and wondered what was going to happen next. When she saw Grayson's eye teeth were protruding as well. Then it hit her.

'*Vampire*'.

She didn't want to believe it. Feeling the hairs come up on the back of her neck, and her chest aching, Violette wished she was home with her family and feeling safe. She didn't know whether to run or stay put.

As the woman wriggled free of Grayson grasp, she saw Violette standing there, just watching, and tried to make a grab for her again, but Grayson pulled the woman away. They both moved much faster than Violette's eyes could adjust to and before she knew it, the women had run off, cursing Grayson as she ran.

"Yeah, that's right bitch, you had better run," said Grayson.

As Grayson approached Violette, he noticed that her eyes had become large, and her breathing was shallow.

With her whole body shaking in anticipation of his next move, Violette felt that this could be her last breath, before she would die. She was in shock.

"Are you alright, Violette?" said Grayson, standing in front of her with his hand on her shoulder.

Her mouth opened to speak but nothing came out. She just nodded instead. Violette's eyes were searching to see where Michael was. She needed to feel safe once more.

"OK. Stay here and I will get you some help," said Grayson.

Out of the corner of her eye, she saw Michael grab the guy the woman was with, and toss him to the ground. When Violette looked at his face it had changed. Michael's eye teeth were protruding now, too. A tremor of terror ran through her body.

Got to get out of here, but where do I go? thought Violette.

"If you know what's good for you, asshole, you had better tell me why you attacked us tonight. Otherwise you will die a painful death, just like your master last year," said Michael, holding him down, face first into the pavement.

He wriggled free from Michael's hold and started raving frantically.

"You will be sorry when my master finds out about what has happened here tonight."

Quicker than it was humanly possible to see, he had disappeared.

Standing there in shock, shaking and trying to taking this all in, Violette noticed Annabelle standing across the pathway. She was calling out to her, "Come over here."

Running over to where Annabelle was standing, Violette said, "Did you see what happened?"

"Don't worry…everything will be OK as soon as we get you out of here." Placing her arms around Violette, she sheltered her from what was going on. After a few seconds Violette felt safe with Annabelle.

By the time the driver came around with the limousine and they all climbed in quickly, Violette was starting to feel faint. Sitting next to Annabelle, she leaned into her shoulder for some support and shut her eyes. She couldn't and didn't dare look at Michael or Grayson because they made her feel uneasy.

Vampires... I want to go home... why me?... Am I going to be next? thought Violette.

Gathering her strength and determination that she had always had, Violette sat up straight and looked them all in the eyes. "So... are you all vampires? Is everyone at your house a vampire?"

They all just stared at Violette, not knowing what to say to her. Michael even tried to place his hand on hers, but she pulled away in apprehension of what he would say or do.

Feeling annoyed, she said in a frustrated voice, "I want the truth, so please don't dick me around by telling me some lies."

Annabelle held her hand and Violette felt a warm sensation and a calming feeling inside come over her. Relaxed, Violette finally fell asleep on Annabelle's shoulder.

Albert pulled the limousine up in front of the Gramaze house, only to find Renee and William waiting for them on the front porch. When the door opened and Annabelle stepped out the car with Violette in her arms, Renee said, "Take her up to Michael's bedroom."

"Yes ma'am," said Annabelle, walking inside.

"Debriefing in the operations room, right now," said William, as Michael and Grayson climbed out the car. He was not very happy about the events that had just taken place.

Standing in the operations room waiting for a reprimanding from William, Michael wondered if Violette would ever look at him the same again. The look of hatred and disgust she had had in her eyes had said it all. He knew that even though she was his life partner, that certain events needed to take place before she would transform into a Lepidoptera, and only then would she understand.

"I can't believe this bullshit…for months the Debauched vampires have not made any attempt to attack us. But tonight of all nights when you are on a date they attack. Doesn't make sense. What the fuck is going on?" said William.

"Maybe I can answer that… tonight when we came back here after dinner, I left Violette alone in my room whilst I went to the kitchen. But when I got back she was gone and I found her down in the basement. She was being called by the queen. She doesn't remember anything that happened, though. She just thought she had fallen asleep. I sort of guessed that she was becoming a Lepidoptera, but I what I didn't figure was the Debauched would go after her straight away," said Michael, ashamed of his actions.

"Why the fuck didn't you tell us about this before you left the house tonight? We would have told you not to go down to the Seine!" shouted William.

"I know this now, William… I just didn't think about it all that much before we left to go there," said Michael.

"Well you really need to start fucking thinking about things before you do them Michael. One day you could lose your life or someone else's over this type of action," said William, heatedly.

"Luckily I had Grayson follow us tonight just in case. But I didn't realise you were coming along as well Annabelle. But I am glad you did, as Violette needed you there to calm her," said Michael.

"There is no luck about this Michael. You really need to sort your shit out," said William, as he banged his fist down on the operations table.

"I couldn't believe the look on her face when she saw what we turned into...she looked so shocked. What am I going to tell her, William? I know it is your choice as our Leader whether we wipe her mind of this evening's events or whether I sit her down and explain everything. But I would like to, if you permit me, to explain our kind to Violette and then if she gets too scared we can wipe her mind. You never know she may just accept who and what we are," pleaded Michael.

William hesitated to answer, and thought about what was the best type of action he needed to take and what was paramount for his family's safety.

"What did you expect? Of course she is going to react like that, you idiot... Go to her now, Michael and explain our kind. But if she gets to terrified, you will need to have Annabelle calm her. Let me know what happens... the rest of you, I want you all to get dressed for battle and see what is out there tonight. Those Debauched fuckers are up to something and I want to know what that is."

"What time does Violette need to be home tonight?" said Renee.

"Adrian told me no later than 1am," said Michael.

"I will give Adrian and Emily a call now and let them know that Violette has fallen asleep on the couch watching a movie with us all. I will ask if it is alright for Violette to sleep here the night," said Renee.

"Thank you Renee," said Michael.

Leaving the operations room and walking down the hallway, Michael heard Annabelle calling out to him.

"Wait, Michael. I want to tell you something."

Stopping in his track, he turned and waited for her to catch up to him.

"Did you want some help telling Violette about us and herself?" said Annabelle, with her eyebrows raised.

"Just how am I going to tell her Annabelle? I don't want her to think we are monsters of some sort," said Michael.

"I was going to suggest that I go in there first and talk with Violette. You must remember I am the only one she hasn't seen with my fangs hanging out and I did calm her. Maybe she might be more receptive to me, and then you can come in later on or we can both go in together. What do you think?"

"I am not sure what to do. Do you remember how you found out and what was said to you, Annabelle?" said Michael.

"Yes I do, and it was so unreal to me. I just couldn't believe that this world even existed. But I did get over it quickly, and that is in your favour."

"OK... I think I need to be the one to tell her. If I need your help, can you come in straight away?"

"Sure, no problem Michael. Just call me in when you need me."

Chapter Seven

Waking from her sleep when she heard the bedroom door open, Violette held her breath as she watched Michael walk into the room and sit down on the bed next to her. As he put his hand out to reassure her, Violette quickly sat up, curled herself up into a ball at the head of the bed and watched his every move. She didn't trust him and was not sure what he had planned for her.

"It's OK, Violette. I am not going to hurt you… remember how I told you that I loved you? Well, that hasn't changed," said Michael, pulling his hand away from her slowly. Hearing her heart beat quicken and listening to her thoughts, he knew she was frightened to be in the same room as him. But he had to try reasoning with her.

Violette didn't say a word. Instead, she sat there just staring at him. She wanted to go home to her foster family and Danielle, and to feel safe once more.

"Violette, I wanted to explain to you about what happened tonight and also about my family, and yourself as well."

"I know what I saw tonight. I don't need you to explain," said Violette, getting off the bed and moving toward the door. "Anyway what do you mean myself?"

Shaking, she tried the door handle. When it opened Violette tried to make a run for it, but to no avail.

Within a blink of the eye, Michael rushed to the door, grabbed her by the arm and pulled her back into his bedroom. Closing the door, he said, "Sit down on the bed."

Violette pulled her arm away from him and ran back over to the bed. "Please... I just want to go home."

"Once you have listened to what I am about to tell you, then you can go home. Alright?"

"Yes," she said, reluctantly.

Michael went into his bathroom. When he returned he had a mirror in his hands.

"What do you need that for?" said Violette, swallowing hard, looking at the mirror.

"May I?" said Michael, indicating he was going to lift her hair off the back of her neck.

She nodded, and held her breath.

"Have you noticed this on the back of your neck previously?" said Michael, showing her the butterfly tattoo starting to form.

"Yes. It's a birth mark," said Violette, looking into the mirror image of her neck. But something was different about her birth mark today. It was now forming a black shape, which she hadn't seen previously.

"It's not a birth mark, Violette."

"Well, what is it then?" said Violette, taking a deep breath.

"When a male Lepidoptera vampire meets his female life partner, the female has the butterfly tattoo already on the back of her neck. But at this stage it is only under the skin and not visible to the naked eye. A bit like a birth mark. Once they feel an attraction for each other, like you and I do, the tattoo starts its transformation. At first the black outline of the butterfly appears, which is exactly what yours is doing. Once they consummate their attraction for each other, the butterfly tattoo begins to colour in and you then become a Lepidoptera vampire. There is more to it Violette, but that is the basics of it," said Michael, watching her reaction to this news.

"Come on… I wasn't born yesterday Michael. That is the biggest load of bullshit I have ever heard. Yes, I agree, you and everyone in this house are vampires. But me… no, I don't think so," said Violette, folding her arms across her body.

"Well technically you are Violette, you just don't know it yet. What I have just told you is true. Vampires have lived amongst humans for thousands of years, without any humans knowing they exist."

"Prove it," said Violette showing her stubbornness.

Even though she was scared, Violette wasn't about to believe what Michael was telling her.

"OK. Do you remember tonight when I found you in the basement and you were about to open a door because you could hear someone calling you?"

"Yes, I do… but how do you know that? I thought that was a dream."

"Well it wasn't…our queen Lepidoptera was down there calling you to come to her so she could enlighten you on our ways and to tell you what happened to your birth parents. But I pulled you back because I didn't think you were ready for that yet."

"What do you mean? My parents are dead, you know that." She felt hurt that he would even bring up her parents. Violette didn't like where this was going at all.

"Technically the parents you thought were your birth parents weren't. They adopted you and told you that you were their child."

"You're lying… I don't believe you," said Violette, with a lump in her throat and tears starting to well in her eyes.

"Think about it… you are a Lepidoptera female vampire and the only way that could happen is if another Lepidoptera has brought you into this world, not your parents who died," said Michael, trying to convince her.

"If that's true, then why didn't they just tell me that I was adopted?"

"I can't answer that. But it could have been because they didn't want you to look for your birth mother."

"That would mean that Danielle and Stephen are not my true blood brother and sister either... this is so unbelievable. Am I going to wake up and find this is all a dream?" said Violette.

She was starting to feel that she didn't belong anymore and that everything she had known was a lie.

"Unfortunately, I am telling you the truth."

Violette sat on the bed feeling numb. Staring straight ahead, and speechless for the first time in her life, she couldn't comprehend what Michael was telling her and didn't want to believe it either. With the thought of being adopted and that her life was a complete lie, she couldn't hold back the tears any longer.

"Are you going to be alright? Say something, anything," said Michael, with a furrowed brow, feeling useless and frustrated.

"I don't know. It's a lot to take in and absorb you know," said Violette with a tear stained face. She ran her hands down her face to clear her mind and try to put things in perspective. "So why is the queen Lepidoptera in the basement, instead of in the house with you all?"

"Because we have to hide her from the Debauched vampires. They know she exists, but they don't know she is here. There also is another reason, but I can tell you about that another time. It's a long story," said Michael.

"I would rather know now," said Violette, intrigued.

Sighing heavily, Michael toyed with the idea as to whether to tell Violette about coven family business.

"OK. I will start at the beginning, as it may make more sense," said Michael, envisaging how things used to be. "Our queen used to be the one in charge of all Lepidoptera's and she ran our coven, here in France. Being that she is a multi-coloured vampire, the queen is very powerful, wise and well respected amongst our kind. More so than any of us. About sixteen years ago, the queen's life partner was killed by the Debauched leader in a battle. At that time the queen was pregnant, and she became withdrawn and isolated herself away from everyone. With William being her second in command, she turned the running of business and the coven over to him. And as of today, William still runs the business in consultation with the queen."

"Oh, wow. So what happened to her baby?" asked Violette, with raised eyebrows.

"Over her lifetime, the queen made a decision to adopt out all her babies. This was so that they could fit into the human world and learn their ways. So this is what happened to her last child," said Michael.

"God, that is awful," said Violette. "So what does the queen look like?"

"She is really beautiful. I will take you to meet her one day," said Michael.

"OK. Who—or should I say what—are the Debauched vampires," said Violette, with a creased brow.

"They are a race of vampires that are evil, Violette. They would suck the life out of each and every human if they had the chance to."

"So are you saying they are evil and your family are re-spectable vampires?" said Violette, trying to make light of the situation. She was confused, as she had always thought all vampires were bad, even if she thought they didn't exist.

"Yes, you could say that, Violette."

"I suppose you had better take me home, as it's nearly 1am," said Violette, looking at her watch and trying to stay calm.

"It's OK... Renee has rung Adrian and Emily and told them that you have fallen asleep on the couch and asked if you could sleep here the night and they have said yes."

"Oh." Surprised by his answer, she wondered why Michael wanted her to stay. Was she fresh meat to him? Only time would tell. He seemed calm enough to her though. But Violette still didn't entirely trust him. Being strong minded, she was intrigued. "I suppose that way we can talk some more, so I can understand about the Lepidoptera's."

"You seem to be taking this well Violette...how are you feeling about all this now?"

"Well... I am a little bit scared still, and I really don't know what to think of this all...but now it's starting to make sense to me. But there is one thing I want to ask you...do you drink human blood to keep alive?" She thought she knew the answer to her question, but needed to hear it with her own ears.

"Yes... but it's not like the movies portray it. We only need to drink human blood once a month and usually we get this from our blood bank supply man we know at the Paris Hospital Morgue."

"Oh. OK." *Well that's a bit different.* "Why did that couple try to attack us tonight?"

"They could sense that you hadn't turned into a full Lepidoptera vampire yet. To taste your blood would be like tasting cocaine to them and it would give them a buzz for hours."

"Hmm, really...so when will I turn into a vampire?" Violette was feeling anxious over something she had never contemplated in her whole life.

"Maybe never. It's up to you, if and when that will happen. You see the female Lepidoptera only turn into a vampire once they make love to their life partner. We have only seen it happen another way once in our life time, and this happened hundreds of years ago. The female Lepidoptera became so angry and enraged that it brought out the vampire in her," said Michael.

"Hmm, so I have two choices; either get down and dirty with you or get really angry. I know which way I will be choosing when it comes down to it."

"Humph...there is no need to rush into anything, Violette. You have plenty of time to think about what you want to do."

"So is making love to a vampire any different to making love to a human?" *Not that I want to do that. I am still a virgin.*

"I have been told that it's not much different at all. But I don't know firsthand as I have never had a life partner before."

Cautious, but starting to feel at ease talking with Michael, Violette was only just now starting to process the information he was giving her. Then it dawned on her. "What year were you born Michael?"

"I was born in 1899. So that would make me 117 years old."

"But you only look about 18, maybe 19 years old." *No that can't be right,* thought Violette.

"This is one of the advantages of being a vampire, you stay young forever. But I suppose the worst thing about being a vampire is you have to move around a lot because people notice if you stay young looking for too long. I used to live in LA, in West Hollywood, many years ago. That is why I said I knew where Century City was, when you told me you lived there."

"Oh, right," said Violette, trying to process his answer. "You have told me how the females turn into Lepidoptera, but how do the males become Lepidoptera?"

"When males are born, they are human and know nothing of the Lepidoptera world. But when they turn seventeen years old, they start to feel like something is wrong with them, and the craving of blood kicks in. Once this happens, usually someone from one of our covens shows them the ways of the Lepidoptera and they provide them with A+ Blood. Eventually, by the time they are eighteen, they are fully transformed and the aging process stops completely. That is why a lot of them look young," said Michael.

"But for me, I am not from the queen's lineage. I was initially born a human, who had a loving mother and father," said Michael, looking off into the distance, remembering the good times he had with his parents. "When I was about twenty years old, we were on our way home from a religious gathering one afternoon, when our horses were spooked by some Debauched vampires. I remember my mother screaming and my father trying to calm our horses down, before our horse-drawn carriage went over and we were driven off a cliff. When I eventually woke from the accident, I was pinned under our carriage, laying upside down, feeling scared. I remember watching my poor mother and father die, as the Debauched sucked the life from them. What I didn't know, until later, was that William saw the whole accident play out and saved me from the Debauched. But the injuries I acquired from the accident were horrific, and I was only given a slim chance to live. That's when William bit me and turned me into a Lepidoptera, and showed me the ways of his coven. In other words, he saved my life, Violette. I have been with William's coven ever since then."

"Oh my God, Michael. That is awful. I am so sorry," said Violette, her words heart-felt.

"It happened a long time ago. But it is one of the many reasons why I hate the Debauched," said Michael.

"I am not surprised," said Violette.

"What else would you like to know, Violette?" said Michael.

"Umm…why does William and a few others look older?"

"It's because they are from the 'First Ones'; where they were transformed from a bite at any age. Once you are bitten back then, you usually stay looking the same age forever. Does that make sense?"

"Yeah, it does, sort of. So is William like some sort of leader or something, because he seems to be always telling you and everyone else what to do?"

"Yes… William is our leader and he is over 3000 years old, and is very well respected in the vampire community. There are only a handful of leaders left in the world now. The Debauched vampires have killed them off over the years."

"3000 years old. Wow, that is unbelievable. Imagine being alive for that long. I bet he would have seen a thing or two in his life time," she said, curiously.

"I would say so. William is one of the very first humans that was bitten by our queen and then reborn into a vampire."

"So explain to me about the Debauched vampires and the First Ones." Violette was thirsty for knowledge.

"The Debauched vampires are ones who feed off humans on a daily basis. They can't seem to get enough blood. They also do merciless things, like selling humans to the highest bidders for money, dealing in drugs at night clubs. These vamps are evil and they need to all be put to death."

Death, thought Violette swallowing hard "Right. I must remember to steer away from them then. Is there any way you can turn Debauched into good Lepidoptera's again?"

"Believe me, we have tried over the years. But nothing good has come of it."

"OK. So what about the 'First Ones'? What happened there?" said Violette, thirsty for information.

"Many years ago, the first family of Lepidoptera vampires, 'First Ones' were slaughtered by humans. At the time when this happened, our queen was out hunting and when she returned home to find all of her family had been annihilated, she managed to escape and hide out until the hysteria died down. Many years later, she put down roots in France, only to find that she became lonely for company of her own kind. Over time she created a new family of her own, but as the years went by, some of the Lepidoptera turned bad, hence this is why we call them Debauched. As it stands now, our queen is the only 'First One' left, and this is why we must, at all times, protect her and keep her whereabouts a secret," said Michael.

"God, that sounds awful. You know just when you think your life couldn't get any worse; I believe it could after talking to you about the 'First Ones'. The queen has had such a difficult life, and come to think of it, so have you all. Especially having to hide your true nature," said Violette, feeling sorry for him.

Hearing a knock at the door, Violette jumped as it startled her.

"Everything alright in there?" said Annabelle, talking through the door.

They both said, "Yes," in unison.

"Great. Just let me know if you need anything," said Annabelle, as she walked away.

"Annabelle has the power to calm you by touch," said Michael.

That explains why I felt so calm when we arrived back here tonight, and why I fell asleep on his bed. Wow, what a nice ability to have.

"Actually each of us has an ability or what you might call a 'power'. Like one of the abilities that I have is mind reading. I can hear your thoughts."

That would make sense, as a few times he did actually know what I was about to say. But I just thought that this was a coincidence, thought Violette, as the realisation hit her that he would have heard all of her thoughts that night whilst they had been talking.

"Wait on, you just said one of your abilities…you mean you have more than one?"

"Yes Violette. But we can discuss me later," said Michael, clenching his fists out of agitation. He just wanted Violette to understand what she was becoming.

"I wonder what my ability will be, Michael?"

"Well it all depends on what colour your butterfly tattoo will be," said Michael, standing and taking the mirror back to his bathroom.

"Oh, OK," said Violette, watching him walk back into the room.

"Would you like to get a drink or something to eat, Violette?" asked Michael.

"Umm…yes please. A nice warm cocoa would be great."

Violette was starting to feel comfortable now. She still felt a bit apprehensive about it all, but was beginning to accept her fate.

"Come down to the kitchen and I will make you one," said Michael, as he held his hand out for her to take.

Violette felt anxious, but she accepted his hand to help her off the bed, because she previously had always felt safe with him. She simply needed to trust him again.

Walking into the kitchen, Violette let go of Michael's hand and stopped in her tracks when she saw Grayson sitting at the island bench. She felt a little apprehensive about being in a room with more than one vampire.

Don't be stupid, they won't hurt you, thought Violette.

Grayson seen the look of terror on Violette's face and read her mind as she entered the room and saw him sitting there.

"It's OK, Violette. We won't hurt you."

Getting up out of his seat, he walked over to her and gave her a hug. She felt a bit intimidated at first, but realised that he meant every word he said.

"Thank you so much for saving me from the Debauched vampires tonight. I will never forget what you did for me and I will owe you both for the rest of my life," said Violette, hugging him back. She couldn't believe that she had plucked up enough courage to say anything to him at all. She was so nervous.

"You're welcome, Violette. We would do anything for you, as we love you like our own," said Grayson, trying to make her feel comfortable.

"Thanks Grayson. That's nice of you to say," said Violette, not realising that she had just become part of a family that would look after her well-being.

"If it wasn't for you, Violette, we wouldn't have found out that the Debauched vampires were still here. We followed them tonight and established where they have been hiding. Once William gives us the go ahead, we will attack them and find out what their new leader is planning," said Grayson.

One thing that Michael hadn't told Violette about yet, was that all vampires could talk to each other through mind thoughts or suggestions.

Michael looked at Grayson and thought, *I don't think Violette needs to know about any of this yet. So can we just keep it quiet for now?*

He nodded.

"I hear you are sleeping over tonight Violette," said Grayson, with a smirk on his face.

"Yes I am. But I am not sure which room I am meant to be sleeping in...not that I am sleepy, yet. My mind is still trying to piece together everything that Michael has told me about the Lepidoptera vampires and how it all works," said Violette.

"Yeah, it takes a bit of getting used to, that's for sure," said Grayson, remembering when he turned. "Actually, I need to go. I'm being called by William to go out on patrol. I will catch you later on."

Frowning Violette said, "Called? I didn't hear him calling you."

"Ah, sorry Violette. William is mind calling us. I had better go," said Grayson.

"Oh… OK. Hey…what if I make you all breakfast in the morning? It will be my way of saying thank you for saving my life. It's the least I can do for what you have done for me tonight," said Violette.

"Sounds great Violette. But if you don't feel up to it in the morning, that's no problem. We are all used to making our own food each morning," said Grayson.

"OK. But the offer is there anyway. Good night and please take care," said Violette, watching him walk out the kitchen.

Placing a hot cup of cocoa on the island bench in front of her, Michael said, "Here you go."

"Thank you," said Violette, placing her hands around the mug.

"You're welcome," said Michael, smiling.

Taking a sip of her cocoa, she started to feel relaxed. "I am feeling a bit tired. Where am I sleeping tonight?"

"Would you like to sleep in my room tonight or would you prefer to sleep with Annabelle in her room?"

Hesitating to answer, she thought about what Michael had just asked her. She had never slept in a boy's room before. "If it's OK with you, I would prefer to sleep in your bedroom. But

I want to make it clear... I will only be sleeping in there, nothing else."

"Sounds good to me," said Michael, sitting next to her at the island bench.

Finishing her cocoa, Violette placed the cup in the dishwasher. With the events of the night and everything she had learned, her body was starting to give way to the tiredness.

"Tired?"

"Yeah," said Violette, nodding her head, yawning.

"Let's go up to my room."

"OK."

"Annabelle has left some of her pyjamas on my bed for you to wear," said Michael, as they walked up the staircase.

"That's really nice of her. I will have to thank her later. Hang on...how did you know that?"

"Mind talking."

"Right..." *That's going to take a bit of getting used to.*

Opening the door to his room, Michael said, "You can use my bathroom if you like."

"Thanks," said Violette, walking over to the bed to collect the pyjamas.

Looking into the mirror after she had changed into the pyjamas, Violette put her hand to her mouth and breathed outwards. Smelling her hand, she realised that she needed to brush her teeth. Once finished, she folded up her clothes and returned to Michael's bedroom.

Looking around, she located Michael on his couch watching TV.

"Hello," said Michael, as she entered the room.

"Hi. What are you watching?" said Violette, trying to seem interested. But in reality she was embarrassed, and feeling a little bit confused.

"Just flicking through the channels. I haven't found anything yet."

"Oh. OK. Well...um...do you mind if I sleep in the bed?" said Violette.

"Sure. I will sleep on the couch then... I might just go have a shower, anyway," said Michael, getting up off the couch.

"OK," said Violette, watching him walk into the bathroom and turn the light on. *Cute ass.* She still felt an attraction to him, even though she wasn't quite sure about this vampire thing.

Smiling at her thoughts, Michael left the door to the bathroom open and turned the shower on.

As Violette climbed into bed and hoped under the covers, she noticed Michael hadn't shut the door to the bathroom. Raising her head off the pillow, she tried to see if she could sneak a peek at him. With his back to her, he took off his shirt and then his jeans, leaving him standing there in his underwear, feeling the water to see if it was hot enough for his shower.

Oh my, thought Violette, averting her eyes away from the bathroom doorway. She didn't dare look any further, for fear of the consequences of her actions. Yawning, she closed her eyes, and tried to think of anything else than Michael. It wasn't easy. Eventually she was exhausted and fell asleep.

The room was in complete darkness, except for the dim light coming from the TV, when Violette woke. Disoriented, she remembered she was at the Gramaze house, in Michael's bed. Turning around to see what the time was on the digital clock next to Michael's bed, she found Michael sitting across from her, on a single seat chair watching her.

"What are you doing?" said Violette, pulling the quilt up to her chin as she sat up.

"You are so beautiful, Violette, when you are sleeping," said Michael, in a quiet voice.

"Thanks... I think. Can't you sleep?" said Violette.

"One of the many perks of being a vamp is that I don't need much sleep."

"Oh, right." *Silly me.*

"How are you feeling?"

"Yeah, I'm good. Still need some more sleep, but I am otherwise OK."

"I mean about being a Lepidoptera and eventually being my life partner?" asked Michael, trying to read her mind.

What am I going to say? Yeah I don't mind... But I do mind, thought Violette.

"I am still getting used to the idea of it all. I do like you Michael, but I am only sixteen years old and way too young to be making decisions on a life partner."

"Would you rather that I didn't tell you about the Lepidoptera? I can erase it from your mind, if that is what you want."

Realising what he was saying, she said, "Erase it from my mind... what... um... I don't think that is a good idea."

"Why not? At least you wouldn't be tormented by it all. I can hear it in your thoughts, you know."

"I would prefer to know Michael. And if you erase my memories, then I wouldn't remember you, and I don't want that. Like I said before, I do like you, a lot, but I am not ready to become a Lepidoptera yet. I would just like to take it slow. There is no rush, is there?"

"No, there is no rush."

"What time is it?"

"It's ten past five in the morning."

"Really? Wow, I would never have guessed that. It's so dark in here."

"Yeah. All the rooms in the house are like this. Too much light for a vamp is not a good sight. Would you like a cup of tea or something else?"

"Um…maybe a hot cup of tea, with milk and one sugar. That would be nice. Thanks."

"One cup of tea coming up. I won't be long," said Michael, walking towards the door.

Smiling, Violette decided to lie back down on the pillow and wait for Michael to return.

Chapter Eight

Opening her eyes, Violette realised she must have fallen asleep again. The last thing she remembered was Michael offering to make her a cup of tea. Sitting up, she looked around the room for Michael but couldn't see him anywhere; but noticed it was twenty-two past nine on his digital bedside clock. Still not feeling comfortable with the events from the previous night, she climbed out of bed and went into bathroom to have a shower to clear her fuzzy brain. Upon opening the door, she found Michael standing there naked. Violette stood there in awe, not knowing what to say and just smiled at him.

Oh my goodness… what a body. He looks so good that I could eat him, thought Violette.

Startled, Michael grabbed a towel from the rail and placed it around himself.

"Oh, sorry Michael. I didn't know you were in here," said Violette staring.

He smiled and pulled her quickly toward him and kissed her lips tenderly. Wrapping his strong arms around her waist made her world shift from feeling worried about what might happen in her future, to felling safe and loved. The attraction she felt towards him was powerful and he knew it, because he felt it too.

"Would you like to have a shower with me?" said Michael, looking into her eyes.

She could feel his penis through the towel as he pressed against her.

"Umm."

"We don't have to have sex in the shower you know. We could just explore each other…would that be OK?" said Michael. *Frangipani, mmm.*

With her head feeling hazy from the strong pull she felt toward Michael, and his vampire scent which drove her crazy, she was very tempted, but at the same time, Violette felt unsure and she stepped back from his embrace.

"Well you have to have a shower anyway. I can smell you from here," he said, smirking at her and trying to make light of the situation. "I could wash your back for you."

Looking down at her hands and fidgeting with them, she sighed loudly.

"OK… but turn around so I can get undressed first," said Violette. *What am I doing?*

Nodding, Michael turned his back to Violette and waited patiently for her to get undressed and hop into the shower.

Hearing the glass shower door open and the water running, he asked, "Can I turn around now?"

"Yes," said Violette, feeling her face turn beetroot red and stepping to the back of the shower to allow him to enter.

Michael adjusted the water temperature, and shut the glass door. Gazing at her beautiful body for only a second, as the room started to fill with steam, Michael swiftly pulled Violette in close to him and kissed her passionately. Caressing her right breast with his hand, he whispered in her ear, "Breathe…"

Violette felt overwhelmed by the sensation of his touch. With her heart beating loudly, she took a deep breath, and tried to steady her nerves. Holding onto the tiled walls for support, she was overcome with excitement as his teeth grazed her earlobe. His persistent soft, wet kisses on her neck continued down her body slowly until he was kneeling in front of her on the shower floor. When he reached her pubic hair, his tongue started to massage her bulb. Speechless, and now holding onto his thick hair, Violette quivered from his touch, when his tongue touched her clitoris. Moaning, she watched him enjoying the tastes of her body. With her whole body feeling like it was on fire from the pure pleasure, his welcoming tongue made her orgasm.

Standing back up, Michael steered her hand down to hold his penis and showed her how to start stroking it. This was the first time she had ever touched a boy's penis, and it seemed to turn her on even more.

It is so velvety soft, yet hard, thought Violette.

Michael whispered in her ear, "Keep going... feels good." He then put his hand over Violette's to show her how to work her hand up and down his shaft.

"Would you like to take this further in my bed?" said Michael, breathing heavily as he kissed her neck.

Violette didn't answer at first. She was so turned on by him and yet at the same time anxious. "I am not sure if I am ready. I have never had sex before."

Michael knew this already from reading her thoughts. Looking into her eyes he said, "That's OK. I can take it slow. If you feel you want me to stop you just have to say so."

She nodded and turned off the shower.

Michael picked her up in his muscular arms and carried her to his bed.

What am I doing? Should I let this continue? thought Michael. He had concerns with how fast this was happening and the consequences of his actions.

"Do you have any protection? I am not on any contraception," said Violette, lying there wet from the shower.

"Yes I have some condoms in my draw next to my bed."

"Are we sure we want to do this?" she said.

"Are you having second thoughts, Vi? Why don't we just lay here and cuddle up instead. Would that be OK?"

She nodded and then cuddled into Michael's chest. "I am not sure I want to become a vampire just yet. But one thing I am sure of is, I feel like I am ready to take our relationship to the next level."

"I would love to take you here and now, but I am happy to wait until you are ready, Violette," said Michael, kissing her hair.

"Knock, knock. Breakfast is ready downstairs for you love birds, if you want it," said Annabelle, through the door.

"Thanks Annabelle. We will be down in ten minutes," yelled Michael.

"OK," said Annabelle.

When Annabelle left, Michael said, "Did you want to go down stairs for breakfast or stay here and get into who knows what trouble?"

"I think we had better go downstairs," said Violette, smiling.

As Violette was waiting for Michael to get dressed, she reached for her phone in her handbag and rang home.

"Hi Emily. How are you this morning?" said Violette, feeling a little bit nervous.

"Good morning, Violette. I am well this morning. How was your date with Michael?" said Emily.

"It was really nice. Sorry about not coming home last night. After our dinner, we ended up coming back to the Gramaze house and watched a movie. But I was so tired that I fell asleep," said Violette.

"I am glad you had a good time last night. But I am also glad that we have made an appointment at the doctors today for you at 1.30pm, considering you are now having sleepovers," said Emily.

"I should be home about lunchtime, Emily."

"OK. I will chat with you some more when you get home, Violette. Bye," said Emily, as she hung up.

Violette wasn't sure what to make of the phone call with Emily. But she had the feeling she would find out just how Emily and Adrian felt about this when she arrived home.

Once they were dressed, Michael and Violette headed for the kitchen.

"Mmm, something smells good," said Violette, with her nose in the air as they walked down the stairs.

Entering the kitchen, she realised that Annabelle had cooked them waffles, pancakes and hot coffee and cocoa.

"Thank you, Annabelle. This is so nice of you. It was meant to be me making breakfast this morning; but I slept in instead," said Violette, sitting on the stool next to Michael.

"That's OK. I know all about sleeping in; especially if you have a great partner," said Annabelle.

Annabelle's life partner had died in battle five years previously by the hands of the Debauched vampires. But she knew how it felt to be in love.

Embarrassed to think that Annabelle knew what they were up to in Michael's bedroom, Violette's face turned three shades of red. Reading her thoughts, Michael shifted closer and held her hand firmly.

Don't worry Violette she doesn't know what we did or didn't do, thought Michael.

But Michael's lips didn't move when she heard him say the words.

Looking at Michael, she twisted her head sideways, *I did hear that, didn't I?*

With an eyebrow raised and a smirk on his lips, he nodded.

How is this possible? thought Violette to Michael. Violette couldn't believe that she could now mind-talk to Michael. It was an amazing experience.

Not sure, thought Michael, shrugging his shoulders.

I wish we had stayed in your bedroom. I am still wet down below, thought Violette, smirking.

My cock is still hard, and would you please stop teasing and tempting me, thought Michael, as he pushed her hand up his leg to feel him through his jeans.

"I think you two need a very cold shower. Even though I don't know what you are mind-talking about, I can see it on your faces," said Annabelle smiling.

"You know we can mind-talk?" said Violette, feeling embarrassed.

"I didn't, but I do now," said Annabelle.

"I have only been able to do it since this morning. I wonder why it's just started happening now?" said Violette.

"I hate to say this…because it's a bit embarrassing, probably, for you both. But you don't have to have sex for this to happen. You just need to bring each other to orgasm, which can happen in other ways, as you know," said Annabelle, with a knowing smile.

"Right," Violette said, nodding.

Feeling uncomfortable, she glanced at Michael and thought, *Beam me up Scottie.*

"Ah… I think we had better finish breakfast and then we can go for a walk in the garden," suggested Michael.

"Sorry… I didn't mean to embarrass you. But you needed to know. It's a great ability and gift to have anyway, Violette. Especially if you don't want anyone to know what you are talking to Michael about," said Annabelle smiling.

"I suppose so. But how far away from Michael can I be for him to hear my thoughts?" said Violette, buttering her pancakes.

"You can be in France and I will hear your thoughts. But once you are in another country I can't hear you or talk to you," said Michael.

"The reason I asked, is because if the Debauched vampires attack me when I am by myself and kidnap me, at least I can mind talk to you and you could come and help me," said Violette.

As they were talking, William walked into the kitchen and he had overheard the entire conversation.

"Good morning."

Jumping when she heard his voice, Violette turned to see William standing in the kitchen.

"Good morning, Mr Gramaze."

"Please… call me William."

"Oh, OK," said Violette.

Pouring himself a mug of coffee, William said, "Violette, I am glad you brought up the Debauched this morning. I was thinking we should probably get you into some training here at our house. We have a training and combat room that you wouldn't have seen yet, and we can train you in some basic fighting and protection skills which will help you if you do get attacked."

Nodding, Violette remembered back to when she was just fourteen years old and the taekwondo tournament she attended and won. She hadn't used her skills in a while, so it would be interesting to see what she could do to protect herself now.

"Also I have decided that one of us, at all times, will guard you, no matter where you go. Plus, we will program into your mobile phone our private telephone number, so that you can ring us if you think you are in trouble," said William.

"Oh, OK. That's very kind of you, William. I just hope that I don't bring too much trouble to your family before I turn into a vampire," said Violette, gulping a breath.

"You let us worry about that, sweet girl. Don't forget you are now family and we look after our family," said William, placing a hand on her shoulder.

"You are too kind, William." *Family... Wow.*

"Please remember Violette, you can't tell anyone outside of this family what you know about us. Not even your sister," said William, seriously.

"I promise I won't say anything to anyone, William. I am very good at keeping secrets," said Violette.

"Also, at the moment the Debauched vampires don't know where we live. So if you ever think you are being followed then you need to let us know, prior to you coming here," said William.

"Yes, Sir. I will remember... so when did you want me to start training, William, and who will be training me?" said Violette, thinking that it would be Michael who would help her with the training.

Hmm... She seems to be OK with all of this Michael. I am very surprised, thought William to Michael.

Michael nodded.

"We can start tomorrow night. The person who will be training you is Kelan. You would not have met Kelan as yet. He will be back from Chicago tomorrow and when you come over tomorrow night I will introduce you. Don't worry about bringing clothes to train in as we will have some here for you, and that way Emily and Adrian won't query you on what you are wearing. You can have showers here so they won't even know about the training," said William.

"Oh, OK. Thanks," said Violette. *He has thought of everything.*

"Can we go now William? I want to spend some time with Violette before she has to go home at noon?" said Michael, impatiently.

"Yes," said William, authoritatively, as he scowled at Michael. "See you tomorrow night Violette, around 7pm for training... Michael ask the chauffeur to give Violette a lift home later on."

"Yes, Sir," said Michael. *As if I didn't already know that.*

"Thank you William. See you tomorrow," said Violette, as she watched William leave the kitchen.

"Well, I had better go too. I will catch up with you both later on," said Annabelle.

"Thanks for the breakfast, Annabelle," said Violette.

"You are welcome."

"Bye," said Violette. Michael nodded, and Annabelle left the kitchen.

"What did you want to do for the next two hours, Violette?" said Michael, as they walked out the kitchen and into the dining room with their breakfast.

Sitting down at their large wooden table, she said, "I don't mind... as long as we can spend time together."

"Would you like to go horseback riding?" said Michael, as he sat next to her.

"Wow you have horses here?"

"Yeah, down the back of the gardens there is a stable and we have twenty horses."

"Cool...but I will need to borrow some jeans and a shirt to go horse riding, as I think it might be a bit uncomfortable going riding in a dress."

"No problem. There are spare clothes in a cupboard down in the stables area."

After they ate their breakfast, Michael showed Violette where the clothes were, so she could choose what she was going to wear. She was dressed within minutes and they then chose the horses they were going to ride.

As Michael got onto his horse, he said, "How good of a rider are you, Vi?"

"Catch me if you can," she said, riding off quickly out the stables and into an open field, with a smirk on her face.

Michael rode off after her. He loved this cheeky side of her and could feel from their connection, just how much Violette was enjoying herself.

At the back of the stables was a large section of the property where they could ride the horses. There were plenty of trees and bushes, and sandy, open ground to ride around on.

As he finally caught up to her, Michael said, "Did you want to stop over there in that meadow? I am sure the horses would like to have a rest and eat for a few minutes."

She nodded. "Hey, you know when we are together and talking through our minds, can the others hear what we are thinking about?"

"No, they can't hear unless you allow it."

"I don't understand…how do I allow it or not allow it to happen?"

"Can you hear me mind talking to you at the moment?" said Michael, hopping off his horse and taking the reins of Violette's horse.

"No I can't…but why is that?" said Violette, dismounting her horse.

"It's because I am blocking you and you are not open to it."

"OK, I get it now. So if I was thinking about kissing you then you would have to be open to me before I was thinking it."

"Yeah sort of like that…it's hard to try and put into words."

"Alright then. What about now. Are you open to me?" *Michael I want to kiss and cuddle into you.*

"Yes, I can hear your thoughts. But my answer is still no. We can fool around; but that's it."

Michael didn't want to encourage Violette as he knew what would happen. He knew she wasn't ready for their world.

"Hey, Michael… Catch me if you can." She ran off into the meadow behind her as fast as she could.

But what she didn't know was that Michael was super-fast. Before she knew it, Michael was in front of her standing with his hands on his hips, waiting to grab hold of her.

"Oh, that's an unfair advantage Michael. Will I have that type of speed when I become a vampire?"

"Yes you will, and many other abilities as well…Violette, can we just enjoy our time that we have left this morning? Did you want to go swimming in the lake over there?"

"I don't have a bathing suit on."

"Who needs them? We can go skinny dipping, if you like."

"Now who is teasing whom?"

Shrugging, Violette stripped off and jumped into the water. "This water is so warm. Why is that?"

"It's actually from a hot water spring nearby."

Michael stepped out of his clothes and dived in under the water. Coming up slowly in front of her, she felt his hardened cock brush the inside of her thigh. Putting his arms around her, he kissed Violette tenderly on her lips.

With her pulse racing, her heart felt like it was going to explode from the magnetism she felt for Michael. *I can't believe how lucky I am to fall for a great guy like Michael,* thought Violette.

"Thanks."

"Hey, no fair. You were listening to my thoughts about you."

"Well as I said; you have to be open to the mind-talk."

"Now listen to what I am thinking." *I just can't get enough of you Violette, and soon I won't be able to stop myself from having my way with you.*

"You are such a teaser, Michael... I think we had better get out of the water and head up to the house. I need to be home soon," said Violette, looking at her watch.

Leaping out of the water with Violette in his arms, Michael put her down gently on the ground. Looking into her eyes he caressed her face with his hand and then kissed her lips tenderly.

As they came up for a breath, she whispered into Michael's ear, "After combat training tonight you are going to have to try to stop me from wanting you so badly. The more I see and feel of you the more I want you."

"It's getting harder and harder to pull myself up now. Maybe I can speak with Annabelle or Renee about what I can do to stop these feelings of wanting you so badly," said Michael, as he put his clothes back on.

"Good idea. I don't think I am ready to become a Lepidoptera, just yet."

Once Violette was dressed, they rode the horses back to the house. Weaving through the trees, Violette all of a sudden felt a wave of sadness come across her. But it wasn't coming from herself. It was coming from Michael. She could feel that he didn't want her to leave.

Walking the horses back into the stable, Michael said, "You go get changed and I will take their saddles off and put them back in their pens."

"Oh, OK. Thanks."

Michael watched as Violette walked into the change room. *So beautiful. Tonight can't come around soon enough for me. Got to keep myself busy during the day to keep my mind off her*, thought Michael.

"OK. I am ready to go now," said Violette, walking over to Michael, smiling.

"Nearly finished. Just need to fill up their water and feed."

"Thanks for taking me horse riding. I loved it."

"You are most welcome," said Michael, winding the hose around the hook. "Would you like a drink when we get back up to the house?"

"Umm, no thanks. I had better get going. Emily will be waiting for me."

"OK," said Michael, taking her hand in his. "I suppose we had better go back up to the house."

"Yeah, I suppose we should. I am looking forward to tonight."

"Why is that?"

"Well I used to do taekwondo when I was fourteen. Will be interesting to see what I remember."

"I think what Kelan will teach you is better than taekwondo."

"Really. Cool."

Walking around the side of the house to the front doors, Violette noticed that the limousine was already parked out the front waiting for her. Michael had previously mind talked to the driver and instructed him on where to take Violette.

"See you around seven."

Pulling her in close, he kissed her lips with endless affection. It took him all his might to release the hold he had on Violette.

"Bye," said Violette, giving him one last hug before she turned and stepped into the limousine.

Chapter Nine

"I'm home," shouted Violette, as she ran up the stairs to her bedroom to get ready for her appointment. She was glad to be home and around some normalcy. She needed the distraction to clear her clouded mind, and if possible, to think about something else other than Michael and vampires.

Stepping into the shower, she placed her head, neck and shoulders under the hot water and enjoyed the way it always made her feel: calm and rejuvenated. With her eyes closed, she remembered the events of the previous night and how in a split second her life had changed. She wasn't sure though if she was ready for a life partner yet, let alone become a vampire. But what she did know was the attraction she felt for Michael was indescribable and nothing like she had ever felt before. Confused and trying to make sense of it all, she finished her shower and changed into some clean clothes.

As she was drying her hair, Emily came into her bathroom.
"Hi Violette. Will you be ready to go in five minutes?"
"Hi Emily. I am nearly ready now. I will meet you in the foyer, if that is OK," said Violette.
"OK dear. Don't be too long then," said Emily, walking out the bathroom.

Placing her hair dryer back in the vanity cupboard, Violette took one last look at herself before she headed down stairs. *Hmm... not a good look,* thought Violette as she retrieved the concealer from her cupboard and rubbed it into the dark circles under her eyes. *Now that's better.* Putting her hair up in a ponytail, she was ready for her doctor's appointment.

Climbing into the limousine, Violette chose a seat next to the window. *I wonder what the doctor will say,* thought Violette, as she watched Emily sit next to her.

"Did you have a nice time with Michael at dinner last night?"

"I sure did. The food was really nice, too."

"So...where did you sleep last night, Violette?"

Looking out the window as they drove along, Violette had to think quickly of a convincing answer. But she couldn't look Emily in the eyes when she replied. "When I woke this morning, I found myself on the couch. Someone had put a pillow under my head and a blanket on me."

"I think you may find that it was Renee who did that, my dear," said Emily, placing her hand on Violette's.

"Yeah... later on I found out it was Renee. She is very thoughtful," said Violette.

"Well, it looks like we are here already," said Emily, pointing to the building, as the driver pulled over into a side street.

Stepping out the car, Violette spotted Annabelle out the corner of her eye standing in the shadows. Nodding slightly to Annabelle to acknowledge her presence, she then remembered what William had said about one of them guarding her at all times. Continuing on into the doctor's office with Emily, who was oblivious to the situation, Violette felt safe, knowing Annabelle was outside keeping a lookout for the Debauched.

"Can I help you?" said the receptionist, when Emily and Violette approached the counter.

"Yes. Violette has an appointment to see the doctor," said Emily.

"As it's your first time to our clinic, could you please fill in this form?" asked the receptionist, handing Violette a clip board with the paperwork to fill in and a pen.

"Oh, OK," said Violette, taking the paperwork. Looking around the room, she chose a seat next to the receptionist desk with Emily. Once she had filled it in, with some help from Emily, Violette handed it back to the receptionist for entering into the computer. She didn't have to wait long before the doctor was calling her name.

"Good morning, Mrs Lachance. What can we do for you today?" said the doctor, sitting down at his desk.

"This is my foster daughter, Violette. We were wanting to talk with you about contraceptives," said Emily, as she sat down in front of the doctor's desk with Violette.

"Ah, well, we would have to do some tests first, and then we can talk about contraceptive treatment for Violette."

Rustling through some papers in his filing cabinet, he handed the forms to Emily. "Here we go. If you could please fill these in."

As Emily filled in the paperwork, the doctor took Violette over to the corner of the room and proceeded to do some tests. Once they had all been done, the doctor asked them to wait in the waiting room for the test results to come back. He also gave Violette some pamphlets to read on sex, sexually transmitted diseases, and contraception.

Forty-five minutes later, the doctor called them into his office again.

"Take a seat, ladies," said the doctor, looking at the test results. "Well, it seems all the results are clear. That's good…so now I can prescribe some contraceptives for you Violette."

Violette could feel her face turning beetroot-red with embarrassment, as the doctor proceeded to tell her about the use of condoms when having sex, whilst he typed out the prescription. She couldn't wait to get out of there.

Handing the prescription to Violette, the doctor said, "Here we go…just always remember to have safe sex, Violette, and you should be alright."

"Oh. OK. Thank you doctor," said Violette, taking the prescription and walking toward the door.

"Yes, thank you doctor," said Emily, joining her.

After Emily and Violette left the doctor's office, they went to the pharmacy next door, to have the prescription filled.

Whilst Violette waited for Emily to pay for the tablets, her mobile phone rang. Looking at the screen, she noticed it was Annabelle. "Hello."

"Don't come outside. Debauched are here. I feel their presence," said Annabelle, in a panicked voice. "I have alerted William, so back up should be here soon."

Walking over to the clear glass windows of the pharmacy, so that she could get a better view outside, Violette's eyes darted left and right, trying to spot the Debauched herself. "I don't see them."

"Get away from the window, you idiot."

Spotting Annabelle across the road waving her hands frantically at Violette to get away from the window, she walked back towards the counter and pretended to look at a jewellery stand.

"Where are they?" said Violette, quietly.

"I don't know. But I feel their presence everywhere. Just stay inside. I will ring you back when it's safe to leave."

"OK," said Violette, hanging up her phone and hoping back up would be there soon. She wasn't sure how long she could keep Emily in the pharmacy though.

"You ready to go dear?" asked Emily.

"Umm…would you mind if I have a look around the pharmacy, Emily? They have some pretty nice things in here," said Violette, hoping she would say yes.

"Sure…but I might just go sit in the car and wait for you, dear. Just come out when you are finished."

"Actually, I wanted your opinion. What do you think of these earrings?" said Violette, placing them near to her ear.

"Mmm, they look lovely dear."

"You don't reckon they look too long?" said Violette, trying to waste time.

"No. I think they look just perfect. Why don't I get them for you," said Emily, taking her purse out of her handbag.

"Oh, that's OK, Emily. I can pay for them myself."

"Nonsense, dear. I won't hear of it. You keep your money. Let's go back up to the counter."

"Thanks Emily. That is so kind of you. But do you mind if I have a better look first before I choose what I want?"

"Sure, my dear."

As Violette chose a wide variety of jewellery to try on, she asked Emily for her opinion, which helped to take up some time in the pharmacy. She felt terrible lying to Emily. But what else was she meant to do?

It wasn't long before Violette's phone beeped with a message from Annabelle. Taking the phone out of her bag, she read the message. *All good now, Vi.*

"OK, I think I like these ones the most, Emily," said Violette, placing her phone back in her bag and walking over to Emily, who had started to look around the pharmacy herself.

"Great, dear. Let's go pay for them and then we can go home."

Stepping into the car and taking her seat, Violette noticed Annabelle across the road in the shadows, along with Michael and Grayson.

You're safe now, my sweet girl, she heard Michael say in her mind.

Thank you, thought Violette, as the car drove off and they went out of view.

On the way home, Violette said to Emily, "Thank you so much for organising the doctor's appointment for me. I really appreciate it. Even if it was a bit embarrassing."

"You're welcome. Better to be safe than sorry," said Emily, smiling.

"Yes I agree…by the way, is it OK for me to go to dinner at Michael's house tonight?" said Violette.

"I can't see why not, dear. But you will need to be home by midnight," said Emily.

"Thanks, Emily."

Violette then let Michael know through mind-talk, that she was coming over at 7 o' clock as planned.

At around 6.45, Violette heard a knock at the front door, and when she opened it, Michael was standing there.

"Hello, what are you doing here?" she said, looking puzzled, but glad to see him.

"Well…I was thinking I would pick you up and drop you back off later, because of you know what," said Michael, in a quiet voice, putting his finger to his lips.

"Oh, I had forgotten about that. Give me a minute and I will be ready to go. I just need to finish getting ready. Lamiae and Emily are in the kitchen if you want to see them."

"OK," said Michael, watching her run up the marble stair case.

Michael walked through the house to the kitchen and said hello to Lamiae and Emily.

"Are you here to pick up Violette?" said Emily.

"Yes, I thought it would be better if I come and pick her up, that way she is not driving by herself at night time when she comes back home late," said Michael.

"That was very thoughtful of you, Michael. Violette is such a lucky girl to have someone like you who cares for her wellbeing as much as you do," said Emily.

"Would you like a drink while you are waiting for Violette to get ready?" said Lamiae.

"No thanks, Lamiae. I am sure Violette won't be long now and I promised William that I wouldn't be too long as well," said Michael.

"Ah, here she is," said Emily.

"Are you ready to go, Michael?" said Violette, smiling.

"Yes, I am ready. You look really beautiful in that dress Violette," said Michael.

"Thank you," said Violette.

"Have a good night and don't be too late," said Emily.

"Don't worry Emily, I will make sure she gets home early," said Michael.

They both said their good byes and walked to the Gramaze house.

When they arrived, the house looked empty. "Where is everyone tonight?" asked Violette.

"They are all out on patrol."

"Oh, OK," said Violette, not realising that it was the norm in this house to be out on patrol.

"Come on," said Michael, putting his arm around her. "I will take you down to the training and combat room where you can get changed into some clothes and padding you will need for tonight's training session."

Placing her arm around his waist, she walked side by side with him to the training room.

As they entered the room, Violette's eyes were over-whelmed with the size of the room and the armoury it had on the wall. Gulping in a breath, she noticed Kelan waiting for her on the soft mattress area. His brown eyes looked her up and down with contempt, and his athletic body made her feel slightly intimidated. Holding onto to Michael's hand, they walked over to him.

"Kelan, this is Violette," said Michael.

"Hello Violette. You ready for training?" asked Kelan, in a deep voice.

"Ready as I will ever be," said Violette.

"Michael, why don't you show Violette where the clothes are and we can meet back here in five," said Kelan.

"Sure. This way Violette," said Michael, walking toward the change rooms.

Dressed, but feeling anxious, Violette appeared from the change rooms ready to do her best. Noticing that Michael had left, and Kelan was waiting for her instead, she walked over to the mat.

"Have you done any sort of fighting or protection training before?" asked Kelan.

"Yes. The last couple of years I have been learning taekwondo and I am a black belt with two dans."

"Anything else?"

"No, that's all."

"Well…that should help you with what I am about to train you in. You see, I will be training you in combat to kill," said Kelan, matter-of-factly.

"What…I couldn't kill someone, Kelan." Her palms were sweating.

"Well, one day you might have to, and the sooner you realise that the better off you are going to be. Your training with taekwondo will help you to protect yourself. But the training I will give you will help you to understand how to take someone down and to really hurt them. Let me tell you a bit about what happens when vampires attack each other," said Kelan.

Sitting on the mat together, Kelan explained about what happened when vampires fought. Violette got a good understanding of why she needed to know how to kill or hurt a vampire. Put simply, it was kill or be killed when it came down to vampire attacks.

As they started to train, Kelan tested Violette's taekwondo skills. When she had had him on the mat more times than he'd had her on the mat, he knew he didn't have to go any further with that type of training. Next was knife and sword fighting. The knife fighting was good but she needed a lot more practise in the sword fighting.

After about an hour of training, Kelan said, "I think that will be all for tonight. Can you come back on Friday night around the same time, for some more training?"

"I will have to ask my foster parents, but I can't see that being a problem. So I will see you Friday, if not before," said Violette.

Nodding, Kelan then headed toward the change rooms for a shower and left her standing on the mat. Kelan was a man of few words and it sure was disconcerting. But he was a good teacher and she was glad to be in his expert hands.

As Violette was about to walk up the steps to the shower room, she could see Michael waiting for her.

"Mmm, not bad for someone who hasn't had any combat training," said Michael. He had watched the whole training session and couldn't believe how good she was.

"It helps when you have been doing taekwondo for a few years. I still have a lot to learn according to Kelan, though," said Violette.

"I had better watch myself then," teased Michael.

She laughed. "I am going to have a shower now. I don't smell too good!" she said, sniffing her clothes.

"You want some company in there?" said Michael, as he pulled her in close.

"That sounds tempting."

"Well what are we waiting for?" said Michael, as he picked her up in his arms. They grabbed her clothes from the change room and went upstairs to Michael's bathroom.

Once Violette got undressed in Michael's bedroom, she went into bathroom. Michael was already waiting for her, and he was naked.

"Just let me wash myself first," said Violette.

"What about if I wash you instead?" said Michael, looking at her indulgently.

"Mmm, that sounds interesting," said Violette playfully.

When they got into the shower Michael soaped up the cloth with a strawberry shower wash, which smelt just heavenly. As he washed her, he caressed and kissed each part of her body. Violette felt her body explode with pleasure as he knelt down in front of her and enjoyed every part of her clitoris.

Gasping as Michael slipped his finger into her vagina and began moving it in and out, she said, "Oh God, Michael, that feels so good. Please...don't stop." Placing her hand over his, she urged him to move faster. She lost count of how many times she orgasmed.

When he had finished, she took the cloth from Michael and started to wash him, caressing his cock back and forth gently. As he kissed her fervently, his breathing increased. Kneeling down in front of him, she started to kiss him, pulling and sucking on his cock, until he came. The pure pleasure they both experienced was indescribable.

Stepping out of the shower, Michael was about to lift Violette up in his arms and take her to his bed to make love, when Annabelle knocked on the door and said, "Your dinner is ready."

"Thanks, Annabelle," said Michael, sighing and rolling his eyes.

"You know, Michael, I am sure she is reading our minds. This is the second time that she has stopped us from making love in your bed."

"Don't be silly Vi, she can't read my mind if I don't let her in," said Michael.

"Yes, but when you think about it, I don't know how to control that yet. So maybe she is reading my mind, and I don't know it," said Violette.

"You could be right Vi. I will ask her later on tonight about it in private, once you have gone home," said Michael.

"It's not a bad thing her knowing though, even if it is embarrassing. I don't want to become a vampire, just yet. Mind you I am finding it harder and harder to resist you. I am sure next time, if she doesn't stop us again, that it will happen," said Violette.

"Then we will have to start being a bit more careful, Vi. I know we both badly want to have sex, but there are consequences, and unless you want to become a vampire, we shouldn't pursue this fooling about, until you are ready," said Michael.

I really do need to speak with Annabelle or Renee about how we can slow our feeling for each other whilst I am human, thought Violette.

After dinner Michael, took Violette home. He knew he wouldn't be able to resist her if she stayed in the same house as him tonight any longer.

Once Violette arrived home, she changed into her pyjamas, put on the TV and fell asleep. She was totally exhausted from the day and night.

Later that night on patrol, Michael caught up with Annabelle. She confirmed that she did mind read Violette's thoughts, but only to help her, not to see what was going on in Michael's bedroom.

Walking along the rooftops in the city and looking down to see if the Debauched vampires were causing trouble, Michael said, "Annabelle, I was wondering if you could help me with how Violette and I go about slowing our feelings for each other? As you would have seen when you were mind reading Violette, she wants me just as bad as I want her, and we are teetering on the brink of making love. But Violette is not ready to become a vampire yet."

"There is one thing you both can do," said Annabelle.

"What is it?" said Michael.

"You know how you both can hear each other's thoughts now? Well, you can do the same thing with lovemaking. When you are in Violette's mind, talking to her, all you have to do is think about having sex with her and explain to her in detail about your lovemaking, and it will feel like you both are having sex at the same time with each other," said Annabelle.

"That actually works?" said Michael, with a raised eyebrow.

"Yes, it does. I have tried it previously and it may not be the same as doing it, but it will feel like you have done it. Caution, you both will need a towel in your bed when you finish, so put one down first," said Annabelle, smirking.

"Thanks Annabelle. You are great," said Michael fist-bumping Annabelle.

"Anytime, bro," said Annabelle, fist-bumping him back.

The next day, Michael sent a text message to Violette and told her to open her mind to him. Once she did, Michael explained about what Annabelle had told him last night.

"It couldn't be that easy, could it?" said Violette, in disbelief.

"What are you doing right now? Are you able to lock the door to your bedroom?" said Michael.

"No one is home at the moment, and yes, I can lock my door," said Violette.

"Do you want to see if we can do this now?" said Michael.

"OK," said Violette nervously. She then shut her bedroom door and locked it. Even though Violette wanted to try this with Michael, she was still unsure if she was doing the right thing. Losing her virginity was huge to her, even if it was imaginary sex.

"You will need a towel under you before we start," said Michael.

As Michael and Violette got into their beds, they started to mind read each other's thoughts. They could feel the excitement and pleasure they were giving each other from their thoughts straight away. It was a strange feeling though. Violette felt like she was dreaming about what they were doing, when she had her eyes closed. After about one hour of love making in their minds, she could sense that the pull she had felt towards Michael had disappeared.

"Do you feel that Michael?" said Violette.

"Wow…yeah. I don't feel the pull towards you now either. So would you be willing to do this again, when the need arises?" said Michael.

"Sure, especially if it feels like this, every time," said Violette.

"I can't believe this actually works. I will have to thank Annabelle for her help," said Michael.

"I think that I will go and have a shower," said Violette.

"Yeah, me too," said Michael. "I need to have a cold one!"

"I hope you don't think I am naïve, but is this something that only happens when you are a vampire or does this happen to humans as well, Michael?" said Violette.

"It only happens to vampires, Vi. We can go for hours once we are excited and aroused," said Michael.

"Something to look forward to when I become a vampire," said Violette, teasing.

"Violette, I need to go. I can hear Grayson telling me that we are needed by William for a meeting in the operations room."

Violette sighed.

"Alright then. I will see you later on tonight."

"Bye," said Michael.

Violette lay on her bed for a while thinking about Michael, and smiled at the lingering warm feeling between her legs, before heading to her bathroom for a shower.

Chapter Ten

With the water cascading over her body washing the soap off, Violette's stomach started grumbling. It was nearly lunchtime and she was absolutely famished after all the exercise with Michael that morning. Smiling, she remembered their sweet encounter through mind talk, and how it made her feel exhilarated.

She turned the water faucet off, and stepped out the shower onto the white bath mat and dried herself off. Wiping the steam from the vanity mirror with the same towel, she couldn't believe how tired she looked, with dark circles under her eyes. As she reached for her concealer in the vanity cupboard, she pricked her finger on something sharp.

"Ouch."

Bending down to have a look at what had bitten her, she realised she had pricked her finger on a pair of scissors which were standing up right in a container. Sucking her finger to contain the blood spillage, she moved the scissors to the back of the cupboard so it didn't happen again. She searched through the cupboard and came upon some plasters and decided to put one on her finger, as this was the only way she was going to be able to stop the bleeding. Looking down at the white bath mat, she saw a drop of blood had landed on it.

"Shit…how am I going to get that out?"

She put the mat under the cold water faucet on the vanity, and scrubbed madly, hoping the blood would come out.

Thank God… it's coming out, thought Violette, continuing to rinse the mat. Hanging the bath mat over the shower glass to dry, she then continued to get dressed.

As she walked out of her bathroom, Violette's attention was drawn to her bed and the fact that it was unmade. Before she headed down stairs to make something to eat for lunch, she decided to make her room look a bit more presentable. She certainly didn't need Emily or Adrian getting any inkling what had been happening in there.

With her stomach grumbling again, Violette made her way down the stairs to the kitchen. As she approached the kitchen, she was stopped in her tracks, when she heard the sound of glass breaking and voices. Instantly she felt the hairs on the back of her neck stand up. Peeking around the corner to see what the noise was, she noticed that there were two huge guys, who she could feel were vampires, and who had broken the glass panel in the kitchen door to get into the house.

Violette ran for her life, hoping they didn't see or smell her. As quietly as possible, she ran down the stairs to the basement, where she hid in the linen closet. Her heart was beating loudly, and she was sure the two bloodthirsty vampires would find her sooner, rather than later. Crouched in the back of the linen closet and shaking she thought, *What am I going to do? I know, I will mind talk to Michael.*

Michael… Can you hear my thoughts? I have two huge vampires in my house, and I am scared. Please… Help me.

But when he didn't answer her, she started to panic. As the sinking feeling set in that she was about to be kidnapped, or worse yet, killed, Violette's heart felt like it was going to jump out of her chest. She wasn't ready to die, not yet. She had big plans for her future and no one was going to take it away from her now. Remembering the combat training Kelan had taught her previously, Violette stood with her legs apart and fists clenched, ready to fight the Debauched vamps as soon as they open the door to the linen cupboard.

Hearing the sound of footsteps coming down the stairs and voices talking, she tried to calm herself. From under the door she could see that a light in the basement had been switched on and shadows were coming towards her. She was definitely in trouble.

Holding her breath, she watched the door open suddenly. They were not going to be able to take her easily. But when she looked up to see their faces, she saw Grayson, and two other vampires, whom she recognised as the security guards from her house, standing there to help her.

"Who else is here Grayson?" said Violette, quietly.

Extending his hand out to help, Grayson said, "Shhh, Violette. Michael and James, another member of our family, are here as well, and they are looking through the house now to find the two vamps. Are you alright?"

"Yes, thanks Grayson. I am just a bit shaken, that's all."

"We just need to sit tight and wait for Michael and James to let us know that it's alright to come out of the basement," said Grayson, noticing her finger with a small plaster on it.

Hmm, this is why the Debauched are here. They can smell her blood, thought Grayson to himself.

Whilst waiting to for Michael and James to come and get them, all Violette could hear above her was fighting and things breaking. After a few minutes, the noise above quietened and then they heard footsteps coming down the stairs.

Grayson pushed Violette behind him, whilst the two other vampires, Bennett and Micajah, stood their ground waiting for whoever it was descending the stairs.

As Michael came into view, down the stairs, Violette started to feel light-headed. Being scared out of her mind had taken its toll on her. Tears flowed freely down her cheeks at the realisation of what had just happened hit her.

Breathing a sigh of relief, Grayson turned to Michael and said, "All done?"

"Yes," said Michael.

Rushing over to Violette, Michael pulled her into his embrace with his muscular arms and held her tight. Having him kiss her on the forehead made her feel like everything was going to be alright. She felt safe once again.

"We have gotten rid of them. Everything will be alright now, babe," said Michael.

Sobbing, she said, "I was so scared. I thought I was going to be taken by the two vampires or worse, sucked dry."

"You're safe now," said Michael, comforting her.

As Violette looked into Michael's eyes, she could feel his pain.

"You have been hurt, show me," said Violette, frowning and wiping the tears from her eyes.

"It's not too bad...vampires heal quickly," said Michael, as he lifted his shirt to show her the knife wound.

"Oh Michael, look at you."

But as she looked at his wound, to her amazement, it began to heal over. Raising an eyebrow, she said, "Wow, that is quick."

"Come on, let's get upstairs and help James clean up the mess before anyone comes home," said Grayson.

"Good idea. I think Emily and Adrian will be home soon," said Violette, knowing the consequences if they came home.

As they entered the kitchen, Violette could see that James was repairing the broken glass panel in the kitchen door and

Lamiae was there cleaning up the mess that had been made from the fight.

"Are you alright dear?" said Lamiae, as she came over to hug Violette.

"Yes, I will be alright Lamiae," said Violette.

Lamiae must know about vampires. I should have guessed she would have known something, thought Violette.

Michael put his arms around her, and said, "Yes, she knows all about us."

After about 30 minutes, all the mess and destruction was cleaned up, leaving no evidence behind that anything had happened.

"What happened to the vampires that broke in?" said Violette.

"They were taken down and killed. They turn into ash and then all we have to do is sweep it up," said James, matter-of-factly.

Frowning, she said, "Right...guys how did the vampires know I was here?"

"They didn't, and when we asked them about it prior to killing them, they said they were just looking for some fresh blood to drink, that's all," said Michael.

"These vamps were bloodthirsty and they would not have stopped killing humans if we didn't stop them first," said James, looking at Violette.

Jumping, when she heard a knock at the back door of the house, Violette looked to Michael for reassurance, as she pulled the curtains back and found William and Renee standing on the other side.

"Hello. Come in," said Violette, pulling open the door.

"Are you alright?" asked Renee, placing her arm around Violette.

"I am now. As for my nerves…well I don't know."

"Looks like the damage has been taken care of," said William to Michael, as he looked around.

"Yes, Sire," said Michael.

Hearing a car pull up at the front of the house, Violette went to the window to check who it was. She quickly ran back to the Gramaze family.

"Shit…it's Emily and Adrian. You all need to go," said Violette, opening the back door.

Following her command, James ,Micajah, Bennett and Lamiae filed out the kitchen door and back to their homes. But before Grayson left he took off his clean polo shirt and gave it to Michael to wear. Michael's was bloodstained from the battle with the Debauched vamps.

"You owe me, bro," smirked Grayson, as he grabbed Michael's bloodied t-shirt out of his hands and scooted out the door.

"We will go into the sitting room, Violette, and pretend that we have just arrived. Maybe you could make it look like you were bringing some cold drinks into the sitting room for us," said Renee.

"Sure. You go, and I will bring them in soon," said Violette, walking toward the fridge.

With vampire speed, Renee, William, and Michael ran toward the sitting room and made themselves comfortable.

Not suspecting that anything had happened in their house as they walked in the front door, Emily and Adrian caught sight of Violette carrying a tray of drinks toward them.

"Where are you going with those, dear?" asked Emily.

"We have company. The Gramaze's," said Violette, indicating they were in the sitting room.

"Oh. OK. Would you like a hand to carry the tray in, dear?" asked Emily.

"No, I will be OK," said Violette, continuing to walk into the sitting room.

As Emily and Adrian walked into the sitting room, William, Renee and Michael all stood up to greet them.

"I wasn't aware you were all coming over today," said Adrian puzzled, as he shook William's hand.

"Yes, I suppose we should have rung first. I just surmised you both would be home and free to have a chat," said William.

"No bother. It's always good to see you anyway. Take a seat, my friends." said Adrian.

"Would you like to stay for afternoon tea?" asked Emily.

"No thank you, Emily. The cold drink Violette has made us is fine. Actually we have come over to talk to you both about Violette and Michael," said Renee, looking to William for support.

"It seems that Violette and Michael have become very close. I know Violette is only sixteen years old and Michael is two years older than her, but we were wondering what your feelings were to Violette and Michael being able to spend some more time together than what they currently are," said William, looking from Adrian to Emily.

"We were wondering when this was going to come up," said Adrian, searching Emily's face for an answer.

"Yes, well, they came to us today to ask for permission. And I think that is it important enough to warrant a discussion," said William.

"Adrian and I have discussed this and it is fine with us. But Violette's study must come before any relationship that is building between them. We can plainly see that what Violette and Michael have is not just puppy love or an infatuation, but a real relationship," said Emily.

"So what can we propose that will fit in and be acceptable for everyone concerned?" said Renee.

"Well...what about if they can only physically see each other after Violette finishes her homework and assignments each day. And on the Saturday and Sunday they can have sleep overs or see each other the whole day and night. That's unless Violette has a lot of schoolwork to do," said Adrian.

"Violette has been an A grade student up until now and we don't want that jeopardised," said Emily.

"That sounds fair," said William.

"Are you both happy with this arrangement, Violette and Michael?" said Renee, looking at them.

"Yes. It sounds great," said Michael.

"Yes. But is Michael allowed to drop me off and pick me up from school as well?" said Violette, excited.

"I can't see that being a problem. What do you think, Renee and William?" said Emily.

"Sounds good...also, I am not sure if you know or not, but Violette was telling us she used to take taekwondo lessons in L.A. Well, we also have an instructor who comes twice a week to teach us taekwondo and other sorts of training, and we were wondering if you would like Violette to join us so she can graduate eventually," said William.

"Yes, we did know she took taekwondo in L.A. If she has finished her school work on those days, then yes, she can go to training. We do appreciate you offering the training towards Violette. We can work out a payment for the lessons later if you like," said Adrian.

"No need to do that, as there won't be any additional cost to what we are currently paying for the lessons," said William.

"Thanks, that's really nice of you both," said Adrian, shaking William's hand.

"Well now that we have got that all sorted, we had better go, as we have guests coming for dinner tonight," said Renee standing.

Holding Violette's hand Michael thought to her, *Do you believe what has just happened?*

I know. My day has gone from Debauched vampires in the house to having a discussion with Emily and Adrian about us. Unbelievable, she thought back.

"It was good to see you both again. We must catch up with you soon for a dinner or something," said Renee.

"That would be lovely," said Emily, walking arm in arm with Renee to the front door.

"Would you like our chauffeur to drive you home?" asked Adrian to William.

"No thanks, my friend. The walk will do us good," said William, shaking Adrian's hand. "See you both soon."

"Yes, soon my friend," said Adrian.

"Au revoir, my sweet girl," said Michael to Violette, as he kissed her cheeks goodbye with passion.

"See you later," said Violette as she hugged him goodbye.

Following Emily and Adrian inside, Violette said, "Thank you so much for organising and agreeing to Michael and I seeing each other."

"You're welcome, dear. We only want what's best for you," said Emily, placing her arm around Violette as they walked to the kitchen.

"So where is Danielle today?" said Violette.

"She is out with Annabelle shopping at the flea markets," said Emily.

"They seem to have become quite close. I am so glad Danielle has found at least one friend to hang out with. I would say she will make a few more friends once she settles into school. You will probably find her social calendar will be full then," said Violette.

"Yes, I would agree. But we have also spoken with Danielle about how important schooling is, and that she needs to get really good grades to graduate so that she can become a sports teacher," said Emily.

"I was going to go make something for afternoon tea. Would you both like anything?" asked Violette.

"No thanks, dear. We will wait until dinner tonight," said Emily.

"Um… Is it OK for Michael to come over tonight to watch a DVD with me?" asked Violette.

"Yes, dear. That will be fine. We still remember what young love is like," said Emily smiling.

"Thank you both for being so understanding about Michael and me. I really do appreciate the confidence you have in us as well. Don't worry, we won't let you down," said Violette.

With Michael coming that night, Violette decided to shower with a nice blueberry scented body wash. But Michael already knew this as he was mind reading her most of the afternoon. She couldn't seem to get him out of her head. Violette knew she was going to have to find a way of stopping him from entering her thoughts all the time.

Hearing his moped pull up outside, Violette ran eagerly down the stairs and to the front door. Opening the door, she was greeted with a big smile from Michael, who pulled her into his arms and tenderly kissed the lips that he longed for.

"Hello, sweet girl," said Michael, as his hand smoothed her hair away from her face.

Her heart melted from his touch as she kissed him once again. "Hello."

"Come on. We had better go inside," said Michael, trying to slow things down.

Nodding her head, they walked hand in hand inside and shut the heavy wooden door behind them.

"What would you like to do?" asked Violette.

"Umm, what about a stroll around the gardens?" said Michael.

"OK. Sounds good." Violette knew the night air was cool outside, but she didn't mind, because she had Michael all to herself and loved the way his muscular arms wrapped around her and kept her warm.

"I won't be able to stay very long Violette. William has instructed me that I am needed out on patrol tonight. So I can only stay for a little while."

"Oh. OK."

"Sorry," said Michael, feeling her unhappiness.

"It's OK. I understand…hey, did you want to go to that night club, 'Fire and Ice' tomorrow night with Danielle and me?" said Violette.

"I will have to let you know, Vi. I have to check with William first to see what the plan is for tomorrow night."

"That's OK. I am sure if you can't come there will be someone in the wings watching me to make sure I am alright anyway. But I would really love for you to come as it would be nice to have a few drinks and dance with you."

"Me too, but I'll have to check with William to see if it's OK for you to go there. It may not be safe for you."

"That never entered my mind. I forgot about the Debauched, just for a second though."

Bloody Debauched. I sure hate them, thought Violette.

"Yeah, I don't like them much either. They spoil all the fun," joked Michael. "Sorry Violette, but I can hear Grayson calling me. I am needed out on patrol straight away. So I had better head off now."

"So soon...bummer... well at least I got to see you for a little while, anyway."

As they were walking to the front door to say their good-byes, Violette said to Michael, "I love you."

"I love you too, Violette," said Michael, hugging her into his chest. "See you tomorrow. If not in body, I will mind talk to you."

He kissed her once again and then rode off on his moped.

Keep safe, thought Violette, watching him ride away from her.

I will, thought Michael back.

Violette smiled.

Chapter Eleven

Waking the next morning and wondering what time it was, Violette yawned as she looked over at her bedside clock, which displayed ten o'clock. With her whole body aching from the combat training Kelan had given her two days before, she dragged herself out of bed to have a shower. Luckily, the weather had turned cold out, so she could wear jeans and a long sleeved top to hide the bruising on her arms and legs.

She hadn't spoken to Michael as yet, which was a bit strange. But it felt good not to have anyone in her brain this morning. As she hopped into the shower, Violette started to wonder if maybe she could find out a bit more about her supposed birth parents that day. She also wanted to know if Danielle and Stephen were adopted or not. Violette didn't know how she was going to approach the conversation with Emily, but she just had to know the truth.

After her shower, Violette went in search of Emily and found her in the sun room. She was sitting having her morning tea and enjoying the little bit sun which was struggling to shine through the clouds.

"Morning Emily," said Violette, as she entered the room.

"Good morning. How did you sleep?" said Emily smiling at Violette.

"Good, thanks. I can't believe I slept so long this morning though," said Violette, as she sat down at the small metal table across from Emily.

"You must have needed it dear," said Emily, sipping her tea.

"Mmm... Emily...umm... I was wondering if I could find out more about my family history," said Violette, apprehensively.

She looked at Violette strangely.

"Why... what did you want to know?"

"There are a couple of things I wanted to know. I have always wondered why Stephen left home at an early age. Or why I have always felt like I didn't belong," said Violette, fidgeting with her hands.

"Are you sure you want to talk about any of that Violette? It's just that some things are better off left alone and not bought to the surface," said Emily.

"Yes, I would like to know...but why do you think it's better if things are left alone?" said Violette.

"I don't...but all the information I have on you and Danielle and your family... well... you may not like what you hear, dear. I just don't want to upset you," said Emily.

"I would rather know, Emily," repeated Violette, with her brow furrowed.

Taking a deep breath, and trying to compose an answer, Emily said, "I think it would be best if I speak with Adrian first, and then maybe later on we can speak about this some more. Would that be OK with you, Violette?

Humph. Well that's not what I expected her to say, thought Violette.

"Yes...that will be fine. I just want some answers, Emily," said Violette, sighing. "Well...I am going to go into the kitchen and make something to eat first."

"OK dear. I will see you later on then," said Emily.

After Violette left, Emily went into Adrian's office, where he was working, and closed the door behind her.

"I think we need to talk."

"What is it, my love?" said Adrian, looking up from his work, worried.

"Violette has just asked me if I could explain to her about her family history. Do you think it's time that we should sit down with Violette and let her know about her family?" said Emily.

"Yes I do. She has a right to know that she and Stephen were adopted," said Adrian. "She is old enough to understand. But I think we should tread lightly. We don't want to scare her away from us."

"I think you are right. I just wasn't prepared for this to happen so soon. Let's go find her."

Emily and Adrian walked into the kitchen and found Violette making some breakfast.

"Good morning, Violette. Can we have a chat about your parents?" said Adrian.

"Sure," said Violette, as she sat down at the island bench with her toast.

"I will start at the beginning of what we already know. And if you have any questions that we can't answer, then we can contact the Department of Child Welfare and ask them, OK?" said Emily.

"OK," said Violette.

"Did your parents tell you that Stephen and you were adopted?" said Emily, anxious of what her reaction might be.

"No. I didn't know that. I have always thought and have been told that they were our birth parents," said Violette. She sat there in shock as Emily and Adrian confirmed what she already knew, but wanted to deny. "Wait on... so are you saying that Danielle wasn't adopted?"

"Yes, that is correct. From what we have read in your records, your parents adopted you when you were one week old and Stephen would have been about nine years old. Apparently, your real birth mother and father went missing and have never been found. On the day they disappeared, you and Stephen had a nanny looking after you, and when your birth parents didn't return home, she contacted the police. It was all a big mystery," said Adrian.

"Unbelievable." *They must have been my first adoptive parents then. Oh, this just gets better. I have been adopted twice and fostered once. Being a Lepidoptera sucks. What more is life going to throw at me now?* thought Violette.

"Is there anything in the records you have, to say why Stephen left and why we have never heard from him again?" said Violette.

"No, sorry, there is nothing at all on that. It only says he left and never kept in contact with his parents," said Emily.

"Oh. OK. So do you know the names of my real birth mother and father?" said Violette.

"That's something that is not in the records, Violette, and we are not sure why that is. It's the same for Stephen as well. Usually the birth mother at least is listed on the birth certificate, but yours and Stephen are blank," said Adrian.

Astonished by what she had just been told, Violette wondered what had happened to her first parents. Were they taken by the Debauched or killed by some sicko? She would never know.

"This is a lot to take in. I do appreciate you both for being truthful to me though," said Violette.

Michael was right. I was hoping he was wrong, thought Violette.

"Was there anything else you wanted to know or discuss, Violette?" said Emily.

"Umm…I can't think at the moment," said Violette.

"OK. We will leave you to ponder over what we have told you…are you certain you are going to be alright?" said Emily, as she gave Violette a hug.

Violette nodded and said, "I don't know. It's a lot to take in."

She could feel tears welling in her eyes. But she held them back.

"Do you mind not telling Danielle for the time being, as I want to be the one to tell her?"

"Yes, that would be OK," said Emily.

"And would you mind if I could go over to see Michael? I just need someone to talk with about this," said Violette.

"Yes dear. That would be OK. But best to ring him before you go over there," said Emily.

"OK," said Violette.

Emily and Adrian both gave Violette a hug and left her to finish her breakfast in the kitchen.

As she ate her toast, the realisation hit her and her tears started to flow freely down her cheeks. Sobbing into her hands, she couldn't believe that her whole life had been one big lie.

Are you OK Violette? thought Michael. He could feel her pain.

I don't know…would it be alright if I could come over to your house for a while? she thought, as she wiped her eyes.

Sure. I will meet you out the front, thought Michael.

As she was about to go out the front door, she felt someone touch her on the shoulder. Violette jumped and when she turned around, Michael was standing there.

"I am so glad you are here," said Violette, her face tear stained. Cuddling into his chest, she felt safe and wanted once again.

"Everything will be alright," said Michael with concern on his face as his arms wrapped around her for comfort. He had read her mind, so he knew why she was upset.

"Where did you come from?" said Violette, looking up into his eyes. *Why didn't I feel him behind me*, thought Violette?

"Shh… there are tunnels connecting our houses and sometimes we use them to get to your house," said Michael, with his finger against his lips.

"I didn't know that there were tunnels beneath the house. I wonder if Emily and Adrian know," said Violette.

"Actually, your house and mine were built by the Lepidop-tera vampires in the early 1800's. But as of about five years ago your house was sold to humans. I don't think Emily and Adrian would know about the tunnels because they were not on the plans when the house was acquired. And even if they did find them, they wouldn't be able to access my house because only a vampire can unlock the doors between the two houses," said Michael.

"Oh. OK."

"I thought I heard voices," said Emily, walking toward them.

"Yeah. I thought I would come and collect Violette," said Michael turning around.

"Oh, that is nice of you Michael. Violette could do with some cheering up, as she has been given some news this morning that was very unsettling," said Emily. She put her arm around Violette shoulders for comfort.

"OK. I hope the news wasn't anything too bad," said Michael, as he looked at Emily for answers.

"I am sure Violette will let you know…so are you both going to walk or go on a moped to your house, Michael?" said Emily.

"We will probably walk. I can have our chauffeur drop Violette back off later," said Michael.

"That would be good. Well, I will see you at dinner time Violette. Don't be late. Was nice to see you again Michael. Take care of my girl," said Emily smiling.

"I will, Emily," said Michael.

"Thanks Emily. See you later for dinner," said Violette, watching Emily walk away.

When they arrived at Michael's house, Violette told Michael all about what Emily and Adrian had told her earlier this morning about the adoption.

"Do you think that maybe my brother Stephen might be a vampire as well and that is why he left?" said Violette, with a raised eyebrow.

"It's not totally out of the question Violette. We could probably look into it if you like. Do you have a picture of Stephen on you, or at home?" said Michael.

"I just happen to have a photo of him in my wallet. Here it is," said Violette, handing the photo to Michael.

Michael took one look at the photo, and he knew straight away who Stephen was. He had stayed at the Gramaze house previously.

"Well…does he look familiar or not to you?" she said, impatiently.

"If it's the same person, then yes, and he has stayed here before. From memory he was from L.A. too," said Michael.

"Do you know where he is now?" said Violette, eagerly.

"No. But I can ask Brock to do some digging on where he is and then maybe we can go and see him, if you want to. Maybe you can talk to him on the phone," said Michael.

"That sounds great. Can we go and see Brock now?" said Violette, excited.

"He is out on patrol at the moment. But I will see him later on and ask him to check into it for you," said Michael.

"Thank you Michael. I can't believe that I might be able to see him again. I have missed him a lot since he has been gone. At least now I know why he left… so where is everyone today?" said Violette.

"They are either training or out on patrol. We have found out what the Debauched vampires are up to, and it's not good. So this is why everyone is busy," said Michael.

"So that means I am taking you away from your job. Sorry, Michael, I should go, instead of taking up your time," said Violette.

"No, no, it's alright…William told me to come and get you anyway. He said that maybe we could give you some more combat training today, as a few of us would be there to help with the training," said Michael.

"Oh, OK. Let's go then," said Violette. She was eager to do some more training, especially after what had happened previously. And it would take her mind off things. "So what are the Debauched vampires up to?"

"We have been informed that they have a lab where they are experimenting on humans to see if they can make a new breed of vampire. They are currently injecting vampire blood into them to see if the blood will change them from human to vampire. We understand at the moment that they haven't succeeded in doing it. But they are very close to making a new type of vampire. One that will be indestructible. Once they succeed, it will mean the end of not only Lepidoptera vampires but also humans as well. Apparently, they are doing all sorts of experimenting. But this is the main one we know about," said Michael, looking worried.

"How did you find out about this?" said Violette. She felt herself shaking. But she was determined not to let this get to her.

"We caught one of the Debauched vampires the other night and we tortured him for information. Before he died, he told us about what was happening and who the new leader of the Debauched vampires was. The leader's name is Nicholas, and he is a real sadistic bastard, who will go to any length to get what he wants," said Michael.

"I hope I never cross paths with him. He sounds like a real scary dude," said Violette.

"Violette, he is also the reason that I won't be able to go to the night club tonight with you. We need all hands on deck to track these vamps down. But if you don't mind, Annabelle will be going with you and Danielle. That way you will have some back-up if someone tries anything. Annabelle is well known amongst the vampires and I would say that no one will mess with her. Also, you will have Christian, who is from Rome, lurking in the background, so you should be safe. Annabelle will introduce you to Christian later on this afternoon, after training," said Michael.

"Maybe we shouldn't go, considering what is happening," said Violette.

"Mmm, I thought the same thing. But William pointed out that we need to keep things as normal as possible. Also, Danielle would probably ask you why you both couldn't go and that could get messy. Better off to go and Annabelle and Christian can keep an eye on you both...let's get going down to the combat room for some more training."

Training was hard work as usual, but well worth it. Violette now had the confidence to wound or kill a vampire. Whether she could actually knife a vampire when it came down to it, only time would tell. After she had a shower and got dressed, she caught up with Annabelle. They made some plans for that night on what time they would go and how they would get there. Violette was excited about going, but at the same time she was a bit worried about what might happen if the Debauched vampires turned up and started trouble.

As they were walking toward the kitchen, a new vampire Violette hadn't even met yet, came out of the door way. Built with a broad, muscular frame, and blonde hair all messed up, he looked about six foot tall.

Annabelle introduced them.

"Hi Christian, this is Violette, Michael's partner."

Bowing, but not taking his eyes off Violette, he said, "Nice to meet you Violette."

"Nice to meet you too. Which city are you from?" said Violette.

"Rome… I believe we are all going to a night club tonight. I want to reassure you that you will be in good hands," said Christian.

With his strong Italian accent, she could tell he had been on this earth a long time.

"Thank you, Christian. I really do appreciate all that you are doing for us," said Violette.

"You are most welcome. I would do anything for family," said Christian.

"Well, I suppose I had better head off home then and get ready for tonight. Do you think you would be able to give me a ride home Annabelle?" said Violette.

Just as she was asking Annabelle for a ride home, Michael came around the corner and said, "I will give you a ride home, Vi."

"Are you sure? I know you are busy. I can just go with Annabelle if you want," said Violette.

"No, that's OK. I wanted to spend some time with you alone, anyway," said Michael.

"OK. See you tonight Annabelle and Christian. What time are you picking Danielle and me up from our house," said Violette.

"Say around 8pm. Does that sound alright?" said Annabelle.

"Yep, that sounds good. See you," said Violette, as she walked out the front door with Michael.

When she was finally alone with Michael, he said, "I want you to be careful tonight, and if things get out of hand, all you need to do is to mind talk to me and I will be there straight away. You just need to remember what you have been taught in the combat training."

"I am sure we will be alright, Michael. They are not going to attack us in front of everyone in a public place," said Violette.

Michael knew that the Debauched vampires didn't care if it was a public place or not. They would take and drain whomever they wanted, and they had previously. Because vampires had speed in their favour, they could take or drain anyone, including Violette and Danielle, in a blink of an eye. No one would be any the wiser. Usually anybody that did see what happened had their mind scrubbed. So it was a big risk.

"Just be careful. Don't even go to the ladies' by yourself. Don't put your drink down anywhere to dance so that it can be spiked. Promise me Violette... I am really worried they will grab you and I will never see you again, and I couldn't bear that to happen. I love you so much Violette. My life is with you now, so please be careful," said Michael.

"I will be careful. You don't need to worry," said Violette. As Michael kissed and hugged her tight, Violette could feel how distressed he was about her going out that night, without him.

"If it's going to be dangerous for me, I can always stay home if you want me to," said Violette.

"No, I don't want you to stay home. You should be OK with Annabelle and Christian. I am probably worrying over nothing," said Michael.

"I love you Michael, and don't worry I am not going to risk anything. The thought of not being able to see you anymore, well, I just couldn't bear it," said Violette.

After Michael dropped her at home, Violette started getting ready for the night. She pulled out of her wardrobe the most beautiful emerald green blouse and some blue jeans to wear that Emily had brought her the previous day. She then went into Danielle's room to see what she was wearing. She had picked out the prettiest blue dress to wear. It had spaghetti straps and a drop waist skirt and looked very nice on her. Then again she always did have nice taste in clothes and looked gorgeous in them.

"Hey sis, did you want me to do your hair for you?" said Danielle.

"That would be great. But I don't want it up in a bun or not covering the back of my neck, because it will be cold out tonight, and you know how I feel about the cold," said Violette.

What Danielle didn't know was that Violette's butterfly tattoo was showing and she didn't want any vampires to see it.

"Hey, no problem. I can put some up, some down, and then put a pretty clip in it if you like," said Danielle.

"That's sound perfect. Thanks, Danielle," said Violette.

As Danielle was doing Violette's hair, Violette expected Danielle to ask her about the butterfly tattoo when she lifted the hair from the back of her neck. But she never said a word. Violette then realised that maybe humans couldn't see the tattoo, only vampires.

By the time Danielle and Violette had finished getting ready, it was about six-thirty in the evening and Emily had called them for dinner.

Sitting down at the table, waiting for Lamiae to serve their dinner, Adrian said, "Girls, as this is the first night club you have been to in France, I wanted to warn you of some dangers you might encounter."

Huh, does he know about vampires? thought Violette.

"Night clubs can be full of drunks and sometimes guys that spike your drinks. So please be careful not to leave your drinks unattended. Also when you go to the bathroom, go in pairs. It's just safer. Always keep together. We do have peace of mind though and are glad that you are going with Annabelle. Because she has lived here and knows how to keep you safe," said Adrian, looking from Danielle to Violette.

"Don't worry Emily and Adrian, we will be OK. And Annabelle told me today, when I phoned her, that her cousin from Rome, Christian, will be coming with us as well. So we will have safety in numbers…we won't be staying out that late, anyway, and we wouldn't do anything silly that would jeopardise our safety," said Danielle.

"We know you both are sensible girls, and will do the right thing. It's just others we worry about, and how they will take advantage of your kindness," said Emily.

"We will be alright. I'm sure," said Violette, knowing she had the Gramaze family to guard her and Danielle that evening.

"Are you getting excited about going?" asked Emily.

"Yes, very," said Danielle.

"Me too. One of my favourite bands 'Train' is playing live. I can't wait," said Violette.

After dinner, Danielle and Violette went back upstairs to do a final check in the mirror on their makeup and hair.

When the doorbell rang, they both ran down the stairs to greet Annabelle and Christian.

"Hi. You both ready to go?" said Annabelle, standing in the foyer.

"Yep," said Violette.

"Sure am," said Danielle.

"Cool. Let's go then. We won't be too late Mr and Mrs Lachance. See you later on," said Annabelle.

"Look after our girls, won't you," said Adrian.

Nodding, Annabelle smiled and said," We will."

"Bye girls. Have a good time," said Emily, giving them each a hug.

"We will. See you later on then," said Violette.

"Bye," said Danielle.

As they stepped into the car, Violette overheard Christian, who was waiting for them in the front seat, instructing the driver on where the night club was and that he was to wait at the front for them to return, once he had dropped them off.

"Good evening, ladies. Are we ready to go now?" asked Christian, as he turned around in his seat to face them.

"Yep. We are all good to go," said Annabelle.

The night air was cold, as the four of them stood in a line waiting for the bouncers to let them in. Violette could hear the band 'Train' had started to play, and couldn't wait to go inside. The line wasn't long and soon enough they were inside the front doors. The night club smelt like stale beer and sweat, and had strobe lights dancing around the darkened room.

As they stood in the doorway taking the surroundings in, Christian said, "I will see you all later." He disappeared to the back of the room to keep an eye out.

"What is that all about? How come he doesn't want to spend time with us?" remarked Danielle to Violette.

"Don't know, sis," said Violette.

"Hey…you girls thirsty?" screamed Annabelle over the loud music.

They both nodded.

"I will go and get us some drinks from the bar. Why don't you both go and have a dance?" said Annabelle, pointing to the dance floor.

"Sounds great, let's go," said Danielle.

It was hot and thick with people on the dance floor as Danielle and Violette joined in the fun. Watching the band play as she danced, Violette enjoyed one song after another. By the time Annabelle arrived with the drinks, they were hot and sweaty just like all the other people dancing.

"Thanks Annabelle," said Danielle.

"Yeah, thanks Annabelle… hey, I love this song," said Violette, listening to 'Train' announce the next song they were going to play.

"De rien, ladies," said Annabelle.

As the night went on, they all danced and enjoyed themselves. Even though it was hot inside the night club, they had lots of fun. Violette remembered what Michael and the Lachance's had said to her about not going to the ladies' alone, or leaving her drink unattended. It sure was good advice, and she made sure Danielle didn't forget about it either.

"I am going outside to get some fresh air," said Annabelle, shouting over the music.

Danielle and Violette both nodded and continued on dancing. But Violette knew Annabelle was going outside to check on things. Annabelle actually knew the bouncer at the door, and she had previously asked him to let her know if any Debauched vampires came into the night club.

They didn't see Christian most of the night, but Violette could feel his presence lurking in the shadows.

As Violette was dancing, she could hear Michael talking to her. He was checking in on her to see if she was alright and that she was having fun.

What a great guy, thought Violette. She always felt warm and loved.

Whilst Annabelle was outside, Violette turned around to see a guy, whom she didn't recognise, staring at Danielle. With her flirty nature, Danielle was looking his way, and had enticed him to come over and ask him to dance.

After dancing for a while he asked Danielle, "Would you like to get a drink and some fresh air outside?"

"Sure. But would it be OK for my friend to come along with us?" said Danielle, pointing to Annabelle over near the door.

When he noticed Annabelle, he frowned. "Maybe another time then." He then walked off into the crowd.

Danielle shrugged her shoulders and continued to dance with Violette.

Violette thought his behaviour was strange as she watched him walk away. A few minutes later, out the corner of her eye, Violette noticed Annabelle had the same guy bailed up near the side door. She had his arm held tight beside him and her face was close to his face, nodding violently. It looked like she was giving him a lecture. He didn't seem amused at all as he pulled away from her quickly and ran for the front door. Looking over his shoulder, he checked to see if Annabelle was following him as he went out the doors.

Annabelle didn't follow, but Violette saw her looking around the room for someone, and when she sensed where Christian was, Violette presumed she was mind talking to him as they both nodded at each other. Watching Christian run off out the front doors after the Debauched vampire, Violette wondered what was about to happen outside.

By the time Annabelle had come back to the dance floor, Danielle had already forgotten about the vampire, and was dancing with another guy, oblivious to what had just happened.

Smiling as she danced, Annabelle leaned into Violette and explained about how a lot of Debauched vampires came to the night clubs hoping that they could get a feed or sex for the night from any human. And just how lucky Danielle had been that she didn't go outside with the vampire.

The rest of the night was uneventful, and before they knew it, the band had stopped playing and the lights had been turned back on. It was time for them to head on home.

As they were about to get into the limousine, Annabelle said to Violette quietly, "Wait...something is wrong." She then went around to the chauffeur's door and found him slumped in his seat, sucked dry by the Debauched vampires. *Bastards*, thought Annabelle.

Violette scanned the area, but couldn't see any Debauched.

Trying not to draw attention to the driver and the fact that he was dead, Annabelle said, "Looks like the driver must have gone for a smoke or something, as he is not in the driver's seat."

"Oh, that's just great. How long is he going to be?" said Danielle.

Christian... where are you? Get your butt here now, thought Annabelle.

Appearing from nowhere, Christian stood next to the car, in front of the driver's window. When he noticed the dead driver, he knew he had to think quickly.

"It looks like I will be driving us home tonight, as the driver has gone home sick. Get in ladies."

"Oh, OK," said Danielle.

When Christian got into the front driver's seat, he pushed the driver over so he could get in and then put the divider up between him and the girls. Then he unlocked the door for them to get in.

As Danielle and Violette hopped in the limo, Annabelle felt the hair stand up on the back of her neck. She knew from experience, it meant Debauched vampires were in the area. She guessed they were probably after Violette. With swift speed, she shut the door to the limo, and scanned the area. Christian had felt it too, and he had noticed six Debauched vampires across the street, standing and waiting to make their move. When Annabelle saw them too, she knew they were outnumbered and were about to take a flogging if they didn't call for back up.

Michael, Grayson, William; I need backup. There are six Debauched here and they are after Violette. Christian and I will hold them off for as long as we can, but we are outnumbered, thought Annabelle.

Yes, we know. I read Violette's mind. We are already on our way, thought Michael.

Christian and Annabelle waited by the locked car in protection mode to guard Violette and Danielle. Their instructions from William were to protect Violette at any cost, as she was what mattered most. As the six Debauched moved with vampire speed, side by side across the street, to the front of the vehicle, Christian said, "What can I do for you, Debauched?"

"We want that succulent one in the car," demanded the one in the middle.

193

"Good luck, fuckers. That won't happen. Not on my watch," said Christian fisting his hands, and flaring his nostrils.

Without notice, four of the Debauched attacked Christian and then Annabelle. They took them both down in one swift move, whilst two of the other Debauched ripped open the doors of the limo and crawled inside.

Danielle screamed as soon as the Debauched bared his fangs.

"No, no! What are you?!" shrieked Danielle, terrified at the sight of his distorted face. But she didn't stand a chance. He was too fast for her vision to comprehend and anticipate what he was up to, as he put Danielle into a trance, which eventually quietened her screaming.

Violette tried to fight the other one off as best she could, but to no avail. He was much stronger and faster than she had expected. Before she knew it, the Debauched had jabbed a needle into her neck. As her world blackened, she slipped into a deep sleep.

Laying their limp bodies in the back of a black SUV, the Debauched quickly closed the doors and sped away from the night club.

By the time Michael, Grayson and Kelan arrived at the night club, they saw that Christian and Annabelle had been rendered unconscious and were lying face down next to the car. Whilst Grayson and Kelan attended to Annabelle and Christian's needs, Michael watched two Debauched who were inside the car, licking the leather upholstery. From the smell in the car, he assumed Violette had tried to fight them off, but was injured in the process, leaving a splatter of her blood behind. The two Debauched seemed to be in a euphoric state from the blood, which made killing them so much easier for

Michael. They didn't even notice when he entered the car and beheaded them.

Pushing the button to lower the divider in the car, Michael noticed the driver dead in the front seat. As he looked out the front windscreen of the car, he saw five more Debauched across the road, waiting and watching. He knew what they wanted and he was in the mood for a rumble. Rising from the car, Michael moved toward them with vampire speed. But as soon as they spotted him, they ran off, knowing that if they didn't leave they would be slaughtered. The Gramaze family were well known for their strength and abilities.

When Michael reached Annabelle and Christian, their bodies were already starting to heal from the beating they took. Alive but semi-conscious, he knew they needed to organise help to get them back home to completely heal.

"Have you called Renee yet?" Michael asked Grayson.

"Yes. They are on their way to come and collect Annabelle and Christian."

"Good…I knew coming here tonight was a bad idea. But instead of forbidding it, I just let her go," said Michael, with his fists clenched, looking around.

"I had a bad feeling all day about this too, bro. Damn them bloody Debauched. I hope Violette and Danielle will be alright. How are we going to find them?" said Grayson, fuming as he watched for any witnesses.

"There are only two ways I can find Violette, and one is to mind talk. But for some reason she is not answering me," said Michael.

"What's the other one?" said Grayson. He knew time was running out.

"Well, because I am attracted to Violette, if she is in the area, I should be able to sense her, hopefully. I haven't tried this before, but have heard it can work," said Michael.

"The others will be able to help find Violette and Danielle. They will be here in a few minutes, bro," said Grayson.

"That's too long... I can feel her pull now, so I need to follow it," said Michael, feeling frustrated.

"OK...I will wait here for the others and we will find you later. Take care, my brother," said Grayson, putting his hand on Michael's shoulder.

"You too, Grayson," said Michael, as he ran off.

Michael followed Violette's pull, until he heard her voice faintly.

Michael, Michael, can you hear me? thought Violette.

Yes. Where are you? thought Michael, impatiently.

I was knocked out when they took me and Danielle. But somehow I have broken free of it. I don't know where we are because the windows have been blacked out. There are six Debauched vampires in this black SUV with us. I am scared Michael, thought Violette.

All of a sudden her neck started giving her excruciating pain. She wasn't sure how much longer she would be able to keep up the pretence of being asleep.

OK.... when you stop and get out the SUV, you need to give me some sort of landmark. I should be able to find you quicker if you can do that, thought Michael.

He could feel her pain but there was nothing he could do to help Violette.

I love you Michael. But if anything happens to me please...

Stop...I won't listen to any of that sort of talk. Just keep quiet and look like you are asleep still. I will be there soon to rescue you, thought Michael.

I wonder why they want us. Do you think we are going to become part of their experiments? thought Violette.

Over my dead body. I will kill each and every one of the bastards if they hurt you, Violette, thought Michael.

Please get here soon, Michael. I am getting scared, and the back of my neck is hurting badly.

I will be there soon. Just do what they ask you to do until I get there.

As Violette slowly glanced around the van, she noticed that one of the vampires in the back of the van with her and Danielle was the same guy that approached Danielle in the night club. The one that Annabelle had got rid of.

Bastard must have been waiting for the right moment to attack with his comrades. I bet they were the ones who killed the Gramaze chauffeur as well, thought Violette to herself.

You know what Michael… These fuckers better watch out when I get out of here. I am starting to feel extremely angry and frustrated with what they have done and I don't think that I am going to be able to hold back the punishment I will deal out. They are going to pay for what they did to your chauffeur and Annabelle and Christian, thought Violette infuriated. Her whole body was throbbing and she could feel her pulse quickening.

I don't think that I have ever heard you talk like that before, Violette. What is going through your mind? thought Michael, worried that she would do something that would get her killed.

But Violette was silent for a few minutes. Then she thought, *Michael, we have just stopped and they are taking us into a house.*

What do you see? thought Michael.

I see lots of trees, and a winding gravel road. The Eiffel Tower is to my right and I can hear a stream of running water near the house. The house we are going into is like an old Mississippi house, like in the movies. Two storeys and has a veranda out the front, and a big tree with a tyre swing, thought Violette, trying to look around without anyone noticing.

Don't worry, my love, I am not far away from you now. I will be there soon, thought Michael.

Once Michael found the house, he mind talked to William and told him exactly where he was, so that they could come and help rescue Violette and Danielle.

I want you to wait until we all get there. Do not go in alone or you will get yourself killed, for sure, thought William.

I will only wait for you to get here as long as Violette is alright, thought Michael.

We are only five minutes away now. Sit tight, thought William.

How are you going, Violette? thought Michael, as he waited for everyone to turn up.

I'm OK. Danielle and I have been put into what looks like cells with locked doors. There are other people in here as well. Michael…there are probably at least fifty humans in here, and some of them look like they could do with medical attention. As I walk around, I notice that some of the women are actually pregnant. God, how sick is this place? These poor people. I think that they are doing more than experimenting here.

Where are you inside the house, Vi? thought Michael.

When we entered the house they put blindfold on Danielle and me. Once they put us in the cells they then took the blindfolds off. So I am not a hundred percent sure where we are, Michael. But I think we are in the basement as there are no windows in here, and it looks like there are stairs going up to a door.

OK. How is Danielle? thought Michael.

She is still in a trance, so she is OK for the moment, thought Violette, cuddling Danielle.

Michael heard cars driving up behind him.

Everyone is here now, Violette. So it won't be long and we will be inside to get you.

OK. Hurry Michael.

William approached Michael and asked, "How are they going?"

Michael explained the situation and where he thought they were being held in the house.

Standing back at the edge of the property, William conducted a search, using his vampire vision, of where the guards were standing, and how many of them he could see. He then gave clear instructions to all Lepidoptera on what their roles were in this mission.

With many Debauched guards standing between them and the house, the Lepidoptera walked towards the house in a line that was impenetrable. One by one, the guards went down as William and his family threw grenades at the guards and tried to burn them with their blow torches.

Storming the house, they found there were a lot more vampires inside than anticipated. The Debauched guards were ready for the attack and were willing to die to protect their leader and his assets. But they were no match for the Gramaze family.

As the Lepidoptera went from room to room, it was soon apparent that either some of Debauched had escaped or had already been exterminated. One thing every Lepidoptera was aware of was that the Debauched vampires didn't have as much strength as usual. It was as if they were drained of their strength very quickly. This made killing them very easy.

Out the corner of his eye, William spotted Nicholas, the leader of the Debauched vampires, escaping out the back door of the house.

William ran off after him and thought to Grayson, *Take charge, and lead us to victory. I am going after the Debauched leader.*

Yes, Sire, thought Grayson.

Once the house was cleared of the Debauched vampires, Michael and Grayson went in search of the locked cells Violette had spoken about. The doorway to the basement had been hidden in a linen cupboard, which made it hard to find. Opening the door, Michael ran down the stairs in search of Danielle and Violette. But what he ended up finding was cell upon cell of humans.

As he walked along looking into each one, he saw many men and women who were skin and bone. Their faces showed the pain of a thousand lashes, and they were all in need of immediate care and medical attention.

"I wonder how long each of these humans have been locked in the cells down here, Grayson?"

"I don't know, bro. This is appalling how they are being kept in these conditions down here."

As each human was released from their locked cell, Michael and Grayson had to wipe their minds of any memory they had of their abduction and torture by the vampires. After they were all given medical attention and nourishment, the humans were herded into a large truck waiting to take them back to their loved ones and homes.

Entering the last cell, Michael saw Violette sitting on the floor at the back of the cell with Danielle, who was still in a trance. She was rocking her back and forward in her arms.

If Danielle remembers anything at all about being abducted by vampires, then I will have to erase her mind as well. I Just hope it doesn't come to that, thought Michael.

"Would you like me to take Danielle?" said Annabelle, as she entered the cell.

"Yes, please," said Michael.

Annabelle noticed that Violette didn't appear well, and that she had an angry, glazed look in her eyes. She knew what was happening.

Bending down in front of Danielle and Violette, Annabelle placed her hand on Violette's arm to calm her and said, "Let her go. I am here to help."

Without hesitation, Violette let Annabelle pick Danielle up in her arms and carry her out of the cell, up the stairs and into a waiting car, where she could be examined.

Kneeling down in front of Violette, Michael leaned forward to push the hair out of her face and to see if she was alright. But as he looked into her eyes, he could see she was changing. Violette had been so angry and frustrated by the events of the night, that it had brought forward her transformation into a Lepidoptera vampire.

Turning her around to look at the back of her neck, Michael could see her butterfly had turned a vibrant red and the black detail was starting to form. This meant that soon she would need to feed for the first time. Michael knew he had to take Violette to the nearest hospital, where he could acquire some A+ blood. Newborn vampires needed to have the right type of blood the very first time they fed, otherwise they turned into a Debauched vampire.

Michael felt Renee's presence enter the room.

"How's she going, Michael?" said Renee.

Michael lifted Violette's hair off her neck and showed Renee that the transformation was starting.

"Violette…are you feeling alright, my dear?" said Renee, kneeling in front of Violette and looking into her eyes.

"I don't feel the best. The back of my neck hurts and I am starting to feel strange," said Violette, rubbing her neck.

Turning around to Michael, Renee said, "It's a long way to the hospital from here. I will take Violette to the hospital for some blood. I think you should stay here, Michael, as you are needed here to help with the clean-up. As soon as I get Violette fixed up at the hospital, we can meet you back at home."

"I agree…thank you, Renee. Please take care of her," said Michael.

"I will," said Renee.

"Renee is going to take care of you, Violette. I will see you later at home. I love you," said Michael, as he gave her a kiss on her forehead. He then ran off to help with the clean-up.

Renee carried Violette in her arms to the waiting car, which Brock was driving. She instructed Brock on where to take them and that it was an emergency.

"Don't worry Violette, I will take care of you. Once we get to hospital, I will help you through the transformation."

"Thanks Renee. I appreciate how good you are to me," said Violette, as she put her head on Renee's shoulder.

"You are welcome," said Renee, placing her arm around Violette.

As Renee comforted Violette, she said to Michael via mind talk, *Can you please find William? I haven't seen him for a while. The last anyone saw of him was when he had gone off after Nicholas.*

I'll look for him now, Renee, thought Michael, thinking he hadn't seen or heard from William in a while either.

Michael tried to mind talk to William, but there was only silence.

After the clean-up was just about done, and all the humans were taken care of, Michael thought to Grayson, *Have you seen William in the last half hour?*

No…I haven't seen him since he went after Nicholas earlier on. Let's go look for him now, thought Grayson.

With vampire speed, Michael searched the entire grounds and even the river that ran near the house, but he couldn't see any sign of William. He mind talked to everyone and asked if they had seen what happened, but most of them said they were too busy to notice what happened once William and Nicholas started to battle.

All of a sudden, a sick feeling came over Michael, and he thought, *Well, if he isn't here, and nor is Nicholas, then Nicholas must have taken William captive.*

Once Michael found Grayson inside the house, he said "When we have finished here, bro, we need to get everyone looking for William. He is missing and I think Nicholas has taken him. I can't seem to mind talk to William either, and I have looked everywhere. There is no sign of him."

As Grayson was left in charge by William, Grayson then mind talked to everyone, *Listen up Gramaze… I want each of you to go over the house, the grounds and anywhere else around here. William is missing.*

It only took about five minutes, and then everyone reported back in saying that they had not found him.

Everyone, except Annabelle.

Grayson…you need to come down by the river, near the dock, as there is something here that might be of some importance, thought Annabelle.

As Grayson and Michael approached the dock, they could see a body lying near the river. Luckily it was not William. It was one of the Debauched vampires, and he was still alive.

Michael grabbed him by the throat and said, "Tell us where Nicholas has taken William."

"No way in hell will I tell you anything. I am dying, anyway," said the Debauched vampire, with a smug look on his face and a determination that he was not going to relay any information on their leader's whereabouts.

"If you don't tell us, then we will torture you for as long as you live, and that could be for the next twenty minutes. Believe me when I say this, that this will be the most excruciating pain you have ever felt," said Grayson, with a smirk on his face, as he grabbed the vampire by his throat.

"Alright, alright... I will tell you. As long as you don't torture me," said the Debauched vampire, with his hands up, terrified. "Nicholas and I ambushed your leader and we drugged him so that he couldn't cause us anymore trouble. Nicholas put him on the boat and was going to take your leader to London."

"Why did Nicholas take our leader instead of killing him?" said Grayson.

But the Debauched vampire didn't answer.

"Tell me, or suffer the consequences," said Grayson, grabbing him by the shirt.

"Alright...please...he needs your leader for our experiments," said the Debauched vampire, cringing.

Feeling his blood rage faster from the hatred he was feeling towards the Debauched vampire, Grayson beheaded him. With the body of the vampire turning to ash straightaway, Grayson said, "Fuckers. They all deserve to die."

Grayson took his phone out of his pocket, and decided to ring Joseph Peteria, a well-respected leader of the Lepidoptera vampires in London. He and William were very close.

"Hello, Grayson. How is everything?" said Joseph, in his English accent.

"We have a situation here Joseph, which I need your help with. Tonight, the leader of the Debauched vampires here in France abducted William, and has taken him to London. We have also been informed that they are planning on experimenting on William," said Grayson.

"Fucken hell. You have my full support Grayson. I will instruct my family to look for William straight away. How did this happen?" said Joseph.

Grayson described to Joseph the events of the night and what had happened with the abduction. But what Grayson left out was the knowledge of a new female Lepidoptera vampire in his family. He wasn't sure if William would want anyone to know yet, being that there hadn't been a new female anywhere for years.

"We will be there in about one and a half hours to your home Joseph, to help out with the search for William. In the meantime, can you please keep me informed on any news?" said Grayson.

"Hopefully I will have some good news for you when you arrive Grayson," said Joseph. He then hung up.

"Michael, I want you to stay in France and look after everything here whilst we are gone. Plus, you will have Violette to worry about, once she gets back to the house with Renee. I will have Annabelle and Christian stay here with you all to look after business as well," said Grayson authoritatively.

"Yes, Sire. But are you sure you don't need me to come with you, Grayson?" said Michael.

"Yes, I am sure...don't forget, you are going to have to come up with a story to tell Danielle and Violette's foster parents. You may want to have Renee call them, as it will sound more convincing coming from her," said Grayson.

"Right. I had forgotten all about the Lachance's." said Michael, realising this had to be done to keep their family secret.

I want everyone out the front, now, thought Grayson to all the Lepidoptera's via mind talk.

Once they were all assembled, Grayson spoke about what had happened to William, and then instructed them all on their mission for the night, which was to rescue William and bring him back home alive.

"Now let's get the fuck out of here."

With all of their cars heading off into different directions from the Debauched vampire hide out, Kelan pressed the detonator trigger. Grayson watched through the window of the van, as the house behind them exploded with a huge fire ball and debris scattered everywhere. Kelan was one of the Gramaze family explosives experts and it was his job to make sure no evidence of what had happened there was left visible.

At least they won't be able to experiment in that house any more, thought Grayson.

You said it bro, thought Michael, as he heard the police sirens in the distance.

Even though William had been captured, and Violette was transforming into a Lepidoptera, at least one consolation was that the Gramaze family had stopped the human experiments which were being carried out by the Debauched and had returned each human to their families.

Chapter Twelve

At the hospital morgue, Renee and Violette waited for the attendant, Charlie, to come back with the A+ Blood.

"How are you holding up, Violette?" said Renee, watching Violette pace the room.

"My skin feels like it's crawling with insects," said Violette, itching her skin madly. "I can hear every human and what they are thinking about. It's so loud that I can't shut it off inside my brain. I've tried putting my hands over my ears to stop the noise but that doesn't work. It just keeps getting louder and louder. That isn't the worst of it, either. I can now hear the heartbeat of every human and the pumping of their blood rushing throughout their veins. My head feels like it's going to explode. Is this ever going to stop?"

Slumping down in the corner of the morgue, she rocked herself backwards and forwards. As she continued to sweat and shake, Violette placed her hands over her ears, and pulled her knees up to her chest, to try and fight off the cravings.

"It won't be long now, Violette," said Renee, placing her hand on Violette's shoulder.

"Please...don't touch me. I feel like I want to rip your head off, Renee," said Violette, with flared nostrils as she looked up through her sweaty hair.

Seconds later, the doors to the morgue swung open, and in walked Charlie with the blood.

"The fastest way to get this into your system is to put it into you via a drip," said Charlie, bending down next to Violette.

"I don't care how you do it. Just hurry up and do it now. I am on the verge of drinking from someone," said Violette through gritted teeth, looking at his jugular vein pulsating.

Charlie could see she was serious, so he quickly retrieved an intravenous drip needle, and inserted it into her arm.

Violette flinched as she felt the pinch from the cannula being inserted into her arm. Waiting for the blood to take effect in her body, she felt the inside of her mouth move. Feeling around in her mouth with her tongue, she realised her eye teeth were now protruding out of her gums.

"How long does it take for the blood to start making me feel not so blood-thirsty and like my head is going to explode?" said Violette impatiently, as she watched the blood flowing into her vein.

"It usually takes effect instantly. I think it's taking longer than usual because we had a long drive here. You just need to give it time to work," said Renee.

Just as Renee said this, Annabelle walked in through the side door into the morgue.

"How you are going there, Violette?" said Annabelle, looking from Violette to Renee.

"Not good. I feel like I want to feed off someone, and I can't stop these noises inside my head," said Violette, shaking.

Annabelle knelt down next to Violette and put her hand on her arm to calm her. Instantly Violette felt the release.

"Thank you, Annabelle. That feels better. I don't know what I would do if you weren't here. I don't think I could have controlled myself for much longer," said Violette.

"You are welcome," said Annabelle, looking at Renee with raised eyebrows.

Once the first bag of blood had finished, Violette started to feel a little better, and bit more in control of herself.

"I can show you how to shut out the noise," said Annabelle, reading Violette's thoughts.

"That would be good Annabelle. It's literally driving me crazy," said Violette.

"You just need to concentrate on clearing your mind and relax," said Annabelle.

"That is easier said than done," said Violette, with an irritated sigh.

Annabelle sat next to Violette on the floor and placed her arm around Violette's shoulder. Pulling her in gently, Annabelle watched as Violette started to relax from her touch.

"Thank you," said Violette, as she felt the wave of calm come across her and the noises quieten.

"Charlie…can you please give us six more bags of blood, because Violette will need this later on tonight?" said Renee.

"Sure. No problem. Only too happy to help," said Charlie. He had seen this happen many times and knew the process.

Pulling her phone out of her pocket, Renee dialled a number.

"Brock, we will be out the front in five minutes. Can you swing by and pick us up?

"Yes ma'am."

"Thanks."

Hanging up her phone, Renee said, "OK ladies…you ready to go?"

Nodding, Annabelle helped Violette up off the floor.

"You OK to walk by yourself?"

"Sure," said Violette.

"Thanks once again, Charlie. I am certain we will see you again soon. Take care," said Renee.

"Anytime," said Charlie, as he watched the three women walk through the double doors.

On the way back to the Gramaze house, Violette stared out the window of the car and thought about the night's events.

Why did I go to that stupid night club? I should have stayed home. Selfish... and now look at me, I'm transforming into something I didn't want to be yet. What an idiot.

"Don't be too hard on yourself Violette," said Renee, placing her hand on Violette hand.

"I can't help it. What happened tonight was all my fault," said Violette.

"Not entirely dear. And if it wasn't for you, we wouldn't have found all those humans who needed our help," said Renee.

"Yeah…do you believe how many humans were down there? The torment that they would have gone through. I wonder how long some of them were missing for?" said Annabelle.

"Those poor people. I am just glad we were able to help them. I remember feeling so scared tonight. Not only for myself, but for Danielle as well. When we were held captive in the cells, all I could think about was that the Debauched vampires were either going to experiment on us or drain us completely of our blood. When I knew there wasn't anything I could do, and I started feeling a sense of uselessness, I became irritated and frustrated. I think in the end that's what tipped me over the edge and started my transformation," said Violette.

"I would say you are right, Violette," said Renee.

"What am I going to do now? Michael told me that it was probably impossible for me to go back and live with Emily and Adrian once I turned. I really don't know whether I wanted this life yet or not."

Tears formed in her eyes as she looked to Renee for a solution.

Renee put her arm around Violette for comfort and stroked her hair.

"Only time will tell, my dear girl. Everyone is different. If you can stand to be around humans, then you will be able to live with them too."

"What am I going to tell them when I don't go home tonight?" said Violette.

"I have taken care of that already. I spoke with Adrian tonight when we were at the hospital, and he said that it would be OK for you and Danielle to sleep over our house tonight. But he wants both of you to be home by lunch time tomorrow," said Renee.

"Thanks Renee. Hopefully that should give me some time to come to grips with this. Is Danielle already back at your house? What is going to happen to her?" said Violette.

"Yes, and she has been made comfortable back at the house. What we are going to do when we get back is take Danielle out of the trance, and see what she remembers. Hopefully she won't remember anything after the night club. That way we can fill in the blanks for her. It should be OK...by the way, don't you go feeling guilty about what happened to Danielle tonight. It's not your fault, at all. The Debauched are the ones to blame for all this," said Renee.

"Yeah, but I did knowingly play a part in this. Danielle is the only real family I have, and I would never forgive myself if anything happened to her tonight," said Violette.

"I would say that William will not be so accommodating next time you want to venture out. I also reckon he might just double your guard," said Renee.

"Besides your house, my house and school, I don't think that I will be going anywhere else for a while. Well, at least until I have fully transformed," said Violette.

Watching the early morning traffic drive by as she looked out the window, Violette felt a surge of energy rush throughout her body. She even thought her sight was different.

"All of a sudden I feel like I could run a marathon. I have so much energy. Is that normal?" she said to Renee.

"Yes. It's the next step in your transformation. You are on your way to becoming a full vampire who will only need to feed on blood once a month, instead of feeling like you want to feed all the time, like you do now," said Renee, smiling.

"This is happening much faster than I thought it would. I suppose the test will be when I come in contact with humans." *I hope I don't hurt Danielle when we are back at the Gramaze house.*

"Don't worry dear, we will be there to support you. Danielle will be safe," said Renee.

"I keep forgetting you can read minds. Thank you. I do appreciate your help," said Violette.

"You are welcome, my dear. That is what family do," said Renee.

It dawned on Violette that she hadn't given any consideration to Annabelle's injuries after the beating she had taken.

"Annabelle…I am sorry. I haven't even asked you how you are feeling," said Violette.

"I feel good. I am just about all healed now. It doesn't take long to heal when you are a vampire," said Annabelle, showing

Violette her body. She had a few cuts and bruising all over her body. But as Violette watched, they were healing in front of her eyes.

"Wow, look at how fast they are healing. I bet there would be a few doctors out there that would love to patent your blood for its healing properties," said Violette.

"Yeah, I suppose so. I have never thought about it like that before," said Annabelle.

"How is Christian going?" asked Violette.

"Actually, he has healed well. No need to worry," said Annabelle.

"That's good. Thank you for saving Danielle and myself tonight," said Violette.

"Well…I didn't save you Violette. They still took you both," said Annabelle.

"Yes, but you protected us from getting hurt. Anyway, you couldn't have done much else. There were six of them and two of you. Not good odds," said Violette.

"I don't think William will see it that way when we debrief," said Annabelle, looking at Renee.

"I am sure William will understand, Annabelle. He knows you were outnumbered and did your best to protect Danielle and Violette," said Renee.

"We'll see," said Annabelle.

"I hope you don't get into too much trouble…can I ask you a favour when we get back to your house," said Violette.

"Yes. What is it?" said Annabelle.

"Well…could I ask you if you could touch Danielle as she is coming out of the trance. Just so that she will feel calm and relaxed," said Violette.

"That is our plan anyway," said Annabelle.

"Oh good. Thank you," said Violette.

As the car approached the house gates, it was apparent to Renee that William was still not at their home because she couldn't mind talk to him. She was starting to get worried. *Where could he be?* she thought. Pulling up to the front door, Renee noticed Michael was waiting for them.

"Annabelle, can you please take Violette into the house? I need to speak with Renee privately," said Michael.

He gave Violette a warm, welcoming hug and said, "I will see you soon."

"OK," said Violette.

Annabelle nodded and helped Violette into the house. Shutting the front doors, Michael directed Renee into the sitting room.

"What is going on and why are you trying to block me out of your thoughts? Where is William?"

"I have some bad news for you Renee…William has been taken captive by Nicholas and we think he is now in London. Grayson and the others have gone to London to see if they can find him. We have also asked Joseph Peteria and his family to help find William. Grayson has vowed he won't leave London until they find William, no matter what shape he is in," said Michael.

Renee couldn't believe what she was being told.

"What can I do to help find my man?"

"At this stage, Renee, you can't do anything. We have to wait to see what Grayson can find out. But there are a few things around here that may need your help, like Danielle and Violette," said Michael.

"Right… OK. But as soon as you hear something please let me know. I am really worried, as I haven't been able to mind talk to William since he has been taken, which is not a good sign," said Renee.

"You have my word. I will let you know as soon as I hear something," said Michael.

"Thank you…why don't you go see how Violette is doing. I just need a few minutes and then I will help with Danielle," said Renee.

"OK. Don't worry, William can handle himself and I am sure he will be alright," said Michael, walking toward the doorway.

"I am sure you are right," said Renee.

Standing in the doorway to the kitchen, Michael listened to Annabelle, Violette, and Christian, who were sitting at the island bench, chatting about the night's events.

When Violette sensed Michael standing there, her eyes lit up with excitement as she turned around in her seat and saw his ragged face. Feeling the electricity run through her veins and the attraction for him as he walked toward her, Violette jumped up out of her seat and ran straight into his arms. With his muscular arms around her, she finally felt safe as she cuddled into his chest.

"How are you? I wanted to make sure you are going to be alright, now that you are a vampire," said Michael, holding her tight.

"I'm alright…I'm a bit tense and shaken though. But I will be OK. To be honest, I am more worried about Danielle at the moment," said Violette, looking up into his concerned eyes.

"Don't worry. She will be alright. Renee will be here in a minute and then we can all go into the sitting room and bring Danielle out of the trance slowly," said Michael, stroking Violette's hair.

"How did everything at the Debauched house go after I left tonight?" asked Violette.

"We took all the humans that were being held captive back to their own homes. It all worked out well. But the house…well…we demolished it. Blew it up, to be exact. They won't be holding anyone captive in that house again. One thing that you are probably not aware of yet, is that William has been taken by Nicholas. Apparently to London. We are just waiting to hear from Grayson on if they have found William or not."

"Oh my God, Michael. That is terrible. I bet Renee is worried out of her mind. Is there anything I can do to help?" said Violette, forgetting her own worries.

"No. Not at the moment," said Renee, overhearing the conversation as she walked into the kitchen. "Until we hear from Grayson, we need to carry on here as usual. That is what William would want us to do…so in the meantime, let's go and wake Danielle out of the trance and see what she remembers."

Entering the sitting room, Annabelle sat next to Danielle on one side of the couch and Violette on the other, whilst Christian, Michael and Renee took their seats across from them and waited for Annabelle to bring Danielle out of the trance.

When Danielle finally opened her eyes, she was surprised by all the eyes on her.

"What's going on? Where am I?" asked Danielle, as she sat up quickly.

"Hello sleepy head. You must have been tired, as you fell asleep in the limo on the way home. Christian had to carry you into the house," said Annabelle, as she placed her hand on Danielle's hand.

"Sorry, that's a bit embarrassing…I only remember getting into the limo. I don't even remember the drive home. I must have fallen asleep straight away, did I? So where are we?" said Danielle.

"We are at the Gramaze house. We were just about to watch a movie when you woke up. Oh, and by the way, I have asked Emily and Adrian if we can both sleep over tonight and they said yes," said Violette.

"Cool. I love sleepovers. I had such a great time at the night club tonight. What about you Vi?" said Danielle, stretching her arms out to the ceiling.

"Me too, sis," said Violette.

Stop touching Danielle and see how she goes, thought Renee to Annabelle.

Annabelle nodded to Renee and pulled back from Danielle.

"What are we going to watch anyway," said Violette to Annabelle.

"*Vegas?*" said Annabelle.

"I love that movie," said Danielle.

"Yeah, me too," said Annabelle.

Seems like Danielle is OK, thought Annabelle.

Excellent. So how are you feeling Violette? thought Renee.

Um...yeah, good...I think. Even though I can hear and feel Danielle's blood pulsating throughout her body, I don't feel like I would hurt her, thought Violette.

"Well Michael and I are just going to go up to his room for a while. I am sure you will be OK with Annabelle. See you later," said Violette to Danielle.

"Oh. OK. No problem. Will catch up with you both later then," said Danielle. She always enjoyed spending time with Annabelle.

"I might go and see what I can cook up for a snack," said Renee, walking toward the doorway.

"I will stay here with the girls and watch the movie," said Christian, smiling at Danielle.

"Catch up with you later on, sis," said Violette, walking toward the doorway.

"Sure," said Danielle. She was too interested in Christian, and didn't even notice them leaving the room.

Walking up the stairs, Violette said, "That went well. I didn't even want to drink from Danielle either."

"Yeah...you showed real restraint, didn't you? I think you should be OK around humans, Violette. But time will tell," said Michael, kissing the side of her forehead. "Have you been listening to all the mind talk around the house?"

"Yes. I can't believe Nicholas and his henchman were able to overpower William, and take him captive. Have you heard anything from Grayson yet?" said Violette, entering Michael's room and sitting down on the bed.

"No, and I hope they find William soon," said Michael, as he sat next to her. "How are you feeling?"

"I actually can't believe how good I feel. It's like I have so much energy and I don't know how to get rid of it. Did you want to go for a run, so I can burn off some of this energy?" said Violette.

"I can think of something else that will wear us out," said Michael smirking.

"Well... I didn't know if it was appropriate, because of everything that had happened tonight," said Violette, looking into Michael's eyes.

"We could just fool around and see what happens," said Michael. He could sense she was feeling nervous, but he could also feel that she wanted him, just as much as he wanted her.

"OK," said Violette. "Maybe we should shut the door then."

"Good idea," said Michael, jumping off the bed quickly and walking toward the doorway.

Michael returned to his bed, and stood in front of Violette with his hands out front. Standing to face him, he gently pulled her in close. As he kissed her neck and grazed her earlobe with his teeth, Michael caressed Violette's right breast through her blouse.

More. Don't stop, thought Violette.

"Your wish is my command," said Michael, unbuttoning her blouse and bra clip, discarding it to the floor.

With the tension building in her body, as his touch consumed her, Violette moaned in sheer delight when his thumb and forefinger elongated her nipple, making it hard, until she came.

Kneeling in front of her, Michael slowly slid her jeans off. Discarding them to the floor he gently pushed Violette onto the bed. As he stood at the side of the bed, looking at her body in wonderment, he thought, *Wow, what a beautiful body. So lovely.*

With speed quicker than the human eye could see, Michael stripped down to his boxer shorts, climbed onto the bed, and laid next to Violette. Kissing her sweet, warm lips passionately, Michael was aroused by every inch of her body. Giving into her scent, he gently pulled her to the side of the bed. With her feet touching the ground, he knelt in front of her and slowly pushed her legs open.

As he caressed her clitoris with his fingers, whilst his pulsating tongue licked her bulb, she felt like her body was falling apart. Scrunching the bedspread with her hands to steady herself, Violette felt his teeth nip at her vagina.

"Please...don't stop, Michael...that feels too good," pleaded Violette breathlessly, as she pushed her vagina into his mouth gently.

Michael didn't answer her, because he was enjoying her smell and taste way too much.

Eventually coming up to stand in front of her, he pulled Violette off the bed and kissed her welcoming lips with a desire that only a Lepidoptera could feel.

Still reeling from the pleasure Michael had given her, Violette reached for his firm cock and started to rub it back and forth. This sheer pleasure was welcomed by Michael, as she knelt down in front of him and slowly took him into her mouth. Teasing him, she twirled her tongue around the head of his penis, and then sucked it with vigour, over and over. Turned on immensely, Michael grabbed her head and pulled his cock in and out of her mouth rapidly. Moments later he stilled in front of her and came.

With a smirk on her face and her body craving more, Violette rose to her feet in anticipation of what would happen next. She was ready and nothing was going to get in her way tonight.

"God, woman, that was too good," said Michael pulling her in close and running his hand down the side of her face gently. *So beautiful*, thought Michael, looking into her eyes. Leaning in, he kissed her soft lips tenderly and she eagerly reciprocated.

When their lips parted, Michael watched Violette lay her sensual body on his bed. With her sensors heightened and aroused by the sweet smell of his body, she pulled him onto the bed and kissed his body in places that delighted every inch of his core. Excited, Violette felt her fangs descended out of her gums. The smell of his blood pulsating throughout his veins was driving her crazy.

"Take what you need Violette," said Michael, reading her thoughts and extending his arm to her.

With a bemused look at him, she sank her fangs into his forearm and drank from him. His blood was nothing like she had tasted before, and made her feel euphoric as it gushed into her mouth. The more she drank, the more she wanted.

You taste so good...I can't seem to stop...what is wrong with me? thought Violette, as she continued to enjoy his lifeblood.

"There is nothing wrong with what you are doing, Violette. Take as much of me as you want," said Michael, monitoring how much blood she was draining from him.

When she had finished taking what she needed from his forearm, Michael said, "Lick the wound Violette. It will help it heal faster."

"Oh, OK. Did you want to drink from me as well, Michael?" said Violette, wiping the blood away from her mouth.

"Not today, Violette. I don't want you to stop your full transformation," said Michael. *But there is something else I would like to do.*

Reading his mind, she smiled and nodded eagerly.

"Are you sure you want to do this?"

"Yes," she said impatiently.

She was ready.

Violette felt a pinching sensation as Michael entered her for the first time. Wet and full of desire for him, she adjusted to his rhythm quickly. As he pulled his hardened penis in and out of her, she felt her world come apart with the unadulterated sensual pleasure. Their love-making seemed to go on for hours, tingling every nerve ending in her body as she had multiple orgasms.

With sweat beading on their foreheads, Michael and Violette were both exhausted and sated as they laid next to each other on top of the sheets looking up at the ceiling.

"You OK?" asked Michael, breathing heavily.

"Mmm… I'm good," said Violette, trying to catch her breath.

"Would you like a cold drink?" asked Michael, turning his head to face her on the pillow.

"That would be nice. I am really thirsty," said Violette, feeling her mouth was dry with her tongue.

Hopping out of bed, Michael put his denim jeans on and said, "I won't be long."

"OK," said Violette, watching him walk over to the doorway.

Whist she waited for Michael to return with her drink, Violette stared at the ceiling, contemplating her future as a Lepidoptera vampire. Even though her life was turning out to be totally different than how she had expected it to be, Violette felt fortunate to have such a wonderful life partner, like Michael, in her life.

"Penny for your thoughts," said Michael, as he entered the bedroom.

"I was just thinking how much my life has changed and will continue to change," said Violette.

"Was there something you wanted to talk about?" asked Michael.

"No. Not really."

"OK," said Michael, handing Violette a cold drink.

"Thank you," said Violette, until she looked down into the cup. "Blood. I was hoping for a cola."

"I can get you a soda later, if you like. But right now you need to keep your blood intake up," said Michael.

"Not sure if I can drink that, Michael," said Violette, looking into the cup and screwing her face up.

"Try…once you take the first sip, you will see it's not that bad," said Michael.

Violette's eyes were focused on Michael as she held her breath and took the first drink. As she pulled the cup away from her mouth, she said, "Mmm…not bad." Taking another drink, she ended up guzzling the rest down quickly. "In fact it tastes so good, that I want more," said Violette, as she licked her lips.

"Just let it settle in your stomach first, Violette," said Michael. He could feel that she was craving blood, so he asked Annabelle via mind talk, to come and help Violette through her thirst.

Startled by the knock at the door, Violette jumped.

"Can I come in?" asked Annabelle.

"One minute Annabelle," said Violette.

Pulling the sheets up and over her body, because she was still naked from their love-making, Violette then said, "OK. You can come in now."

"How are you feeling?" asked Annabelle, as she sat next to Violette on the bed.

"Umm…I am starting to feel agitated again. What I would really like is some more blood to drink," said Violette, fidgeting and fighting back her bloodthirst. "Is that normal?"

Annabelle placed her hand on Violette's arm and within seconds she could feel Violette relaxing again.

"Thank you Annabelle."

"You are welcome. Part of the female transformation process is the craving of blood, Violette. But also we need to let you try to use your abilities. What colour is your butterfly, Violette?" said Annabelle.

"It's red. Why do you ask?" said Violette worried.

"OK. That means your ability is strength and also the power to change the thoughts of others…so…I know what we can do. We need to go and see Danielle. If you can get her to change her mind through mind control, then that should help with the transformation process," said Annabelle.

"OK. So basically if I use my ability on Danielle, then I won't feel like this?" said Violette.

"Yes. But we will also need to get you some more blood as well to drink," said Annabelle.

"OK."

"Thanks for your help Annabelle," said Michael.

"No problem at all. Come on, why don't you get dressed, Violette and we can go down to see Danielle," said Annabelle.

Danielle was sitting in the kitchen with Christian at the island bench when Annabelle, Michael and Violette walked in.

"Hello, sis. What you up to?" asked Violette.

"Just having a hot drink and then I was thinking about going off to bed," said Danielle.

"Oh. OK. Hey… Would you like a jam and cream dough-nut?" said Violette, sitting next to Danielle at the island bench.

"Yeah, I would love one," said Danielle.

But Violette already knew this was one of Danielle's favourite cakes. Violette then spoke to Danielle's mind. *Say that you hate donuts.*

"You know what Violette…when I think of it…I'm not a big fan of donuts," said Danielle, screwing her nose up.

"No problem. If you feel peckish, there is plenty to eat in the fridge," said Violette.

"Thanks. But I am all good for now," said Danielle, picking up her hot drink.

How do you feel now? thought Annabelle to Violette.

I feel a little bit better, thought Violette.

Good. Now I want you to go down to the combat room and do some strength fighting with Michael. It will probably get rid of some of the energy you have as well… Just excuse yourself to Danielle, thought Annabelle.

Violette nodded.

"So what are you and Christian going to do for the rest of the night?" said Violette.

"I will be going to work soon," said Christian.

"Well…I was going to ask Annabelle if I could borrow some of her pyjamas and then go to bed. I really feel tired all of a sudden," said Danielle yawning.

"Yeah, that's no problem Danielle," said Annabelle.

"OK… I will see you in the morning then," said Violette, giving Danielle a hug. "Good night."

"Night, sis," said Danielle, hugging her back.

"Follow me and I can get you some pyjamas and show you where my room is, so you can have a sleep," said Annabelle to Danielle.

"OK. Night everyone," said Danielle, walking towards the doorway with Annabelle.

Chapter Thirteen

In the combat room with Michael, Violette could feel that her senses were heightened and her strength had increased with every punch she threw.

"You won't hurt me no matter how hard you punch or kick me. So give it all you've got," said Michael, teasing her as he held her down on the mat. He knew she wasn't showing him her full potential.

"OK. But you will be sorry," said Violette, kicking him off and holding him down on the mat firmly.

Smiling up at her, he said, "That's better. Now we can begin some real fighting."

Pushing her off quickly, he stood up in a defensive stance and raised his fists up, ready to fight her.

Jumping to her feet with a big smile on her face, Violette said in a playful manner, "Bring it on."

Over the next hour they trained hard, and Violette felt a bit more in control of herself and her cravings. Michael was even surprised at how good she was at combat fighting.

"OK. I think that might be enough for one night. I'm exhausted. Let's head for the showers," said Violette, taking a step back from Michael and wiping her brow.

"Are you sure? How you feeling now?" said Michael.

"I feel better. Much better in fact. Annabelle was right."

"That's great. I can't believe how much better you are at fighting. You will be ready for combat in the field sooner than I thought."

"Yeah…but I don't think I could kill anyone Michael. It's just not in my nature," said Violette.

"You will when it comes down to it, Violette. It's either kill or be killed. But I wouldn't worry too much about that yet," said Michael, as he put his arm around her. "Let's go have a shower."

"OK," said Violette.

As they were coming out of the shower room, Renee came rushing in and said, "They have found William. Grayson is bringing him back home now."

"I am so glad for you, Renee. I was so worried," said Violette, walking over to Renee and giving her a warm hug.

"Me too," said Renee, sighing.

"Is he going to be alright?" said Violette, anxiously.

"He should heal fast as long as Nicholas hasn't done anything to him," said Michael.

"I am going to go and set up our room for William, so he can rest up when he gets back," said Renee.

"Did you want some help?" said Violette.

"No dear. I will be fine. But thank you for asking anyway. See you both later on," said Renee.

"OK. Let me know if you need anything," said Michael, watching Renee walk out the combat room.

"Thanks, Michael."

"With everything that has been going on, I forgot to put away the weapons we used. Give me a minute," said Michael.

"Would you like some help?" said Violette.

"No. I won't be long," said Michael, kissing her forehead.

As she waited for Michael to come out of the weapons room, Violette spotted Danielle making her way into the combat room.

"Hi, sis. What are you up to? I thought you were going to bed," said Violette calmly. She didn't need Danielle walking into the room any further.

"Yeah, I did go to bed. But I couldn't sleep. So I decided to take a walk around the house. I sort of got lost," said Danielle, looking around.

"Oh, OK. What about I take you to the kitchen and we can make a hot cocoa," said Violette.

"No thanks. I am not thirsty. What is this room used for?" said Danielle, looking around.

"They use this room to learn about taekwondo and other forms of martial arts." said Violette.

"OK. The Gramaze have such a nice house… hey, what do you think of Christian?" said Danielle.

"He seems nice," said Violette. She knew where this was going.

"He has such a great body, and, oh, wouldn't I love to touch that?!" said Danielle excited.

"Danielle…looks aren't everything. You know he is from Rome, don't you, and is only visiting for a while," said Violette matter-of-factly.

"Yeah, I know. But when is he going back home?" said Danielle.

"I don't know. Why don't you go and ask him?" said Violette.

"OK. Do you know where he went? When the movie finished he just seemed to vanish and I am not sure on where he is," said Danielle.

"Didn't he say he had to work tonight?" said Violette.

"Oh yeah. That's right," said Danielle. "Do you know what time he usually gets back?"

One in the morning, thought Michael to Violette, as he eavesdropped on the conversation.

"Michael said about one in the morning," said Violette.

"What…when did he say that?" asked Danielle, confused.

"'Oh…um, I mean, I think he will be back about one," said Violette. "Sorry. I guess I'm tired."

Hey babe, you need to get Danielle out of the combat room. We don't want her seeing the weapons, thought Michael to Violette.

Yeah, I know. I am trying, thought Violette.

"OK. Maybe I can catch him when he gets back then. I might just go and see what Annabelle is doing," said Danielle.

"OK. Once Michael gets out the shower, we are probably going to head off to bed now ourselves. See you in the morning, sis," said Violette.

"Oh, right. Good night," said Danielle.

"Grayson has just told me that they are only minutes away from the house. We should ask Annabelle to take Danielle up to her room and they can watch a movie or something up there," said Michael, walking back into the room, after putting the weapons away.

No need to ask me. We are on our way to my bedroom already and I will try to make it a movie that is loud, so she can't hear anything, thought Annabelle to Michael and Violette.

Thanks Annabelle. Please take care of her for me, said Violette.

I will. No need to worry. How are you going now? said Annabelle.

I'm feeling good now. Thanks for your help, said Violette.

You're welcome, said Annabelle.

Glad for William to be home and in one piece, Michael and Violette eagerly headed upstairs to greet him.

As the front door sprung open, Grayson and Micajah were on either side of an unconscious William, carrying him in. His face and clothes were sodden and bloodied, and his beaten body was covered in bruises. He looked barely alive.

Taking in a quick breath with her hand to her mouth, Renee watched Grayson and Micajah carry her beloved, sweet man past her. With tears forming in her eyes, Renee couldn't believe the state he was in. William had been in battles before, but had never come home like this. Something was different.

"William. My poor man."

He was alive and that was all that mattered to Renee.

When Violette saw the look on Renee's face, she immediately walked over to her and gave her a comforting hug.

"God, he looks awful," said Violette, with her brow furrowed, knowing she was partly to blame for how William was.

"He should be alright, Violette. Don't worry too much. Vampires heal quickly," said Renee, watching Grayson and Micajah carry him up the stairs. But Violette heard the uncertainty in her voice and wasn't convinced.

"I need to be with William. I will see you later on."

Violette watched as Renee followed the others up the stair case.

"He has been through a lot of pain and suffering at the hands of Nicholas, so we need to get William into bed and hooked up to some blood to start the healing process," said Bennett to Renee, as they walked up the stairs.

"Yes, I know," said Renee nodding.

Grayson and Micajah carried William into his bedroom and laid him down on the unmade king size bed. Bennett and Renee followed them into the room and shut the door behind them.

Michael watched and listened to Violette's thoughts as the expression on her face changed when the door shut.

"Don't worry…he will heal in the next couple of days. Renee will look after him."

"What can I do to help?" said Violette.

"At this stage, you won't be able to do much at all, except for giving them your support. And I am sure once William has healed, he will be thrilled that you have become a part of the family," said Michael.

"I wish there was more I could do. I feel useless just standing here waiting," said Violette.

"Please don't worry, my love. Like I said, it will just take a couple of days and he will be back on his feet," said Michael, wrapping his arms around Violette for a hug. "Let's go for a walk. I am sure you have many questions about our world still, and how to deal with being a new vampire."

"I do have some questions," said Violette.

But she was more worried about William than becoming a vampire herself.

"Come on, then. Let's go outside," said Michael, placing his arm around Violette's shoulder and directing her to the back patio area.

Sitting at the top of the brick paved steps, Violette leaned on Michael's shoulder and stared straight ahead into the darkness of the garden area. She liked that it was quiet there, and even though she knew Michael would be reading her mind, he kept silent, so she could gather her thoughts. But there was something that Violette noticed straight away as she sat watching the night sky.

"I don't feel the cold anymore, even though it's chilly out tonight."

"That is because when you are a vampire you don't feel cold or heat. Your body always stays the same temperature," said Michael.

"Really…fantastic. I probably do have a lot of unanswered questions, Michael. But at the moment I only want to know one thing: are vampires able to go out in the full sun?" asked Violette.

"We can go out in the day, but the sun needs to be behind the clouds. Otherwise we can start to burn, blister and then die. As long as the full sun is not on us, then we are OK."

"Oh. OK…what am I going to do about going to school? Most humans just love to sit in the sunlight and soak up the sunshine," said Violette.

"Let's not think about that now, Violette. We can deal with that when it arises," said Michael.

"OK," said Violette. But she was worried about it. And pretty soon she would have to deal with it, as the weekend was nearly over. "Can we go back inside now?"

"Sure. Would you like to go up to my bedroom and maybe we can watch some TV?" said Michael.

"Sounds good. I am getting a bit tired anyway."

Standing up, and placing his hand out in front of him, he took Violette's hand and helped her to her feet.

Walking up the stairs to Michael's bedroom, Violette asked, "Do vampires sleep or stay awake?"

"Well, it depends on who you ask. Some vamps say they don't sleep at all. Then others say that they only need a little bit. It's really up to the individual," said Michael.

"I wonder what I will be like…at the moment I usually love my sleep, and can't seem to get enough of it sometimes," said Violette.

"Time will tell Violette. Just let it takes its course," said Michael, opening the door.

As Violette cuddled into Michael's shoulder whilst they watched TV, she couldn't help but contemplate how much her life had changed forever and about what things she would have to give up in turn for being a Lepidoptera vampire.

Eventually sleep came knocking, and she dreamt of what the new day would bring.

Chapter Fourteen

Alone in their bedroom, Renee knelt down beside the bed and watched her man rest peacefully. Stroking his forehead, she realised he had a high temperature, and decided to retrieve a wet flannel from their bathroom. As she sat down next to the bed, William opened his eyes.

"How are you, my darling?" said Renee, placing the cool flannel on his forehead.

"I am weak, but I will be better tomorrow my love," said William, in a soft, hoarse voice.

"Is there anything I can get you to make you feel more comfortable?" said Renee, looking into his eyes.

"Yes, there is something you can do for me. You can lie down next to me and just cuddle me. I have missed you so much, my love. For a time there, I didn't think I was ever going to see you again," said William. Even though William was a warrior, and a leader, he was also an affectionate man, just like all the other Gramaze family men, who appreciated having a life partner.

"You're home now, my darling, and that's all that matters," said Renee, lying next to him.

"Renee can I ask you…?" said William.

"You don't have to ask me for that. You know you can have my blood whenever you want some," said Renee, sitting up and placing her neck near his mouth.

William was usually gentle, but tonight he was like a savage, as his fangs tore into her flesh and sucked the blood from Renee's neck.

Panting as he pulled away, William said, "Sorry, my love. I don't mean to be so rough. I can't seem to get enough of your blood tonight."

"It's OK. Your body is trying to heal, William. So it would be expected that you need some of my blood," said Renee, looking into this radiating eyes and reading his thoughts. "Would you like me to get you some more A+ blood from the fridge and hook it up to your drip?" said Renee.

"Yes, please," said William.

"OK. I won't be a minute," said Renee, as she kissed his lips and then headed for the door.

When Renee left the bedroom, William's head started to pound and his whole body was shaking and sweating profusely with the pain from the severe beating he had taken from Nicholas's henchman. As his breathing became rapid in the darkened bedroom, William became restless and needed to release his feelings of bloodlust. He couldn't wait for Renee to return, as he would need every drop of blood they had to get past this thirst.

Taking the blood from the fridge, Renee could feel William's extreme pain from their life partner connection. He was close to bloodlust and she knew it. *What can I do?* she thought. She couldn't bear to see William like this. Renee knew she only had one option. Pulling her mobile phone out of her pocket, she dialled the number of the only person she knew could help William with her ability: Susan.

"Hello. This is Renee. I need your help to heal William. Can you come to us now?"

"Yes, I can be there within the hour, my friend. Tell William I am on my way," said Susan.

"Thank you," said Renee and hung up.

Susan was a Lepidoptera vampire who had the ability to heal and she had been good friends with Renee and William for at least fifty years. Renee also knew that William had to get better sooner rather than later, if he wanted to keep the Debauched vampires under control, otherwise they would take over the world. As William was their leader, he needed to be in the operations room devising a plan to stop the Debauched vampires, not lying in a bed in extreme pain and thirsting for blood.

Returning to their bedroom with a bag of blood, Renee changed the empty bag which was on the stand and sat down next to William on the bed.

"Thank you for organising her to come and heal me, my love."

"I hope you don't mind me contacting Susan," said Renee, handing William a cup of blood to drink.

"No...that's OK. I know you did it out of affection for me...thank you for the blood. It should take the edge off the cravings," said William.

"You are welcome. Susan should be here soon, so hopefully she will be able to heal your mind and body," said Renee.

"Don't count on it. The way I am feeling at the moment is not something I am used to, and it's very hard to keep it at bay. The last time I felt like this was when I first became a vampire. I am not sure I can contain this thirst I have. Renee...I would suggest you leave me to my thoughts, as I don't want to hurt you," said William.

"I won't leave you William. I know you wouldn't hurt me. Not intentionally anyway. But I will go and get you some more blood to drink," said Renee, hoping off the bed and walking toward the door.

As she opened the door, Renee found Susan standing there. She was just about to knock on the door when Renee opened it.

"Hello Susan. Thank you for coming so quickly."

"Anytime. That's what family is for," said Susan.

"Come in, Susan," said William.

"What seems to be the problem, William?" asked Susan, as she approached the bed. But once she neared him, she could see he was not his usual self. Instead, he looked weak, which she put down to the beating he had taken.

"I have been tortured by the Debauched, and not in the conventional way, either. I am close to bloodlust. Can you stop these uncontrollable feelings?" said William, as he watched Susan sit next to him on the bed.

Realising William wanted to suck her dry, Susan put her palm on his forehead and started the healing process. As William relaxed and closed his eyes, he soon forgot about the bloodlust and fell asleep. It took Susan most of the night to help William recover enough, so he could call a meeting with his family the next morning.

As the daylight appeared through the crack in the curtains, Susan sat on the bed feeling exhausted from all the healing she used on William throughout the night.

"Renee...would you mind if I could take a nap some-where? Could I get some blood brought into me as well? I am feeling a tad weak this morning from all the healing," said Susan.

"No problem, Susan. It's the least I can do," said Renee. "Come this way, and I will show you to your room."

"Thank you," said Susan, following Renee out of the bedroom and into a room where she could rest and regain her strength. She knew she would be needed again later in the morning to do some more healing for William, as he was not fully recovered yet.

"Make yourself comfortable in here, Susan. I will be back in a minute with some blood for you," said Renee.

"OK. Thanks," said Susan, sitting on the bed and taking her shoes off.

Within minutes, Renee had returned to Susan's room.

"Here we go. Some blood and I thought you might like to have a shower, so I brought you in some clean clothes to wear," said Renee, handing her the outfit.

"Thank you, Renee. You are so thoughtful."

"Well…I will leave you to rest. I need to go and see how William is doing and get him ready for the meeting this morning. I will catch up with you later on," said Renee, giving Susan a hug.

"Thank you, Renee. Tell William I will come and see him later on," said Susan.

"OK," said Renee walking towards the door.

Entering their bedroom, Renee heard the water running in the bathroom, and assumed William must be having a shower. Walking into the steam-filled bathroom, she noticed his dirty, bloodstained clothes, from the night before, scattered on the floor. Placing them in the washing basket next to the vanity, she watched William's silhouette in the shower. Opening the shower glass door, Renee found William with his hands out in front of him leaning against the tiled wall of the shower with the water cascading down his shoulders, soaking up the water. She could feel from their connection that he was not himself.

His bloodlust was gone, but his strength hadn't returned, which was disconcerting to Renee.

"I am losing my abilities as a Lepidoptera," said William, as he turned his head under the water to face Renee.

"How is that possible?" asked Renee, with a furrowed brow.

"I have been drugged by the Debauched. Possibly something experimental," said William, turning the taps off and grabbing his towel he had previously placed on the side shower screen.

"Bastards...what can I do to help you, my love?" said Renee.

"Nothing...Susan has said she will try some sort of healing ritual on me later...but she isn't quite sure it will work. The only other thing I can think of is to go and see our queen," said William, drying himself off.

"Oh, right. What about in the meantime?" said Renee.

"Rest...but first I need to dress and then speak with our coven this morning. I have already ordered everyone to assemble in the operations room in ten minutes. We need to devise a plan of attack to stop these fuckers," said William.

One thing William was worried about, was if he could keep up the façade in front of his family this morning. He wanted to show he was still in control.

"Don't worry, my love. You will do fine," said Renee, reading William's mind.

Composed and in control, William stood at the head of the table in front of his family for the first time since his capture.

"This morning we need to talk about a few things...firstly though...I would like to welcome our newest family member, Violette," said William, walking over to Violette and placing his arms around her for a warm, welcoming hug. As soon as

William hugged Violette he felt a surge of strength hit his body. *What the fuck was that?* thought William to himself. Everyone in the room clapped, bringing William back to his senses.

"Thank you," said Violette, feeling like her face had turned beetroot red.

"You are welcome to join our meeting this morning, Violette. But I warn you, what you hear in here may shock you, until you get used to the way of life we are living," said William.

"Thanks William. I do appreciate your offer. But for today I don't think I will join the meeting, as Emily and Adrian are expecting Danielle and me home," said Violette.

"Not a problem. I would like to catch up with you later on tonight, though," said William seriously.

"OK," said Violette. *I wonder what that is all about?* she thought. She gave a nod to all in the room and then left to find Danielle.

Michael met Violette outside the operations room and gave her a cuddle.

"I will see you later on. Are you feeling alright today?"

"Yes, surprisingly, I feel really good. You go back to the meeting, Michael. I will catch up with you later on tonight," said Violette.

"OK," said Michael.

He gave her a quick kiss goodbye and then went back to the meeting.

When Michael entered the operations room, William was discussing his abduction.

"As you all know, yesterday I was attacked and drugged by Nicholas, who took me to his operations in London. When I came to, I found myself chained and locked up in one of the cells they had underneath their mansion. Not only did I endure continuous bashings with chains, but they also gave me electric shocks whilst I was in water up to my waist. They thought by torturing me that I would give up the locations of all the Lepidoptera operations worldwide. But they were wrong. When they figured that I wasn't about to give up the information they required, they decided to pump me with some sort of experimental drug," said William, looking around the room at each of the faces in his family.

"Fuckers…they will pay for what they have done," ranted Grayson.

"Yes, they will. Anyway, when I was left to rot in the cells, with no guards watching me, I unlocked the cell door and went searching around their huge house to see what I could find out about their operations, and who was involved in the experimenting. One room in particular, which was at the back of the house, had a computer set up, where I found out what type of experiments they have been performing and where some of their operations are around the world. Luckily, I was able to print out a list of all of this information. The reason I have assembled you all here this morning is to advise you that I have spoken to all our counterparts around the world, and they are all willing to help us exterminate the Debauched in their locations."

As William looked around the room, he only saw a thirst for destruction of the Debauched, on the faces of each one of his coven.

"Tonight we will attack their operations here in Paris. Our counterparts around the world are going to do the same thing, at the same time as us in their cities. That way there is no way any of the Debauched operations can inform the others of the attacks planned. Our plan will be to get out as many humans as possible and send them back to their homes without any knowledge of us. Once they are all out, we will kill or torture any remaining Debauched vampires, and blow all their operations sky high. Them fuckers won't know what happened to them."

The Gramaze family coven cheered as William said, "Are you ready?"

"We will be ready, Sire," roared Michael.

"Today we will all do some combat training and get our equipment and weapons ready for tonight. I don't want anyone leaving the house today, as there is too much to organise. Is that understood?" said William.

They all nodded and agreed.

"Michael, I will send over Susan and Renee to guard Violette and her family today. We can't spare you, so please make Violette aware of this," said William.

"Yes, Sire," said Michael.

"Before you all go there is something else I want to discuss…I won't be coming with you all tonight into combat. It seems that the drugs that were injected into me have now taken away my strength. I will be staying here, and if there is any information you need, I can relay it back to you. Whilst you are out in the field tonight, I have asked Grayson to be your leader of operations. So follow his every move and instruction," said William.

"Is there anything that can be done to get your strength back?" said Annabelle.

"At the moment, we are not sure. Susan is staying for a few more days. So I am hoping her healing power may be able to give me my strength back. I am useless at the moment without it. In fact, hour by hour I seem to be losing my other abilities as well. I would say that this is what the Debauched vampires have been experimenting on. If they can turn all of us back into humans then they would be able to take over, and the human population will cease to exist after a while," said William, watching the shock on the faces of his family.

"Fuck…I couldn't even imagine what it would be like to be human again," said Bennett.

"We are going to mutilate these motherfuckers tonight Grayson. I certainly don't want to turn back into a human," said Micajah, with flared nostrils.

"Well, that's what the plan is tonight. We will attack and annihilate them all so that they can't experiment on anyone any longer," said Grayson.

As William was about to close the meeting, the big TV screen in the operations room lit up with a video feed of the Brussels operations vampires. Vincent was the Brussels leader, and he and William had been good friends for a few hundred years.

"William, I wish to speak to you and your family about the attack tonight," said Vincent. "Is this true that the Debauched have been experimenting on our own kind as well as humans?"

"Yes…it's true. I am living proof of that. I stand here today to tell you that I have been experimented on and that I have lost some of my strength and other abilities," said William.

"Is there any cure for this?" said Vincent.

"Not that I know of. This is why I want to put a stop to it. We don't want any more of our kind becoming human again…because…well, you know the ramifications of what will happen. The fuckers have to go down and they go down tonight, Vincent," said William authoritatively.

"I totally agree, William, and you have our full support, my friend," said Vincent. "Would you like me to send anyone from here over to help you with the attack tonight?"

"Yes, that would be great. We could do with the help as we are low in numbers here," said William.

"I will send over my most trusted men then, William," said Vincent.

"Thank you. I do appreciate this, Vincent," said William.

With that the screen went blank and William said, "We had all better get into the combat room to do some training. When the four Brussels soldiers arrive I will send them down to the combat room, Grayson, for you to instruct them on our plan of assault."

"Yes, Sire. It will be taken care of," said Grayson.

As Michael was walking down to the combat room with Annabelle, he said, "I wonder who will be coming from the Brussels operations tonight?"

"I was actually thinking the same thing, Michael," said Annabelle.

"You know Violette's brother, Stephen, he is from the Brussels coven," said Michael, as he remembered finding out from Brock a few days before about Stephen's whereabouts.

"No. I didn't even know she had a brother," said Annabelle, with raised eyebrows. "Hang on…I think I have actually met him."

"Yeah, we both have. He came over last August, to help out with the queen's protection," said Michael.

"Yeah, that's right," said Annabelle nodding. "I remember now."

"Violette and Danielle haven't seen him for years. But at this stage I don't want to get Violette's hopes up, just in case he doesn't come. So don't say anything to Violette. Just keep your thoughts to yourself, if you know what I mean, Annabelle," said Michael.

"You have my word, Michael. My lips are sealed," said Annabelle, standing in the doorway of the combat room.

"Thanks…you go in. Don't wait for me. I am just going to let Violette know that Renee and Susan are guarding her today and tonight," said Michael.

"Right," said Annabelle, nodding and walking into the combat room.

Violette, thought Michael.

Yes.

I wanted to let you know that Renee will be protecting you during the day and Susan will be guarding you during the night. The rest of us are getting ready to take down the Debauched tonight, thought Michael.

Oh, OK. Please be careful, thought Violette.

I will...well... I have to go. Bye, thought Michael.

Bye.

Chapter Fifteen

Hearing the front gate creaking as it opened inwards, Emily looked out the window of the sitting room to see a car pulling up to the house. She knew it was Danielle and Violette returning home from the Gramaze house, as they had texted her earlier to let her know they were on their way.

"The girls are home Adrian," said Emily, standing at the window.

"Good. Ask them to come in here," said Adrian, putting his newspaper down on the wooden coffee table.

With her heart beating fast, Violette's eyes opened wide when she saw Emily waiting for them on the front porch, with the door open. It was one thing to feel comfortable around Danielle and not want to suck her dry, but how was she going to conceal her thirst in front of Emily and Adrian? *This should be interesting*, thought Violette, as she alighted from the car with Danielle.

"Hello, girls. How was your night?" said Emily, giving them both a hug.

"It was such a great night, Emily. Thank you for letting us go. I have such sore feet and legs today though from all the dancing last night. Oh and the band, they were to die for," said Danielle.

"How about you Violette? Did you have a good time as well?" asked Emily.

"Um…yeah, the night was excellent. I couldn't believe how good 'Train' were. But like Danielle, I have sore feet and legs too from all the dancing we did last night. Actually, if you don't mind, Emily, I am just going to have a sleep for a while as I am exhausted," said Violette, yawning and trying to make an excuse to get away from Danielle and Emily, because she could feel the agitation was starting again. She needed to try and calm herself. *Breathe, Violette. Breathe.*

"Actually, before you go have a sleep, we need to have a chat in the sitting room," said Emily, indicating the way.

"What about?" asked Danielle, with raised eyebrows.

"Adrian is waiting for us. We don't want to keep him waiting," said Emily, not even answering her question.

Adrian as well. Shit, thought Violette, clenching her teeth and trying to calm herself.

Following Emily into the sitting room, they stood next to the couch waiting for Adrian to speak.

"Sit down girls," said Adrian, patting the couch.

Sit down… I don't think so. Oh fuck, I can hear their blood running through their veins…mmm, they smell good, thought Violette, licking her dry lips. She continued to stand, but Danielle sat in front of him.

"We wanted to speak with you both about your schooling," said Adrian looking from Danielle to Violette, as he took his reading glasses off. "As these last couple of years are important and this is your final year, Danielle, to obtain your baccalaureate, we would prefer if you girls don't partake in any further night clubbing or staying out late. In fact, we would like you to make a start on your studies today."

"Oh, really? Can't we make a start tomorrow?" said Danielle, in a less than enthusiastic voice.

"I am a bit exhausted, Adrian. I was going to have a sleep for a while. Would you mind if we could make a start on our school work tomorrow?" asked Violette.

His jugular vein looks so inviting. Just drink from it then...no! thought Violette as her eyes widened and her mouth felt dry from lack of saliva.

"This is exactly what I am talking about. You are both tired from your night out, so you don't feel like studying," said Adrian with creased eyebrows.

Both girls looked away from Adrian to Emily, swallowed hard, but said nothing.

"Oh...OK...I suppose it will be alright if you both can make a start tomorrow. But I don't want to hear any excuses. You girls have had your fun and now it's time to get on top of your study. And that is starting tomorrow morning. Are we clear?" said Adrian, in a stern voice.

"Yes, Sir," said Danielle.

"Thanks, Adrian. That would be good," said Violette. She could feel herself starting to shake and sweat. Violette didn't know how much longer she could hold off. Her thirst for blood was all she could think about.

"OK. Off you go girls. We will see you both later," said Emily.

"See you both later," said Violette, just about running out the room and up the stairs.

As Violette entered her darkened room and shut the door, she felt a presence.

"Who's there?" she said, nervously with her fists clenched beside her.

Renee came out from inside the wardrobe. "It's just me, Violette. Sorry to startle you. Are you feeling OK?"

"Oh, thank God you are here Renee. I am starting to feel like my head is going to explode again." She then noticed what Renee was holding onto—a blue cooler bag. "Please tell me you have some blood in there for me."

"Yes, dear," said Renee, as she opened the cooler bag and pulled out a bag of blood for her.

Violette yanked it out of her hands fast and tore it open. As she gulped the first bag down, her body started to calm itself once again. And instead of feeling like she wanted to drain someone of their blood, she now felt back to normal again. As normal as she could be anyway, considering she was a vampire.

"Better now?" said Renee, watching Violette's reaction to the blood.

"Yes thanks, Renee. But how did you know?" said Violette.

"I could hear your thoughts, dear," said Renee.

"How much longer will I feel like this?" said Violette.

"Each Lepidoptera is different, my dear. Some take one week, and others take a couple of days. For you it may take a bit longer, because you are around humans. Usually when a Lepidoptera is transforming they are not in contact with humans. So until you are fully transformed you need to be careful around humans. As soon as you feel the agitation coming on, you need to drink some blood. This should help to soothe the transition from human to vampire."

Violette sat on her bed thinking about how much she was going to dread the next few days. She certainly needed a lot of self-control.

"Well, I will be off Violette. I am just going to check on William and then I will return soon, to protect you," said Renee.

"OK. Thanks Renee. No need to hurry. I'm sure I will be alright…oh, how is William going?" said Violette.

"Not good. We are hoping that Susan will be able to eventually heal him. But it's not looking good at the moment," said Renee.

"My thoughts are with you both. Take care of him, won't you," said Violette, as she gave Renee a warm hug.

"Thanks Violette. I will," said Renee, walking towards the window. "If you need anything just mind talk and we will come. OK?"

"OK," said Violette, watching her jump off the balcony.

Renee was anxious to get back home, so with vampire speed, she took the tunnels that connected their homes.

As the night drew near, Violette was starting to get anxious about what might happen that night. She had mind talked to Michael during the day and he had told her about the planned attack on the Debauched.

Since her transformation had started, Violette could usually hear all the mind thoughts of the Gramaze family. But there had been nothing. Not even from Michael. The silence was killing her and she just had to see him. Even if only for a moment to tell him how much she loved him.

Violette sensed Emily was in the sitting room by herself, and as she walked down the marble staircase, she made a bee-line for her.

"I am just going to ride my moped over the Gramaze house to see Michael, if that's OK, Emily," said Violette, standing in the doorway.

"How long will you be, dear?" said Emily, looking up from her newspaper.

"Not too long. I should be back for dinner," said Violette.

"OK. Well, drive safely," said Emily smiling.

"Bye," said Violette.

Entering the garage to get her moped, Violette tensed as she noticed, out the corner of her eye, that there was a guy waiting in the shadows. Her first thought was to run, but she knew she wouldn't get far, so she decided to pretend she hadn't seen him. *Where are you, Susan?* thought Violette.

There was no answer.

As she gingerly walked over to her moped, the man came into the light, and she straight away sensed he was a Debauched vampire. He stood about seven feet tall and his muscular body shaped the shirt he wore as he stood in front of her with his fists clenched and his jaw rigid. Violette knew he was not someone she could attack and win. Maybe the time had come where she would have to fight to the death. *Why hasn't Susan shown herself?* thought Violette.

"If you know what's good for you, you will keep quiet. Come with me. My leader is waiting for you," said the sentinel, in a Parisian accent.

"I am not going anywhere with you, asshole. So you had better be off… now… before I belt the living crap out of you," she said, with her nostrils flared and her breathing rapid.

"Don't make me laugh… if you don't come with me now, I will kill your human family, bitch," said the sentinel.

Violette realised from his demeanour that he was not playing around. He really would kill them if she didn't do what she was told. As she contemplated what to do, she felt something stab her. Looking down, she found he had shot a dart into her arm. Pulling the dart from her arm, her eyes widened as everything blurred and eventually blanked out. Violette slumped to the ground in a heap as the sentinel rang for a van to pick them up.

Violette jumped as she woke feeling panicked. *Where am I?* she thought, as she looked around the darkened room. She had been placed, by the sentinel, on a mattress on the carpeted floor, in what looked like an old storage room, because of the boxes that lined the walls. Remembering she had been drugged by the dart in her arm, Violette rubbed her head as the pounding had started again. Agitated by her own stupidity to once again get taken by the Debauched, she felt weak and didn't seem to have some of her Lepidoptera abilities. She tried the door to see if it would open, but realised it was locked and there was no way out. Four walls and no windows. Spotting a light from under the doorway, she called out to see if anyone would come to the door, but no one came.

Think, Violette. What to do, thought Violette anxiously. *Michael…Michael. Can you hear me?*

Yes, my love. How are you? thought Michael. As soon as Michael asked her the question, he could sense from their connection that something was wrong.

I have been taken by the Debauched vampires and I am not sure where I am, thought Violette, knowing if Michael couldn't find her that she would die.

I can't believe this has happening again. How many more times are these bastards going to take you before you fully turned into a Lepidoptera vampire? Are you alright, Violette? thought Michael.

Yes, I am OK, for the moment. But before you try to find me, you need to ring Emily and tell her that I am staying over for dinner. Before I was taken I told Emily I was going to see you for a while and would be back for dinner, otherwise she will worry, thought Violette.

Yes, yes, we will ring her. But what were you doing out alone? You have been warned about this Violette. And now look what has happened; exactly what we told you would happen. You have been taken again, and God knows what they will do to you this time, thought Michael.

I'm sorry Michael. I thought Susan was outside guarding me, so I thought it would be alright to come over to see you one last time before you went out on the mission tonight. I was worried that I wouldn't see you again, thought Violette.

Shit... that means Susan has been... fuck, I hope she is OK. So you didn't see her at all, Violette? thought Michael.

No, I haven't seen her. I tried mind talking to her, but she didn't answer, thought Violette.

Whilst Michael and Violette were communicating about what they could do, Renee rushed into the combat room and said to Michael, "We have just had a phone call from Susan. The Debauched have taken Violette."

"Yes I know. I am talking with her now and she confirmed that they have taken her," said Michael.

"Grayson, what can we do?" said Michael.

"We need to ask Violette if she can find out where she is. I would say she will probably be at the same place we are going to attack tonight," said Grayson.

"Do you reckon they have taken her for insurance or just taken her to experiment on? I am also wondering if they knew we are coming tonight," said Michael.

"That's a good question," said Grayson. *If they know we are coming, then someone has told them and that would mean we have a traitor in our house,* thought Grayson to himself.

"Tell Violette that we will be there soon to get her out," said Grayson.

"Yes, Sire," said Michael. *Did you hear that Violette?*

Yes. Please hurry Michael, thought Violette.

"Attention everyone... I will give you two minutes until we depart and then we are all out of here to attack those sons of bitches who dare to take one of our family members," said Grayson.

Entering the combat room, William headed over to Grayson with the soldiers from Brussels.

"Grayson, the four soldiers are here from Brussels. I have already gone through the plan of attack with them. So they are ready to go," said William.

"Everyone…you all remember Jack, Stephen, Theodore and Harrison from the Brussels coven," said Grayson, gesturing to the four men, and looking around the room.

The four vamps just nodded their heads towards all of the Gramaze family.

"We are ready to rumble when you are, Grayson," said Jack.

"Our first mission tonight is to rescue Violette," said Grayson, looking around the room. "So let's do this then." *When is that girl going to learn that it is dangerous to go out without protection?*

Everyone grunted and nodded in agreeance as they ran out the combat room and into waiting vans at the back of the Gramaze property.

"Bring her back alive, Grayson. And bring honour back to this family," said William, as he stood beside the van and gripped Grayson's arm and hand with force.

"Yes, Sire. I intend to," said Grayson.

What a courageous family I have, thought William to himself as he watched them drive out of the driveway. He couldn't have been more proud of his family than he was at that moment.

"I wish I was going with them tonight, Susan. I feel useless doing nothing here," said William, watching their taillights fade into the night darkness.

"You're not doing nothing here tonight William… actually you are the go-to man tonight instead of Brock. And that is a very important job for their mission… anyway I need to start some more healing on you so that you are ready for when they all return. So let's get started," said Susan, walking back inside arm in arm with William.

On the way to the Debauched hide out, Michael thought to Violette, *We won't be long, my love. Stay safe until we arrive.*

I will try, thought Violette.

As they were driving along Michael could feel Violette's pull. But it wasn't coming from the direction they were heading. It was to the north of where they were going.

"Violette is not in the house we are going to blow tonight. I can feel her pulling me in another direction. Do you mind if I take Harrison and Stephen to go and rescue her? Once I have her safe, we can meet you at the intended target house to help with the fallout," said Michael to Grayson.

"Are you sure, Michael?" said Grayson, with a creased brow.

"Yes, I am sure," said Michael.

"Alright. But please be careful. These fuckers obviously don't give a rat's arse about our kind, only their experiments."

"Thank you, Grayson," said Michael.

"Harrison and Stephen, you are going to go with Michael to rescue his life mate, Violette," said Grayson.

"As you wish, Grayson. We are only too happy to help out wherever we can," said Stephen.

As the SUV stopped on the side road and the three of them jumped out the back of the van, Grayson said, "Keep in touch and let us know what happens to you all once you're inside."

"Don't worry bro, we will," said Michael, shaking Grayson's hand.

Michael, Harrison and Stephen all had speed and invisibility on their side, so once Michael felt Violette's pull again, it was easy to get onto the property where she was being held. From the outline of the trees that surrounded the house, Michael sensed that there was only four Debauched guarding Violette inside the house. His plan of attack was simple: kill them all.

"Harrison, you go around the back and come in through the back door to surprise them. Stephen, you come with me through the front and we will exterminate these fuckers. If you get into any trouble, call. Any questions?" said Michael.

Both Stephen and Harrison stood silent. They were soldiers and ready to give their lives for others, no matter what.

"OK, let's go," said Michael.

Walking around the side of the house, Harrison noticed that a Debauched was sitting outside on the back steps having a cigarette. Picking up a small piece of pipe that was lying on the ground next to the house, Harrison threw it across the field and into the side of the shed. Hearing the loud bang, the Debauched jumped to his feet quickly and walked towards the shed. With his back to Harrison as he looked around, the Debauched didn't know what hit him when Harrison snuck up behind and decapitated him. As his body turned to ash, Harrison said softly, "One down, more to come."

Running back to the house, Harrison slowly entered the house through the back screen door. By the time he had looked through the back half of the house, he came across Michael and Stephen.

"Four Debauched down. Stephen, I want you to start looking through this place to find out if they have any intel on the experiments that we can use on further assignments," said Michael.

Stephen nodded and went off to see what he could find.

"Harrison, I need you to stand guard so we are not surprised by any vamps hiding out somewhere," said Michael.

Harrison nodded and ran off to check the house and outside perimeter.

Feeling her pull, Michael quickly searched the entire house, room by room for Violette. Running down the basement stairs, he came to stand in front of a door to where he felt Violette the most. Unlocking the door with his mind, he rushed inside, only to find the room was empty. Once he was inside the room her pull became more intense. Feeling the walls for a hidden panel, he sure enough came across a part of the wall that clicked open when he pressed it. Only a vampire could get this hidden panel open, as the walls were made of thick steel and could only open from one side of the wall.

As the door opened, Violette said, "I am so glad to see you Michael."

"Are you alright?" said Michael, giving her a hug.

"Yes," said Violette, tears welling up in her eyes.

"We need to get you out of here before any other vamps turn up," said Michael, taking her chains off.

"OK. I am sorry I have caused this headache for you," said Violette, as Michael helped her up the stairs.

"We will talk about this later… upstairs I have two soldiers from Brussels here with me. I will introduce you in a minute."

"What about your mission tonight?" asked Violette.

"Once we get you out of here, we will join Grayson and help destroy those Debauched fuckers," said Michael.

Walking up the stairs with Michael, Violette thought she was seeing things as she neared the solid built soldier from Brussels at the top of the stairs. Rubbing her eyes, she took another look. Was her mind playing tricks? Was her brother really standing in front of her?

"Stephen…," said Violette.

"Yes, that is my name. Have we met before?" said Stephen, looking at Violette.

"You don't remember me, do you?" said Violette.

"No. Sorry, miss. I don't know you…except, you have the same name as my little sister," said Stephen.

"Look closer at me, silly. I am…"

She didn't have to finish the sentence because Stephen realised he was standing in front of his little sister. Picking her up and whirling her around, he kissed her hair and hugged her tightly.

"Violette…it's really you. What are you doing here? Oh God, how I have wished to see you again one day. What about Danielle?" said Stephen, eager to find out how her life had been. They had been close as children, and he sure had missed his family.

"Sorry guys, we have to get out of here. Time for chatting later. I can hear some cars pulling up outside," said Michael, looking out the window and seeing headlights coming towards the house.

"Can you walk, sis?" said Stephen.

"I feel weak. I am not sure," said Violette, looking up at her brother.

Stephen picked her up in his strong arms and said, "Let's get out of here."

Meeting up with Harrison outside, who was waiting near the shed at the back of the property, Michael, Stephen and Violette continued to move at vampire speed through the trees and onto the road, so that they could meet up with Grayson.

Grayson… we have got Violette and are on our way to you, thought Michael.

Great… stay where you are. Renee will pick you up in a moment and bring you all to us.

It wasn't long before Renee turned up. At first, Michael thought the van might have been the Debauched vamps, but soon realised through mind talk that it was Renee instead.

Pulling the car up next to them, Renee said, "I see a car coming in the distance. Get in and hold on, guys. It could get a bit rough here." As she sped away, Renee kept checking her side mirrors for any Debauched. Luckily, the car she saw in the distance soon turned off.

"I wouldn't want to be in their shoes, as their master won't be pleased that they've let such an important prisoner escape," said Michael, glad that he, once again, had foiled the Debauched plans.

Chapter Sixteen

"I can't believe my little sis is a Lepidoptera too!" said Stephen, putting his arm around Violette's shoulder.

"It only happened recently. Up until then, I didn't even know this world existed. But I now understand why you left and never came back," said Violette.

"Yeah, it's a bit hard to return home when you feel blood-thirsty. So...Michael is your life partner... you couldn't have made a better choice, sis. I have been in battle alongside Michael previously, and he is one strong and determined vamp. God...it's so good to see you Violette. I have so much to tell you," said Stephen, thrilled to have the chance once again to see his sister.

"I can hardly put my arm around you now. Look at you...you have muscles upon muscles. Been working out, huh?" teased Violette. "I have missed you, big brother. I will have to fill you in on what's been happening since you left home, when we get back to the Gramaze house."

How am I going to tell him that our parents have died? thought Violette.

"We are nearly at the target's house. You must prepare for battle," said Harrison, interrupting Stephen and Violette's conversation.

Stephen nodded to Harrison, and checked his weapons for readiness.

"Violette…stay in the van with Renee. You don't have enough combat experience yet to help us. We don't want you getting yourself killed," said Michael, sitting across from Violette in the back of the van.

"But…"

"There are no buts about this. Don't argue. Just stay here!" shouted Michael.

Violette didn't know what to say. She was not used to this side of Michael that she hadn't seen before. With her eyes looking down to the floor, she swallowed hard and just nodded.

With his teeth clenched and his nostrils flaring, Stephen looked across the van at Michael with disgust in his eyes. He didn't like the way Michael spoke to his little sister. But Stephen knew it wasn't his place to say anything, even if he didn't like it. There were ranks amongst Lepidoptera, and Stephen knew he was at the bottom of the ladder and still had a lot to learn. Remembering back to when he first became a Lepidoptera, Stephen had compassion for how Violette would be feeling completely useless, as she wasn't able to help fight the Debauched.

As Renee pulled over to the side of the road, Michael, Stephen and Harrison jumped out the car to greet Grayson.

"Stephen and Harrison, I need you both to go around the back of the house and try to get inside. You need to keep in touch as to what is happening with you both at all times. Are we clear?" said Grayson.

"Yes, Sire," they both said and ran off around the back of the house.

"Michael, I want you to stay with me and we will smoke some of these motherfuckers. The others are spread out fighting the Debauched," said Grayson.

"No problem. Let's go," said Michael, walking towards the house.

Armed with blowtorches ignited and ready to exterminate, Grayson and Michael were confronted by four Debauched who attacked them from behind. As Grayson and Michael struggled for control with the four vamps, Annabelle and Brock came from behind them and torched the Debauched vamps. As their bodies turned to ash, Annabelle high-fived Brock, who was standing next to her, and said, "Take that you motherfuckers."

We have just killed six more of these bastards, and now we are inside, Grayson, thought Stephen.

We are nearly done out here. Do you need any help inside? thought Grayson.

It seems pretty quiet in here. We should be fine, thought Harrison, as he looked through the house room by room.

Clear the way, my brothers, as I am coming in to lay the charges, thought Brock.

Grayson…you need to come in here. You won't believe what we have found, thought Harrison.

Grayson headed over to where they were and found Stephen and Harrison in a part of the house he didn't know existed. Underground there were handmade brick and concrete tunnels that had water running through the centre of them. The stench was of an unbearable odour of sewage. As they walked down the tunnels further, rats scurried about everywhere trying to nip at their boots, until they were kicked away. Rounding a bend in the tunnel, Grayson couldn't believe what he was seeing: cages filled with vampires.

What the fuck. Are these Debauched or Lepidoptera? thought Grayson to himself.

Even though his senses told him that these were vampires, his brain was saying otherwise. With their steel hand cuffs on and chained to the cell floor, Grayson conducted a quick inspection of each of the vampires, and found track marks on their arms.

Looks like William wasn't the only one they were experimenting on, thought Grayson to himself.

After determining which ones were either Debauched or Lepidoptera, Grayson was disturbed to find that none of them had their strength or abilities that a vampire usually had. In fact, they were more like humans than vampires. As he walked further into the tunnels, Grayson came across a female Lepidoptera vampire he knew.

"What has happened here to you all, Sophia?" said Grayson.

"They have held us captive for months. Injecting us daily with some type of drug. Most of us have lost our abilities and are turning into humans," sobbed Sophia. Her head dropped as the words came out of her mouth.

"Fuckin' bastards. They are going to pay for this," said Grayson.

"What would you like us to do?" said Harrison, standing next to Grayson.

"Let me talk with William first," said Grayson, taking his phone out of his pocket and walking back upstairs.

"Sire, as you probably already know from all our mind talk, we have found at least twenty-five vampires in the tunnels below the Debauched house. What would you like us to do with them?" said Grayson.

There was a silence on the phone as William thought long and hard on what his decision would be.

"I want them all brought here. Even the Debauched," said William.

Grayson couldn't believe what he was saying.

"Even the Debauched... I don't want to challenge you William, but are you fucking crazy? We don't want them bastards in our operations," said Grayson.

"You will do as I bid, Grayson. I will send a truck to collect them all and bring them here. Make sure each of them is securely chained prior to putting them in the truck," said William, heatedly.

"Yes, Sire," said Grayson. Even though he didn't like William's choice, he knew his place in the chain of command was to obey, and not to question why. Hanging up his phone and placing it inside his jacket pocket, Grayson walked back into the tunnels to give his family the news.

Everyone... listen up, thought Grayson to his family. *I have spoken with William, and he is going to send a truck to collect all the vamps, even the Debauched, and take them back to our operations.*

What the fuck? We have the queen there. Why would he jeopardise her safety? thought Michael.

Grayson heard others protesting as well.

Just fucking do as you are told. Don't question my authority," thought Grayson, with his nostrils flared, as he started to unlock each cell.

Knowing it would take time for the truck to arrive, Grayson instructed his family to go from cell to cell, unshackle the vamps and get them ready for transport.

The truck arrived within thirty minutes and one by one the vampires were herded like sheep into the truck and shackled, so they couldn't escape or cause trouble. They were to be taken to the Gramaze house, where it would be decided whether they would live or die.

"The house is clear of Lepidoptera…once you are finished laying the dynamite, we will meet you by the roadside, Brock," said Grayson placing his hand on Brock's shoulder.

"Yes, Sire," said Brock. But Brock knew he would need to do one final search of the house to check for Lepidoptera or humans first.

Whilst Renee and Violette waited in the van, Violette felt like she needed to feed again. Luckily for her, Renee had remembered what it was like to become a new vamp, and she bought along with her some blood which she stored in a cooler bag for Violette.

"God Renee, you think of everything," said Violette, taking the blood from Renee.

"This is what happens when you have been around for a few hundred years on this earth. You learn to read people and how things are going to turn out," said Renee.

After Violette finished the first bag of blood, she started to feel better.

"Thanks, Renee," she said, placing the empty bag in the cooler bag and wiping her mouth.

"You are welcome," said Renee, who was listening to all the mind talking going on. She was proud of her family for the work they had done tonight.

"Is everything alright?" asked Violette.

"Yes dear. They should be back soon," said Renee, keeping watch from the front driver's seat.

Just as she said it, the car door opened quickly and Michael jumped in. He didn't look too happy at all, and was filthy from head to toe.

"It's all over. The Debauched vamps have been exterminated. We will be ready to go in about five minutes. We are just waiting for Brock to set the charges now," said Michael, sitting next to Violette.

"Is Stephen riding with us?" asked Violette.

"No. Stephen is going back in another car. He has been injured and needs medical attention. You will be able to speak with him and see him back at the house," said Michael.

"Is he going to be alright?" said Violette.

"Yes, he will be fine. But for now we need to get him back to the house to heel," said Michael.

"What about you, Michael? Are you OK?" said Violette, placing her hand on his hand.

"I am fine," said Michael, folding his arms across his chest and staring straight ahead. He was not in the mood for niceties, and he knew there would be ramifications for Violette trying to leave her house without a guard. William would not tolerate her lack of caution and reverence for their kind.

What is your problem? thought Violette to Michael.

He didn't answer. Instead he gave her a sideways glance, with flat lips and flared nostrils, that told her not to bother questioning him about anything else.

As they were driving off, there was a huge explosion, which shook the whole car. Looking through the window, Violette could see that the house had exploded and was now a fire ball, with lots of smoke and debris in the sky.

Arriving at the Gramaze house, Violette waited for Stephen at the front door by herself. She couldn't wait to hug him and squeeze him tight. As his car pulled up, Harrison and Jack helped Stephen get out of the back of the SUV. His t-shirt was blood stained at the front, and with his face screwed up, he looked like he was in severe pain. Violette couldn't help herself;

she ran over to him and gave Stephen a hug. She didn't want to let him go.

Harrison and Jack stood back and watched as Stephen and Violette hugged and became reacquainted as a family. Neither of them had seen affection like this, between a brother and sister, for a long time.

"I will be OK, sis. I just need to rest and then I will heel from the knife wound," said Stephen, stroking her hair.

"I don't want to lose you again, Stephen," said Violette, with tears welling in her eyes.

"You won't," said Stephen, trying not to reveal his pain.

"Come inside, Stephen, and we will get you looked at," said Annabelle interrupting them.

Standing back, Violette watched Harrison and Jack help Stephen inside the house. Following them to a room that had been set up with medical equipment for any wounded soldiers, she stood in the doorway, leaning up against the frame, and waited for Annabelle to help treat Stephen for his injuries.

As she stood in the doorway, Michael came up behind her, and placed his arms around her shoulders. "Don't worry. Injuries like his don't take long to heel," said Michael, feeling her concern for Stephen.

Turning around, Violette cuddled into his chest, and took a deep breath.

"I'm sorry I snapped at your earlier," said Michael.

"That's OK. I understand why," said Violette, taking a step backwards and looking into his eyes. "Thank you."

"What for?" said Michael.

"For coming to my rescue once again. I am so sorry Michael for the trouble I have caused tonight. I am still getting used to all of this, and it may take me a while before I learn that I need to have a guard if I go out of the house," said Violette.

"Yes, you will learn or you will be k—"

Violette interrupted. "Don't say it. I know."

She was already ashamed of herself for causing so much trouble.

"I am sure William will want to speak with you later," said Michael, watching Annabelle walk towards them.

"He's all yours, Violette," said Annabelle, indicating to Stephen as she walked out the room.

"Thanks, Annabelle," said Violette turning around.

"I will leave you two to catch up. But when you are finished, you need to debrief with William," said Michael.

"OK. Thank you. I will catch up with you later, then," said Violette.

Michael nodded and walked away with Annabelle.

Walking into the room, Violette noticed that Stephen was the only one in the room. *I am so glad no one else was hurt or was killed tonight*, thought Violette. As she reached Stephen, who was lying on a kind of hospital bed, Violette could see his abdomen area had been bandaged up, and he was sleeping. Sitting in the chair next to his bed, she placed her hand in his and held it firmly. With her tears starting to flow freely down her cheeks from the happiness of finding him, she knew it was only a matter of time before he woke and would be healed. As she lay her head on his bed, waiting for him to wake, she felt his hand stroke her hair. Looking up, she saw him smiling at her. He was finally awake.

"Hi there, little sis," said Stephen, smiling.

"How are you feeling?" said Violette, smiling back at him.

"Better," said Stephen, sitting up. He patted the bed for her to sit down.

"That's good," said Violette, taking a seat.

"What are all the tears for?"

"I am just so happy to see you."

"Me too, sis. How is Danielle?"

"She is good. But she is not one of us."

"When did you both move to France?"

"Umm, I think about eight months ago."

"So the Lachance's are good to you both?"

"Yes…before we talk about anything else, there is something that I need to tell you," said Violette sadly.

"Don't worry you don't have to tell me. I know about Mom and Dad. I did come to the funeral you know. But you would not have seen me, as I had to hide," said Stephen, holding Violette's hand.

"Do you know how they died?"

"Yes… I hunted the killers down, Violette, and they got what they deserved," said Stephen, matter-of-factly.

Violette was shocked by his comments. But her head was telling her that those carjackers did deserve what they got.

"I think I would have done the same thing to them if I could have, Stephen. I remember feeling so lost and angry at them for taking Mom and Dad's lives, that I wanted to kill them too…God, I never thought that I would ever see you again, Stephen. Since Mom and Dad died, our lives have changed so much."

"I am sorry you and Danielle have had to go through all of that without me. But I wouldn't have been able to look after you, anyway. You know, vampire and all."

"That's OK. I understand. So Michael said you have been living in Brussels."

"Yes. I have been there ever since I left home. When I first started noticing that I was craving blood, I met the Lepidoptera vampires in LA. They showed me the ropes, so to speak. After a while I moved to Brussels, and the leader there asked me to stay. As time has gone on, I have grown to know them as my family."

"Must have been hard for you. But I do understand now why you didn't return home."

"When did you become Lepidoptera vampire, Violette?"

"It only happened to me a few days ago. I am still transforming and learning at the moment."

"What about Danielle? How is she?"

"Danielle has adjusted well to living in Bagnolet. She is a real socialite."

"How do you know that Danielle is not a Lepidoptera?"

"I asked our foster parents, Emily and Adrian, to check our records and they told me that you and I were adopted, and Danielle was our parents' biological child."

"That makes sense."

"Danielle doesn't know anything about the Lepidoptera world, so if you intend to see her, then you can't mention the vamps."

"Sorry, but you can't tell Danielle that I am here, Violette. I don't want to try to explain to Danielle why I haven't kept in contact. It's just all too hard."

"I promise, Stephen. I will leave it to you to tell Danielle when you want to, if you do at all."

"So what about you, little sis? How are you coping with being a Lepidoptera vampire? Are you able to be around humans without wanting to suck their blood yet?"

"Surprisingly, I am going really well with it. Actually, it's a lot easier than I thought it would be. So how long are you staying in Bagnolet for?"

"I am not sure, Violette. It depends on if William will need me any longer to help out here."

"Do you think you would want to stay here at the Gramaze house if William asked you to stay?"

"I'm not sure. I would really have to think about that because I have a good life with my Brussels leader and family. I also have a partner, so I would have to talk it over with her."

"Wow...I never even thought about the fact that you would have a life partner."

"Yeah...she is so wonderful. I do love her so much, and she me."

"So life has been good to you then?"

"Not too bad, sis."

There were so many questions that they had for each other. But for Stephen, there was one question that hadn't been answered yet.

"Violette...what colour butterfly do you have on the back of your neck?"

"It's red, I think. Why did you want to know?"

"OK. Can I have a look please?"

"Sure."

As Violette turned around and lifted her hair, Stephen took a look at her tattoo and said, "Your butterfly is changing colour. At the moment it is red. But it also has a bit of blue, and green as well."

"Really? What does that mean?"

"It..."

Before he could answer, they were interrupted by Michael walking into the room.

"Stephen, if you are feeling up to it, William would like to see you in the operations room to debrief about tonight."

"Yes, I am good to go," said Stephen, jumping down off the bed. "I will catch up with you later on, Violette."

"OK," said Violette, as she gave him a warm hug.

After Stephen left the room Michael said, "Is that true? Your butterfly has changed colour? Can I have a look please?"

"What is so important about the colour of the butterfly I have, Michael? And why are you and Stephen so interested in it?" said Violette frowning.

Should I tell her or just brush it off as nothing, thought Michael.

"I don't want any bullshit either. I deserve to know," she said annoyed.

"OK, OK. History tells us that if a female Lepidoptera has the multi coloured butterfly on the back of her neck, then she will have all the Lepidoptera abilities and will be very powerful. This will mean that if you are not protected by our family, and the Debauched vampires claim you as one of their own, then they can breed with you. Our queen has informed us that this sort of inbreeding would create a breed of Debauched vampires that will be indestructible and very hard to kill. In fact, there hasn't been a multi-coloured Lepidoptera vampire born into our world for thousands of years, Violette," said Michael.

"Why was I chosen to be one of the most powerful of all the Lepidoptera vampires?" asked Violette.

"I am not sure why."

"What colour butterfly does the queen have?"

"She is multi-coloured," said Michael. It then hit him. *Violette is a princess to our kind. Wow...my life partner is royalty,* thought Michael.

"If we are the same, what does this mean for me, Michael? I am starting to get nervous," said Violette.

Michael stepped forward and embraced her in his warm loving arms.

"Don't worry, my love, I won't let anything happen to you...but we will need to inform William about this, as it will have a big impact on our family. You can't tell or show anyone your butterfly tattoo until William tells you to do so, Violette."

"What, not even my own brother?"

"When I say anyone, I mean it. You are not safe until William decides what to do."

"I get it, Michael. Can we go and see William now?"

"Sure. Let's go."

Chapter Seventeen

Walking down the corridor to the operations room, Michael and Violette watched Stephen coming out.

"William would like to see you both. I am going to call my partner and then go and recuperate in my room. So I will see you later on."

Violette hugged her brother and said, "OK. See you later then."

William was waiting for them both at the head of the table when they entered the room.

"Sit down both of you, as we need to talk. Firstly, I want to see this for myself," said William, matter-of-factly, as he walked over to Violette.

What Michael and Violette didn't know was that whilst he was debriefing Stephen, William had been listening to them talk about the multi coloured butterfly tattoo on the back of Violette's neck. Without even asking what he was talking about, she just showed him her butterfly tattoo.

"Unbelievable," said William. He was excited, as he knew what this could do for his family. "I haven't seen one of these for thousands of years. I can't believe you have been chosen. We will need to call a family meeting, so that everyone is informed of how honoured we are to have you here, Violette. I am not sure what Michael has told you about being a multi-coloured Lepidoptera vampire, but you are very rare... Michael, I want you to go and round everyone up for a meeting."

"Yes, Sire," said Michael.

As Michael left the room, William said to Violette, "My dear, I will need to take you downstairs later on tonight to meet our queen. She will need to talk with you about your powers and how to take care of yourself and others," said William.

She nodded.

I am not sure I am ready for this, thought Violette to herself.

As everyone casually walked into the operations room, unaware of the importance of the meeting, William said, "I want everyone to sit down at the table, as I need to discuss something with you all that is of great importance to our family."

Once they were all seated, he continued.

"As you all know, Violette has just become a Lepidoptera vampire and the newest member of our family. What I am about to show you is to be kept in this room and never to be spoken about to anyone outside of our family or this house. Violette, I would like you to stand up and show everyone your butterfly tattoo on the back of your neck," said William, proudly.

As Violette lifted her hair to show everyone her butterfly tattoo, she heard everyone gasp, and start saying how lucky they all were to have her as our family member now. When she turned back around, they were all lined up, ready to give her a hug or congratulations. At this stage, Violette didn't really understand about how important she was to the Lepidoptera. It was all a bit overwhelming. But it felt nice to be a part of such a loving family again.

"Alright... sit down everyone, as we need to discuss this further. The first thing that I would like speak to you all about is: if I find out that someone that is in this room does divulge this secret to anyone outside of this family then they will have me to deal with. What you don't realise, is that by telling others about Violette, that they could also be bringing death to our family. I don't have to tell you all of the importance of this, as the Debauched vampires would try to kill each and every one of us to get to Violette. In fact, we now need to make sure that Violette is guarded at all times. Violette, you will need to remember that if you want to go anywhere, that you will need one of us with you. Because if you are taken by the Debauched vampires, and believe me they will try, you can kiss goodbye your life as you know it," said William sternly.

"Yes Sir, I do understand the importance of this, and I promise to keep your family safe always," said Violette.

"Stephen, Harrison, Jack and Theodore, you are sworn to secrecy. And I want you all to swear on your Brussels leader's life that you will not divulge anything you know about Violette," said William.

"You have our word, Sire," they all said.

"Now, the second thing I want to discuss is our mission tonight. I will need each and every one of you to debrief with me individually later on. But first we will hear from out counterparts around the world on how they went with their missions," said William, turning on the big communication screen.

The screen came alive with all of their counterparts around the world that attacked at the same time earlier that evening.

"Hello my good friends. Please tell us one by one, how each of you went tonight, and if you need any help from us with the clean-up," said William.

They all told their stories of how easy it was to defeat the Debauched vampires. Most of them said that they didn't have too many of their family members that were wounded.

"We will need to look into this a lot further, my friends," said William.

"It seems the Debauched were experimenting on themselves," said Vincent.

"That doesn't make sense," said William.

"I know, especially as they kidnapped humans and vamps to do their experimenting on," said Vincent.

"Did anyone see Nicholas at any of the houses around the world?" asked William.

They all said no.

"It seems the motherfucker escaped once again. I just wish I knew what he was up to. But I guess we will never know until we catch the bastard," said William.

The Brussels leader said, "Do you still require my family there to help clean up, or can we organise to collect them from Paris?"

"If you wouldn't mind, Vincent, I would love to have them stay for one week, as we do have a bit of a clean-up here and it would be good if we had them to help out," said William.

"That will be my pleasure William, but please look after them," said Vincent.

"I will treat them like my own family. Thank you Vincent," said William.

The meeting with the other worldly leaders went on for another thirty minutes, and then they all signed off.

As they all were finishing up with the discussions of the future of their family, William said, "I think someone is at the front door. Annabelle, could you please go and see who is there?"

"Yes, Sire," said Annabelle.

When she opened the door, it was Emily and Adrian, and they were there to collect Violette.

"Hello, Emily and Adrian. Come in and I will get Renee and William for you," said Annabelle.

"Thanks, Annabelle," said Adrian.

As Emily and Adrian waited at the front door, Violette, Michael, Renee and William came from the operations room to meet them.

"What is going on here?" said Adrian, exasperated.

"Michael, Violette, can you please give us a minute with Emily and Adrian?" said William.

"Yes Sir," said Michael, taking Violette by the hand.

Violette frowned and followed Michael to the kitchen. *What's going on?* thought Violette to Michael.

I don't know. I am guessing they want some privacy to talk about us, thought Michael to Violette.

Oh, OK, thought Violette.

"Why don't we take this into the sitting room?" said William, gesturing for Emily and Adrian to walk through.

"I think that might be a good idea, William," said Adrian.

Entering the sitting room, William said, "Take a seat my friends."

"I need an answer to my question, William. What is going on?" said Adrian, taking a seat on the sofa, next to Emily.

"What do you mean?" said William.

"It seems that whenever Violette says she is coming over here, that she ends up either sleeping over, or staying late. Why is that?" said Adrian.

"You know what young love is like my friend…they just can't seem to spend enough time together," said William.

"Yes, we understand that. But we all know, that that is not the only thing going on here. Has her transformation taken place?" asked Adrian.

William's eyes widened, as he took a deep breath and contemplated what to tell Emily and Adrian. Even though Adrian was a warlock and he and Emily had always connected supernatural beings with each other, William wasn't sure they needed to know that Violette was a Lepidoptera princess.

"Yes. Her transformation has taken place. I would say that is why Michael and Violette's attraction to each other is more apparent now than before. They are life partners," said William.

"Yes, we thought so too. But I have a question...why, out of all the Lepidoptera's that we have reunited you with, has Violette's been so secretive? Usually you are up front about the transformation. What is going on?" said Adrian.

William looked at Renee, who was sitting next to him, and then to Emily and Adrian.

"You are correct, my friend. But this situation with Violette is not a normal transformation to Lepidoptera. We have not seen a female Lepidoptera for hundreds of years, only males. You can attest to that," said William.

"Yes, but I feel there is more to this story. I am not stupid, William, and I think you owe it to me and Emily to tell us the truth," said Adrian, folding his arms over his chest.

William's nostrils flared, as he stood up and walked over to the window. Looking out into the garden, he said, "I want both of your assurance that this information I am about to tell you, will never be disclosed."

"You have our word," said Adrian, looking at Emily and then to William.

As William informed Emily and Adrian about Violette, and how valuable she was to their Lepidoptera coven, he watched the shock and realisation on their faces, of how important she would become to their race.

"Something you will both need to consider as well, will be to agree to Violette to come and live with us. We can protect her better here than at your house. In fact, there have already been incidents at your house, twice now, that you wouldn't be aware of," said William.

"Why haven't you informed us of the Debauched attacks?" asked Adrian, with a furrowed brow.

"In hindsight, I now think that maybe we should have informed you. At least you could have put up some wards around the house, so the Debauched didn't detect Violette. But what is done is done…so what do you think about Violette moving in here?" said William, standing near the sofa.

"That is something we both would have to think about. Violette is only sixteen, and as we have stated previously, she needs to finish her schooling first, with good grades. As you know, being a supernatural creature, doesn't always mean you can get a free ride in life. And I don't think you have even thought about Danielle and how this will affect her," said Adrian.

"Yes, there is a lot to consider and we do agree that this is not a situation where you can decide tonight. Violette is already becoming a part of our family and we do love her like our own daughter already," said Renee, calmly.

"At the moment, we just want to take Violette home with us," said Emily, looking at Adrian for support. "A decision doesn't have to be made straightaway, does it?"

"No, it doesn't…but you will need to put up a protection ward so that the Debauched don't seek her out. I will have a guard protecting her as well, each day and night. So between us, she should be OK, until you make your decision. But I warn you… the first sign of any trouble and I will be forced to take matters into my own hands. Am I making myself clear?" said William.

"Crystal... well, we had better be on our way," said Adrian, standing and helping Emily to her feet.

Approaching the front door, Adrian and Emily noticed that Michael and Violette were already waiting for them.

"You ready to go, Violette?" said Emily.

"Yes," said Violette, as she read Emily's thoughts about her pending living arrangements. With a raised eyebrow, she looked at Michael and smiled.

You hear that, Michael? thought Violette.

Yes, thought Michael.

This has not been confirmed. Don't get your hopes up, thought Renee to both of them.

Michael and Violette nodded.

Walking out to the car, Michael thought to Violette, *See you later on my love. I will be the one guarding you tonight.*

She gave Michael a hug good bye and said, "See you tomorrow after school."

"I will miss you... oh, and have a good day at school tomorrow," said Michael.

"Thanks for having me over tonight, Renee and William," said Violette.

"You are welcome, my dear," said Renee.

Violette then mind talked to them all, *Who will be guarding me tomorrow at school?*

We will let you know later on, Violette. I need to draw up a list of who can guard you, and at what times of the day and night, thought William.

Driving away from the Gramaze house, Violette realised that her life had changed forever, and there would be very interesting times ahead.

The End of Book One.

Check my website for when my next book in this series
will be published. www.susanhoddy.com

Acknowledgements

This book would not be here, resting in your hands, or on your e-reader if it weren't for the following people. I owe all of them my deepest appreciation

My daughter, Samantha Hoddy, and my fiancée, Michael Houston. I could not have written this without your continued support and love. You have both always told me to never give up on your dreams. Thank you Sam and Michael.

My editor, Rebecca Freeman, whose continued advice and support has provided me with a much needed calming strength to keep going. Thank you, Rebecca.

Several friends, and family members, whom read my manuscript and gave me feedback on what they wanted to see in the storyline and book cover. Thank you all.

My book cover designer, Laura Moyer from the Book Cover Machine, who worked tirelessly to provide me with a truly awesome cover design. Thank you, Laura.